Spelldriver

Magic & Mixology Mystery Series, Volume 6

Gina LaManna

Published by LaManna Books, 2019.

This is a work of fiction. Similarities to real people, places, or events are entirely coincidental.

SPELLDRIVER

To my husband, family, and friends. :)

Special Thanks:

To Alex—For feeding me breakfasts and coffees while I raced to finish these edits! я тебя люблю!

To Christine—For inspiring The Quilter's name.

To my family: Mom, Dad, Kristi, and Megan—for already spoiling the newest member of the LaManna family!

To Rissa Pierce—For your support from the very beginning, especially on this series!

To Stacia—For all the detailed spreadsheets and intricate notes that make this series possible.

To Ruthie—For helping to name this book!

To Janice—For inspiring The Quilter's special talents.

To my friends, especially all of LaManna's Ladies, thank you for a wonderful 2018 and start to 2019!

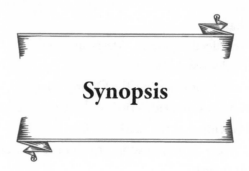

Synopsis

With a wedding on the horizon and her father tucked safely away in prison, the future is looking bright for Lily Locke. Unfortunately, life on The Isle is never calm for long... and when a Ranger is killed brutally in plain sight, Lily and her fiancé—the renowned Ranger X—find themselves hunting a murderer more ruthless than any they've ever encountered before.

However, unraveling the killer's intricate plot isn't Lily's only problem. She has a cousin who is nowhere to be found. A dangerous hunter has escaped from prison. Ranger X is all but obsessed with his latest case, and Lily worries it's consuming him entirely.

Despite it all, Lily must make a decision that will affect not only her life, but the life of the man she loves more than anything else—and once it's done, there's no turning back...

Chapter 1

"**D**on't peek!"

I kept my eyes closed tightly and faced the general direction of the woman's voice. "How am I supposed to decide on a dress if I can't see it?"

"I said don't *look*!" Wanda snapped. "This is my job, and I'm good at it. If I wasn't, would anyone purchase wedding dresses from Wanda's Weddings?"

"Probably not."

Wanda sniffed as if her point had been cemented. She maneuvered behind me and adjusted the newest dress in ways that had me wincing as she pinched my sides, tweaked at my stomach, and yanked at my arms. The light hum of fairy wings intensified.

"Are you sure the fairies don't need a break?" I asked as one of them gasped for air. "They've been fluttering for quite some time."

"They're tough," Wanda said. "They trained with Glinda. Working at Wanda's Weddings is a walk in the park."

I wasn't sure I believed her. The four tiny creatures assisting Wanda were all retired Forest Fairies from Glinda's small army, and most of them were wheezing as they tilted veils and plucked at sleeves and straightened trains until Wanda clucked with perfection.

At least, I imagined she would cluck when perfection occurred. At this point, finding the perfect dress felt like a pipe dream. I had a better chance of getting Ranger X in a dress than I did of finding one that Wanda approved of for my body type, whatever that meant.

"Okay, fine," Wanda said with a dramatic sigh. "You may now open your eyes."

I opened my eyes and found four forced smiles glowing back at me.

"That's, ah..." Mimsey said with a cough.

"Exactly!" Poppy chirped. "It's very..."

Zin scrunched her nose. "Interesting?"

"It's awful," Trinket said finally. "It looks like you dressed up as a marshmallow for Halloween. After it was destroyed by a fire."

"Gee whiz," I said. "You all paint such a beautiful picture."

"Turn," Wanda said, completely undeterred. "I think it's a work of art, but they might have a point. The dress sort of swallows you whole."

I spun to face the mirror and was unable to keep my eyebrows at a normal height. They seemed intent on creeping higher and higher until they just about disappeared into my hairline.

The dress was definitely *interesting*. It puffed out in all directions with a skirt that didn't just swallow me, it devoured me. It flounced up so high my face was barely visible above layers on layers of chiffon. An added cathedral-style veil—currently supported by heavily perspiring fairies—had me feeling like I was a forgotten balloon, floating in a lonely journey across the skies.

"You would definitely stand out," Wanda said. "It would be the talking piece of the ceremony."

"Because she looks like someone plugged her into a Lite Brite," Trinket mumbled. "Is she glowing?"

"Those are the newest beads to hit Wanda's wedding dresses," Wanda said happily. "We captured lightning bugs and bottled their essence. Then we infused them into the beads—"

"And vomited them onto a dress?" Zin murmured.

"The beaded pattern is very intricate," Wanda said. "Lily will be glowing from here to the mainland."

"In other news," Mimsey said, tapping a finger against her lip. "We might need to hand out sunglasses at the ceremony."

"I think I'm going to pass on this one," I said, squinting as an entire row of beads lit up with a vicious burst of light. "It's not good to blind the guests."

Wanda heaved another breath that made it sound as if the world was ending. "I'll pull another from the racks. Give me a moment. While I'm in the back, why don't you sit in this dress and get a feel for it? You might be surprised to find it's growing on you."

"It's definitely growing all right," Mimsey said as Wanda disappeared in a swish of black and white pantsuit. "I can barely see your eyes anymore."

I blew hair out of my face, glancing around anxiously to make sure Wanda was truly out of earshot. Wanda, of Wanda's Weddings, was tall and slender and dressed like a high fashion model from the pages of Vogue. She wore ruby red cat glasses with sparkly red shoes, and her earrings dangled down to her ribs. Her hair was cut short and stylish, and her pantsuit had shoulder pads so large she had to twist her body to make it through the doorway.

Her shop was just as festive as her attire. Tucked onto Main Street on the eastern side of The Isle, Wanda's Weddings boasted a cute little storefront in a two-story Victorian. It had turrets and a fresh coat of Painting Potion sprayed onto the outside, but there was no masking the ancient creak of floorboards or the whisper of wedding dresses as they brushed against the breeze coming in through the lopsided front porch.

Inside the shop was all white fluff and sparkle. Full length mirrors cast sometimes stunning, sometimes horrifying images back at me, while an entire wall of tiaras and veils and glittering jewelry sparkled under the purposefully brightened lights.

"I agree with Mimsey. That dress is definitely growing on you," Poppy pointed out. "I mean, it looks like it's breeding tulle by the minute. Pretty soon I'll have to throw you a life raft just to keep you from suffocating."

I laughed, tried to maneuver into a seated position, and failed. I settled for standing and extended a hand toward one of the fairies holding up my veil. With a grateful wheeze, she alighted on my palm, looked me in the eye, and gave a disheartened shake of her head.

Over the last few weeks, I'd hemmed and hawed over the idea of a wedding during a season of life as volatile as this one. I'd just learned that my father had survived a battle that should have ended his life, which meant he'd be back for me. Sooner or later, he'd find a way to torment my very existence.

I'd also learned my mother had been an assassin. A wild shift from the kind, loving stories I'd heard about her. Then again, the file declaring her as such had come from Liam—a man I still wasn't sure I could trust. After all that had happened over the past few months, some alliances were growing stronger while others had turned precarious.

Not last, and certainly not least, was the contract between me and my father that still remained intact. In a desperate moment, he'd tricked me into signing an irrevocable magical pact that would grant him custody of my first-born son.

The very thought of giving up a child, even one that didn't yet exist, had me panicking whenever the notion crossed my mind. To combat the fear, I'd simply focused on one truth over the last few weeks, adopting it until it became fact. Ranger X and I could never have children. There was no way around the pact, and the truth was, I'd die before giving a child to my father.

It was the only solution that had presented itself as foolproof. While it hurt to realize X and I would never grow our family beyond two, I'd already spent time grieving and was determined to seal my fate for good. After all, so long as X and I had each other, the rest would work itself out. There was nothing wrong with a family of two.

"The Isle to Lily," Wanda said, reappearing quite suddenly at my side. "I've got another option for you. Chop-chop."

I coughed in surprise. The fairy on my palm leapt to attention, launching into flight at the return of her boss and winging around drunkenly until she plowed straight into my hair. As I fished the fairy out, I glanced at Wanda and the dress draped over her arms while the fairy made herself comfortable lounging across my cleavage.

"*This* one has a very real-looking mermaid's tail. With a hint of magic," Wanda drawled, "it will move and twitch as you walk. And if you get into water, it will be enchanted to work in a very realistic way."

"Excuse me?" Poppy raised a hand. "Why would Lily be getting into the water on her wedding day? In her wedding dress?"

"Why do fish fly?" Wanda asked. "I don't know, but I am prepared for every scenario. Now, fairies—unzip, unbutton, undress."

I yelped as the fairies set to work unzipping, unbuttoning, and undressing. I could've sworn they also pinched, prodded, and poked me as they worked, showing their displeasure with my lack of decisiveness. Then again, it wasn't entirely my fault that I hadn't chosen a dress yet. I didn't want to look like a marshmallow or a drowning mermaid on my wedding day, and those seemed to be the extent of my options thus far.

Indeed, the next dress proved to be quite scaly. It itched on the inside and shimmered on the outside, and it was next to impossible to remain standing while wearing it. To go along with the whole mermaid design was a corset that knitted so tightly up my back I felt lunch from last Tuesday working itself back into my esophagus. Not to mention the fact that the entire top half of the dress was designed to look like a set of seashells.

"I think I'll pass," I said. "Maybe we should take a break and—"

"Nonsense," Wanda said. "The mermaid scaling is made from the finest artisan designers in the country, and... Lily? Where are you going?"

I teetered, tottered, and tipped backward thanks to a tail that flapped all on its own. Only Zin's quick reaction time kept me upright.

I forced a smile at Wanda. "What were you saying?"

She blew air out of her nose so fast it whistled. "I'll find another option."

The fairies set back to work stripping me to my underpants. I'd learned that modesty didn't exist when it came to Wanda's Weddings.

Just then, the door to the shop opened, and I dove for the dressing room, greedily grabbing for my clothes in case the incomer was a stranger, or a male, or really any person at all.

"Lily?" a soft voice called out. "Don't worry. It's me."

I poked my head out from behind the door, clutching the fabric of my sundress in front of my body like a shield. "Who is it?"

"The Quilter."

The answer came swift and sure, so confident that it gave me pause as I scanned the woman who'd entered the store. She had a certain timelessness to her features, despite the fact that her hair was frizzled and gray. Her eyes crinkled happily, accentuated by violet eyeliner, as she studied my face with an expression of pure joy. She wore a knitted dress with thick straps that floated down toward her knees and looked entirely too warm to be worn in a tropical climate.

"Oh, don't worry about me. There's a nice breeze," the woman said, moving her knees so her dress swished. "It's like a tank top sweater with ventilation. I made it myself."

The peculiar woman wore a floral scarf around her head that did only a partially decent job of holding her hair back. The rest of it frizzed out around her head in an uncombable looking halo. Even more curious, however, was that she appeared to know me. I was most confident I'd never seen her before.

"Sorry, and you are?"

"The Quilter," she said again, as if it were a regal title to be used like king or queen. "I've come with your package."

"What package?" I asked. "Sorry, but I don't think I—er, ordered anything."

She laughed, the sound light and tinkling. "Nobody orders from me, darling. The orders fulfill themselves. I sensed you might need this."

For the first time, my eyes were drawn away from the woman herself and toward the parcel she hugged to her chest.

"It seems you might need a bit of clarity," she said carefully, her eyes twinkling. "In addition to something warm. Nobody likes to prance around naked. Unless the breeze is warm and the moon is full. Then I quite enjoy it."

"I agree," Mimsey said. "It's not a lot of fun dancing naked when the breeze is chilly."

"Mom!" Poppy said. "Stop."

"It's quite liberating, actually," The Quilter said. "You should try it sometime."

After an uncomfortable pause, Poppy glanced over toward her mother. "Tell me you and Gus don't go prancing around in the buff together. If you do, I'll need a schedule of your activities so I can stay away from fields and prairies during the full moon."

"Of course I don't do that with Gus." Mimsey's cheeks flushed pink. "It's a female thing."

"It's a witch thing," Zin muttered. "Yet again, I'm glad I'm not a witch."

"I'd rather be a blood intolerant vampire than have to bang a drum around a fire in the nude," Poppy said. "The gastrointestinal distress is well worth it."

"I'm a witch," I pointed out, "and I don't bang drums in the nude."

"Give it time." Mimsey patted my shoulder. "You'll come around."

The Quilter kept a quirky smile on her face throughout the whole exchange, moving closer to me as the conversation grew louder. In offering, she extended the parcel once more. "It's yours."

"But..." I hesitated, saw sheer determination in her eyes, and accepted the package. "Thanks."

"Go on, open it," Poppy said. "I love presents!"

I glanced at The Quilter, who gave a gentle nod, a soft smile creasing her eyes into a permanent sense of contentment. Taking that as permission to open the package, I untied the thick velvet ribbon that kept the brown paper secured shut.

As the wrappings fell away, I found a blanket in soft browns and greens spilling onto my arms. The earthen-toned blanket was heavy, smooth against the skin. It felt like butter as I wrapped it around my shoulders.

"You made this?" I gaped. The blanket was large and fell to my feet. If I cinched it around my chest, it was long enough to be a dress. "It's incredible. Thank you. But how did you know I'd need it?"

"Goes with the territory," she said, humming a little ditty. "I'm pleased you like it, but then again, I knew you would."

"Are you psychic?" Poppy asked. "What *are* you?"

"Does it matter?" The Quilter asked lightly. "Let's just say... I know things. Like when people need guidance in the right direction. My blankets are woven with bits of spells and a taste of magic."

"Where can I get one?" Poppy stepped forward, her eyes glued to the blanket as she reached a hand forward and ran the comforting fabrics beneath her fingers. "These would make excellent gifts."

"Gifts. That's all I ever give," she said demurely. "There's no option for special orders or purchases. Well, it's time for me to go. Enjoy, Lily. I hope it brings you the clarity you seek."

Before I could thank her again, the bell was tinkling at the front of the shop and the door was swooping shut behind The Quilter's chunky sweater dress. Through the full-length windows spanning the front of the shop, I watched her frizzy hair bounce down the porch.

"Peculiar," I said. "Have you guys seen her before?"

Zin, Mimsey, and Poppy all shook their heads. Trinket, however, stilled.

"Trinket?"

"I know of her." Trinket didn't bother to turn around from the rack of discount wedding dresses she'd been examining.

"Feel like expanding?" Mimsey prodded her sister with an elbow. "You can't just say something like that and leave us to wonder."

Trinket faced us, her expression unreadable. "Yes, I can."

I blanched at the chilliness in Trinket's voice. "Should I be worried by the fact that I'm wearing her blanket? She did say it's been woven with spells and magic. It doesn't feel harmful, but..."

"I wouldn't be worried," Trinket said briskly. "Here's Wanda with another option."

"What is that ragged thing?" Wanda demanded, her blood red lips parting in a surprised 'O' at the sight of the blanket wrapped around my body. "Get it off. The next option I have is a—"

"Lily?" Zin's voice cut through Wanda's instructions. "A moment, please?"

I hugged the blanket tighter and followed Zin to a corner of the shop. She elbowed her way through the rack of clearance dresses and pulled me into a quiet hallway that led to a small office and an employee restroom at the back of the store.

"Urgent message," Zin said. "You're needed at Ranger HQ."

"Oh, thank God."

Zin just stared at me.

"Oh, you're serious?" I sank backward against the wall. "I thought maybe this was a made-up ploy to help me escape Wanda's clutches."

Zin raised her hand, gestured to the Comm. "It's Ranger X. He asked specifically for you. Practically begged. I think something is wrong."

I felt the blood drain from my face. "Tell them all I'm sorry. And tell Wanda to put this on my tab, will you?"

I grabbed the first bridesmaid dress from the clearance rack I could find, noted the price, and slid my body into it. The Quilter's blanket was nice and all, but I couldn't traipse across The Isle and enter Ranger HQ with merely a blanket wrapped around me.

"Did he say what his call was in reference to?" I asked, the worst fears leaping to the front of my mind. I worried it had something to do with my father. "Did he hint, or..."

"I don't know, Lily. I'm sorry. Go, okay? I'll take care of Wanda for you." Zin spun me around. "On second thought, are you sure you want to wear that? Don't forget shoes."

I glanced down, barely having processed the dress as I'd shoved it over my head. To Zin's credit, the thing deserved to be on clearance. The dress was neon orange with pink taffeta sleeves that puffed like floaties around my arms. Yellow trim flowers ran along the bottom. It looked like something Mimsey might pull off, but certainly not me.

"No time," I said. "Grab my stuff for me, will you? Don't forget my Comm. Or my blanket. Or my—"

"I got it." Zin grabbed the blanket from my hands and shoved me toward the emergency exit. "Now, move."

Chapter 2

I snuck down Main Street and kept to the edge of the path, skirting the crowds to avoid unnecessary questions. Because there would definitely be questions about this dress. I had plenty of them myself. Thankfully, someone inside Ranger HQ had a portal waiting for me by the time I reached The Forest.

I practically skidded through the HQ entrance to the front desk where I found Elle, the beautiful, centuries old fairy responsible for manning reception. Her hair glittered a hot white and her eyes shone with a piercing blue that flattered her pale skin.

"Hi," I gasped, sliding against the desk. "Thanks for letting me inside. I got a message from X to meet here. Know anything about it?"

She gave a succinct nod, though I couldn't tell from her expression if she knew the nature of the meeting. Raising her hands, she scrolled down a paper log with silver nails that had been enchanted to glisten and gleam when the light glinted off them.

"He's waiting for you in the lounge," she said with a hint of amusement that I chalked up to my bad clothing choices. "Your arm, please."

I extended my wrist and let Elle take it in her hands. She pressed the cool touch of her thumb against my inner wrist and held it there for a long moment, leaving a dusting of magic that would provide me access to the appropriate zones.

When she let go, she smiled and nodded over my shoulder. "Take the first left. You'll find him at the end of the hall."

Ranger HQ had a strikingly modern interior, all black hallways and shiny chrome finishes. The rest of the facility was bathed in white, white, white and glass, glass, glass. The space had been constructed as a fortress and looked like an art display. The sandals I'd swiped from the rack at Wanda's squeaked loudly as I reached the first doorway and eased my way into the darkened hallway.

I strode to the end of the hall as Elle had instructed. Letting myself through the only door in sight, I paused for a breath as I entered a lounge and found two figures waiting for me. Unlike the stiff conference rooms with their severe black lines, this space had been carefully orchestrated to project relaxation. A white couch curled along one wall while several Zen plants lined the windows along the far end. A few modern chairs were pressed against a bright orange table that was eerily close in color to my dress.

"What's wrong?" I managed, coming to a stop. "Hettie? What are you doing here?"

My grandmother curtsied toward me. "Well, madam, may I first say you look fabulous in your orange dress?"

"No, you may not," I said. "I mean, thank you. But what's going on? Who died?"

Ranger X seemed frozen in place, so my eyes slid back toward Hettie.

"Well, Bill Yonkers died two weeks ago, and his family still hasn't buried him—but I'm not sure why that's any concern of yours," Hettie said. "He was like three hundred years old."

I glanced at Ranger X as his lips moved, muttering something about age that was likely directed at Hettie. My grandmother was no spring chicken if we were talking exact numbers, but in mind, body, and magic, she was more like a fresh twenty-one-year-old witch who'd just learned she had powers.

If there was anything positive about my grandmother's warped view of age, it was that her outfit was even wilder than mine. Hettie wore bright blue biker shorts that would have needed censoring if she appeared on television, and a bright pink zip up sweater in some sort of velvet material that looked rough to the touch.

She completed her outfit with shoes that had little wheels on the heels. As I struggled to process the scene, she sailed across the room and crumpled into my arms, pretending she'd wanted a hug when really she was just holding on for balance.

"Okay, I'm missing something here." Once I righted Hettie, I stared down Ranger X. "I ran across The Isle dressed like this. You pulled me out of a fitting for my wedding dress. I thought I'd find you comatose and bloody."

Ranger X raised an arm and scratched at his head, his ginormous bicep covering his face in a strategic maneuver. When he lowered his hand, I caught a glimmer of sheepishness sliding across his features.

"There *is* an emergency," I said softly, "isn't there?"

"As a matter of fact, there is," Hettie said. "The emergency is that I wasn't invited to your dress fitting."

"Yes, you were," I said. "I told you last week."

Hettie paused, tapped a finger against her head. "That's right. I guess I got caught up in the flowers. Well, even better that this one got interrupted. Now I can go to the next one."

"Where's the fire?" I was beginning to lose patience and glanced at X. "Do you have an emergency?"

"It's more of a dilemma," X said carefully. "In my defense, I didn't say it was urgent. And there *was* blood."

I glared at him. "And the dilemma is?"

"Oh, spit it out," Hettie said, giving Ranger X a smack on the shoulder. "Your fiancé doesn't like the flowers I picked out."

"Don't tell me this is about flowers." I sized my grandmother up carefully. "Where's the blood?"

"Not on me," she said. "It was an intern."

"Your grandmother sent an intern to the hospital because she brought illegal flowers into Ranger HQ," X said in a rush. "There were five types of carnivorous plants in her bouquet, a sprig of nightshade, and one flesh eating variety of poison leaf that she concocted in her garden."

"What are you planning, a wedding or a funeral?" I turned to my grandmother. "Is the intern alright?"

"He'll survive." Hettie raised purple-tinted eyebrows. "I told him to wear gloves. They don't teach kids any discipline these days."

"He was trying to arrest you thinking you were a terrorist," X said. "And frankly, I was about to let him."

"Until he passed out and the Bloody Bloomer nearly ate his face off," Hettie said. "That was a close one. That's what I call my flesh-eater. Created to scare off intruders from The Twist."

"That's horrifying," I said.

"And illegal," Ranger X pointed out.

"Well, aren't you two spoilsports," Hettie said. "I guess I'll go back to the drawing board and start all over."

"No." I extended a finger toward Hettie's chest. "You'll do no such thing. You're off flower duty."

Ranger X made a sign of the cross.

"And you're not off the hook." I swiveled my finger toward him. "We need to talk, mister."

"Well, I'll leave you two to mingle," Hettie said. "I should be on my way. You're going to take care of that arrest warrant thingy the intern threatened me with, aren't you?"

"There's no arrest warrant." Ranger X sounded exasperated. "I told you that already. But this really is your last warning."

"Perfect," Hettie said. "But I'm gonna tell all my friends I was arrested."

X struggled to maintain his composure as Hettie leaned backward on her heels and popped a wheelie right out of the lounge. I could hear her blading down the hallway, followed by a muffled thump. She hadn't yet learned the art of braking.

"Look, Lily—"

"Did it really eat an intern's face off?" I spun to face Ranger X. "Or was that an exaggeration?"

Ranger X gave a non-committal shift of his weight from one foot to the other. "I got there in plenty of time. It wasn't fatal."

I winced, raised a hand to my forehead, and pinched away the stress. "I knew this wedding was going to be a bear to plan."

"Is that why you're wearing..." Ranger X searched for a word. "That thing?"

My eyes did a vicious roll around my head. "It's because Zin told me you sounded desperate. I thought there was a real emergency, so I threw on the first thing I could find and fought my way out of Wanda's clutches."

"I'm sorry. But I didn't know what to do with your grandmother."

I shook my head. "Well, I suppose I owe you a slight thank you. My dress fitting was not going well. It was a somewhat welcome escape."

"Is *this* dress..." Again, Ranger X hesitated as he scanned my attire and searched for polite vocabulary. "Is it still in the running?"

"No! This is an on-sale bridesmaid's dress," I said. "I had to grab it while sneaking out of Wanda's shop. It was like bootcamp in there. Nothing fit, everything was ugly. Wanda is a... well, she's a witch."

Ranger X softened. For a man of his size and stature, that was no small task. I was average height for a female, and Ranger X stood a solid half-foot taller than me. His shoulders were as broad as most boulders and just as solid, tapering down into a trim waist that boasted a stomach with more abs than I could count.

He wore a suit this afternoon, and I took a moment to appreciate the view. His meticulous attire was offset by the unruliness of his hair—midnight-black locks that flopped over his tanned forehead and hung just above his dark eyes. The combination was startling.

My frustrations were crumbling, and he knew it. All it took was a single look from Ranger X and I could feel the exasperation slipping away.

"Stop doing that," I growled. "I want to be angry."

X gave a soft laugh. "Does this help?"

He crossed the room in two strides. By the time he reached me, his hands were outstretched. Gripping my cheeks in his warm palms, he pulled me toward him and pressed his lips to mine in a hungry kiss. It didn't matter we'd spent last night together, or the night before that, or the one before that. The fire between us seemed only to burn brighter as time wore on.

"On second thought, I think this dress looks cute on you," Ranger X said as we came up for air. His finger toyed lazily with the puffy pink around my biceps. "I like seeing you with a little frill."

"It was the first thing that jumped out at me."

"I can see why."

"And it was cheap," I said with a shrug. "I told Zin to have Wanda to put it on my tab."

"So, you don't mind if it gets ruined?"

I could see Ranger X's mind clicking through various uses for the mountains of chiffon that made up a small solar system around my waist. My neck reddened with heat. To mask the embarrassment, I leaned in for another kiss, which Ranger X took full advantage of by lifting me by the bottom and letting my legs circle around his waist.

"How about a long lunch?" he asked. "I've missed you."

"Since breakfast?"

"It's been a long morning."

"I'm interested."

"Shall we get going?" Ranger X gave a seductive crook of his eyebrow. "Or I suppose my office has a lock on it..."

"*Shit*," interrupted a voice. "I'm so sorry!"

I whipped around at the expletive so fast I heard my neck crack with the effort. Scrambling, I elbowed Ranger X somewhere near the neck and hiked the taffeta down past my bottom as he dropped me to the floor.

A young Ranger stood in the door and bowed his head. "I'm so sorry, sir," he said, not making eye contact. "I didn't mean to interrupt—Elle said I'd find you here, and I hadn't realized..."

"It's fine," I said, even though the Ranger hadn't spoken to me. He had yet to look at my face, but I couldn't say the same for my other body parts. "I was just going to head out, anyway. *Er*, bye. See you at home."

Ranger X reached out, rested his hand on my shoulder and squeezed. "Ranger L, I don't believe you've met my fiancé. This is Lily. Lily, meet Ranger L."

I extended a hand, well aware my cheeks were a furious shade of pink. "Pleasure to meet you. I've heard great things about you."

"You have?" Ranger L asked.

"No," I said. "But I'm very nervous. I'm sure if Ranger X actually talked about work at home, I'd have heard great things."

Ranger L finally cracked a smile. He was an inch shorter than me but sturdily built. He also smiled quicker than most Rangers I'd encountered, and I took an instant liking to him.

"I just wanted to check in with you before I head out for the day," Ranger L said. "I'm off until next week."

"Enjoy your time away."

"Thank you, sir." Ranger L gave a friendly nod in my direction. "Nice to meet you. Congratulations on the engagement."

Once he left, I turned to Ranger X and rested my head against his chest. "I guess the moment is ruined?"

"Not for me." His hand slid to the back of my neck and rubbed in a way that had me melting like gooey chocolate right into him. "The moment's back."

"Except..." I sniffed, pulled back. "You smell a little...funny."

Ranger X coughed. "Things a man loves to hear from his bride."

"I'm sorry, but..." I stifled a gag. "Seriously, what is that?"

Ranger X took a step back, raised his shirt to his nose, and inhaled. His eyes immediately watered as he cursed. "It's the Pollycock Powder."

"I still don't understand."

"Hettie's invention. She registered it in '97. It smells like a sewer system. The pollen gets on you and the stench worsens over time. I'm sorry, I'm going to have to shower—it must have been in her bouquet." He sighed. "Why did you put your grandmother in charge of flowers?"

"I thought it would be harmless!"

"Hettie?"

I shrank. "You have a point. But hey, while you're off cleaning yourself, can I look through the Ranger Archives?"

"What for?"

"I want to find information on my mother," I said. "If she really was an assassin, maybe there will be something in the files that points to her. Or the Core. Or something. I just have to believe there's a way to find out more information about the sheet Liam gave us."

"It requires a special pass to get into the archives."

"How about you get me one of those special passes?"

Ranger X looked at his shoes. "You're not making things easy on me. I'll have to run it through the system—it'll take me a few minutes, and at best I can probably get you an hour on a guest pass."

"I'll take it."

"You'll owe me," Ranger X said. "Are you sure you don't want to pre-pay by joining me for a long lunch in the shower?"

I leaned forward, inhaled, and fell into a coughing fit that sent tears streaming down my face. "Rain check?"

Chapter 3

Ranger X led me to the archives, a sweeping room filled to bursting with texts and maps and papers in neat stacks. Old wooden desks filled the right side of the room like rigid little ducklings standing in line. Behind them, rickety chairs with a layer of dust offered a reprieve from the hours spent roaming the aisles and poring over the endless titles living on the shelves.

After a quick exchange with the grumpy fairy behind the desk, Ranger X secured me temporary access to the archives. I handed over my arm to the fairy in charge who unhappily touched his thumb to my wrist in the same way Elle had earlier, allowing me passage into the restricted area. After our exchange was complete, I leaned in to peck Ranger X on the cheek.

"Best of luck," he said. "I'll see you after?"

I nodded, struggling not to breathe. The Pollycock Powder's scent continued to grow worse by the minute. "Thank you."

"Anything that's not specifically related to your mother—"

"—I never saw it." I plugged my nose and waved him off. "I'll meet you at the bungalow."

Ranger X leaned in for an embrace, thought better of it, and settled for a swift brush of his lips against my forehead. "Please don't get into trouble."

"I'm in a library," I said. "How bad can it be?"

"Archives," the fairy corrected from the desk, his hearing impeccable in the near silent chamber. "You're in the archives. The library is a floor up. Your time has begun, Ms. Locke."

I gave a last look to X. He smiled, gave a cheeky little salute, and then left me alone with one grumpy fairy and millions of manuscripts.

"Files," I murmured to myself. "Where do I start?"

"What are you looking for?" The fairy pushed a pair of glasses further up his nose, clasped his hands together and cracked his fingers. "I might be able to help. My name is Giovanni."

I hesitated, trying to find a way to use his expertise without giving away information about my mother. Liam had given us that file as a strange sort of engagement gift, and I was under the impression that it wasn't meant for the public eye.

"The history of the Rangers," I said. "Initiatives, personnel, really anything. In particular, I'm wondering if there have ever been women involved in the program."

Giovanni frowned. "Your cousin is the first woman Ranger we've ever seen on the island. If you'll recall, a few things changed when you showed up around here."

"Zin getting a spot in the program wasn't because I showed up."

"I'm just saying..." Giovanni waved his arms. "Rules used to mean something. They were strict before you arrived, and now..."

More arm waving. I had a feeling that Giovanni wasn't a huge fan of mine. "I still don't believe the Rangers operated in a vacuum. Look at Elle—she's not a Ranger, but she's instrumental to the program."

Giovanni sighed, adjusted the thick gold chain around his neck. "This way."

I followed the fairy toward an entire wall dedicated to the real heroes of The Isle. The Rangers, the people who'd essentially donated their lives to keep the rest of the islanders safe. People who had given up just about everything to protect their own.

"Personnel," Giovanni explained briefly, tapping a finger against a shelf. "The Rangers will all be listed on this shelf. Other staff members have a wall over here. Each Ranger has a file. You might find a few of them will be locked, but there's nothing I can do about those."

"How do I get them unlocked?"

"You don't," he said. "You're a guest. You're lucky to be here at all. Most of this isn't available to the public eye."

I decided not to press my luck and thanked Giovanni. He obviously didn't care that I was the Mixologist or engaged to Ranger X, which was fair. But my heart was already sinking, wondering if the information I needed would be in one of the locked files I wasn't allowed to touch. Something as essential as my mother's involvement in The Core wouldn't likely be available to the general public.

I bit my lip, reached for the first book, *A History of Rangers*, and began skimming through it. Continuing on, I flipped through one folder after the next, making a snap judgement call on the usefulness of a document's information in seconds. It was possible I'd miss something important by using this method, but with an hour on the clock, I didn't have time to lollygag.

As soon as he'd released me into the archives, Giovanni had flipped over a huge hourglass filled with a shimmering pink sand. Every time I glanced over, the bottom half grew fuller while the top slimmed to dangerous levels.

"Finally," I muttered, locating a gold mine as I found one sheet that listed every Ranger to have ever gone through the program.

To my dismay, however, I quickly realized that there were no real identifying pieces of information. Sure, there were medical terms and specializations, for example, Ranger J had broken his collarbone when he was five and Ranger H had a violent allergy to Pollycock Powder. I wrinkled my nose at the very mention of it and wondered if maybe we weren't all a little allergic to the foul-smelling pollen.

Unfortunately, there weren't any references at all to the Rangers' real names. I scanned the list until I reached the latest additions and found that Zin had been dubbed Ranger Z. In time, I figured, as her title caught on, the general public would slowly forget her real name. In twenty years, only a select few would know her carefully guarded secret, and by the time she was retirement age, she'd be nearly anonymous.

The same went for rest of the Rangers on the list. Without a way to connect the letters to names, I had no way of telling if my mother was mentioned in the list at all—maybe not as a Ranger specifically, but as someone who may have been involved with the program. Frustrated, I shoved the book back onto the shelves.

"I wasn't lying to you," Giovanni said. "There were no women in the Ranger program prior to Z."

"Maybe not, but that doesn't mean I'm giving up."

"If you wouldn't be so stubborn, maybe I could help you."

"Look, I know my grandmother helped with the Ranger program in some way. She has a trophy upstairs," I said, swiping dust from my forehead as I inhaled the distinct scent of old paper. "Where would I find information on her?"

Giovanni's eyes lit with the challenge. "If only you'd said something sooner, I could've spared you the blood, sweat and tears—"

"There are no tears."

"—most of the sweat, I guess," Giovanni corrected.

"No blood."

"Here we go," he said, raising a small fist and giving a knock on a thick book titled *The Women Behind the Rangers*. "I believe this is where you might have some luck."

"What the heck sort of book is this?" I asked, holding it up. "It feels very sexist."

"It's historical."

"Well, it's not necessarily true anymore."

"Then don't look at it," Giovanni said. "I didn't bring it out to have a theological discussion, nor am I interested in having this debate with you."

Scowling, I flipped open the book to a random page near the end, surprised to find my face taking up one entire page. Following the illustration was an article titled "Lily Locke: Mixologist". Beneath it was a list of my qualities, attributes, and skills. Along with my weaknesses.

"I am not indecisive," I muttered to nobody in particular. "And my knowledge of the magical world has increased dramatically over the last year or so. I mean, everyone else my age has had over twenty years head start on me."

Giovanni deflected my glare with the shrug of his shoulders. "I didn't write the article. I'm just the keeper of the facts."

While the part of me that was a glutton for punishment wanted to keep reading the article in all its sordid detail, the logical side of my brain told me that I had to keep moving. The timer kept running whether I was arguing with Giovanni or not, so I wisely shut up and flipped backward to a time period in which my mother had been alive.

"Hettie," I muttered, scanning a finger over my grandmother's section. Not only had she been married to the former Mixologist, but she'd been involved with the Rangers in her own way, as well. Her section was longer than mine and filled with all sorts of misdemeanors and warnings that I tried to memorize and promptly forgot.

In between Hettie's page and mine was a much slimmer list of women—some of them I recognized from my time on The Isle, but most were unfamiliar. Most had been prominent before my time. When I reached the page in the book that should have covered the year of my birth, I paused.

Nothing.

Not even a locked file. The year was scrawled across the top and the rest of the sheet was blank. The next page kicked off the year after and began with a woman named Elizabeth Prowess, a woman who'd fallen in love with a Ranger. A quick scan told me her story had ended in heartbreak when she'd moved away from The Isle and married someone else due to the restrictions on Rangers and relationships during that time.

Before the blank page was a list of attributes for a woman named Mariah Troy. There wasn't much information on her save for height, weight, eye color and the like.

"Giovanni!" I called for the fairy, my voice rising. "There's a blank page here."

"Like I said, I didn't write the book."

"I know, but it doesn't feel right." I hesitated, flipping forward and then back. "As far as I can tell, every other year has an entry."

"Is the file locked?" Giovanni asked. "There will be an illustration of a key at the top."

I shook my head. My confusion must have piqued Giovanni's interest because he flitted over and peered at the book.

"Very curious," he admitted. "There must not have been any women of note this year."

"I just can't believe that's true."

"I didn't mean at *all*," Giovanni said crossly. "I meant within the context of this book."

"Every other year has at least one entry. Most of them have tons."

"Well, there's bound to be a boring year here and there." Giovanni feigned disinterest, but he didn't immediately leave my side to return to the desk, nor did he tear his eyes from the page. "I'm sure it's nothing. Speaking of nothing, time's up. Did you find what you needed?"

"No! Obviously not. Can I have just five more minutes?"

"Rules are rules," Giovanni said. "Ranger X promised me you wouldn't be difficult."

With that, Giovanni closed the book. I dawdled, glancing at the name on the cover beneath the title: Brandon Bates. I filed that name away, along with Ranger H's allergy and Ranger J's broken bone history and my grandmother's list of arrests and warnings.

I wasn't happy to be leaving the archives so quickly, especially not when I sensed there was more to be unraveled. At the same time, I wasn't sure the answers lay in the pages of a book. As somebody smarter and more famous than me had once said, only the victors wrote history.

And it appeared that whoever won the battle had written my mother right out of the book.

Chapter 4

My grudging exit from HQ spit me out on the edge of the woods not all that far from the hut Ranger X called a home. I swung by on my way to the bungalow and let myself inside, calling a greeting to make sure he wasn't running late. When only an echo returned, I locked up and completed the trek home.

I took the quickest route, skirting the scenic path for a seldom-used dirt trail that wound between the sugar-sand beach and the bright pops of color visible from The Twist. The water lapped against the shore beneath a clear blue sky. Gentle, warm rays of sun kissed my shoulders while a light breeze brushed the hair from my face. Another perfect day on The Isle.

I kicked off my sandals and let my toes sink into the sand when the dirt path ended on the beach. The bungalow loomed pink and purple ahead, practically glowing with cottage ambiance. A white porch with peeling paint sat out front, adorned with wicker furniture on the left half and a squeaking swing next to the hammock on the right.

My bare feet padded over the sand-scattered floorboards as I climbed the stairs and let myself in through the front door. I landed in the storeroom, a most glorious space filled with precious vials and beakers, vats and cauldrons, glassware and eye droppers. Inside the containers sat all varieties of herbs and spices—everything from the normal (rosemary, sage, and lavender) to the exotic (dried firebirds, dehydrated mermaid scales, and powdered unicorn horn).

I breathed in the dusty smell of just-burnt wood and noted the smoldering embers in the fireplace despite the beautiful day outside. Gus must have been up early this morning, working by the light from the logs. The scent of coffee mixed with lemon verbena and sugar hovered in the air. I exhaled slowly, content to be back. I loved staying at Ranger X's, but there was nothing more comforting than the potion-laden walls of my own home.

"Can you fix him?" Gus growled. "He's making me nauseous."

I smiled at the old man bent over the table in the center of the room. He had one foot perched on a bench and was squinting into a cauldron no bigger than a coffee cup. "Good morning to you, too."

"It's afternoon, and it ain't a good one," Gus said. "Fix that fiancé of yours. He reeks. I had to restart the fire to try and smoke him out."

With a glance toward the hearth, I found Ranger X standing sullenly before the embers, hands clasped in front of his body as a frown curved his lips downward.

"I feel so very welcome in your home," X said dryly.

"Gus..." I turned toward him.

"Pollycock Powder, huh?" Gus sniffed. "You've got to figure out something to strip the scent."

"He smells..." I paused. Now that I'd taken a moment to actually concentrate on what my senses were experiencing, I caught a whiff of the disgusting powder.

"Yeah," Gus said. "I made coffee and burned your enchanted logs to cover the scent because he refused to wait outside."

"I showered. Twice."

My gaze swiveled to X. "You do stink."

"Unless you can fix me, you're stuck with it."

I sighed. "Give me a few minutes."

Gus stepped back and smugly stared at his handiwork. On the table before him sat several neat little piles of different ingredients. "Thought you might say that."

I studied the stacks for a moment, my brow furrowed in concentration as I mentally flipped through the pages of *The Magic of Mixology*. Gus had forced me to memorize the gigantic book of spells that contained detailed information about every ingredient under the sun, along with the combinations that could make the island implode or dissolve with one wrong Mix.

"No," I said. "I'm not Scent Stripping my fiancé."

Gus shrugged. "Do you have a better option?"

"What does that mean?" Ranger X asked. "It doesn't sound so bad."

"It's not if it works correctly, but the potential side effects are awful. I'm not testing my first attempt at the potion on you."

Gus wrinkled his nose, tapped his cane against the floor. "Suit yourself. I'm evacuating the premises until the stench is gone."

"Do it," X said. "I trust you to make the potion successfully. I can hardly stand myself."

I considered for a moment, then moved closer to the table. My fingers trembled, my heart raced. I distinctly pictured the page in the huge manuscript that stated side effects could include permanent loss of smell, excessive boils, or even death. Then again, most potions listed death as a potential side effect to cover all bases and potential lawsuits.

However, the second I reached the table, my fingers stopped trembling. I sat on the bench and let the familiar sense of calmness wash over me. In a way, I was never happier than I was when sitting in my storeroom preparing to mix a potion. My favorite thing in the world was spending time with Ranger X, and that was the closest I'd ever come to matching the feelings I experienced at the mixing table.

Meeting Ranger X had made me a believer in a little thing called soul mates. Being the Mixologist felt almost the same way. I couldn't shake the sensation that I had been born to be the Mixologist. I belonged here on this island, in this bungalow, learning the craft under

Gus's tutelage. It was the only place on earth where I could sink into something so deeply the rest of the world faded away.

Even spending time with Ranger X felt different; I could feel stressed and angry, nervous and excited, distracted and loving. But there was something entirely absorbing about the art of Mixology. I lost feelings of concern and frustration, let myself be sucked entirely into a portal of concentration.

Before I knew it, my fingers moved between the ingredients Gus had prepared. I knew he was right; this was the best, fastest, and safest way to rid Ranger X of the Pollycock Powder. Even the book had stated that Scent Stripper was a way to combat the pollen's sickening smell. And as nature took over and my hands flitted together, combining lavender with poppy seeds and rose oil with rock sugar, I knew it was right.

"There," I said, brushing my hands against my dress. "It's done. We just have to wait until it boils, and we'll be good to go."

I looked up, blinking at X and Gus when there was no response. I might've been coming out of hibernation for how aware I was of my surroundings. Gus had migrated across the room to the coffee pot and Ranger X stretched his legs by pacing around the room.

"How long was I out?" I asked.

"Twenty-eight minutes." There was a note of lightness to Gus's words. "You beat the recommended preparation time by seven minutes."

I smiled happily. "Felt like it was all of three minutes."

"Not for me." Ranger X scratched at his arms. "It's getting worse. I'm going to kill your grandmother by the time this wedding is over."

Gus grunted in agreement.

"Then we should get married soon to avoid that," I said, pushing the bench back and standing. "I don't think Hettie's planning to go out that easily."

"Apparently not," X muttered, "seeing as she's got an army of flesh-eating plants on her property."

"How's the intern by the way?" I asked. "Will he be okay?"

"He'll live." X looked pained. "How long does it take to boil that thing?"

"Enough time for me to run upstairs and change."

"And here I'd thought you were joining Glinda's fairies," Gus deadpanned. "They wear that sort of thing, don't they?"

I glared at him, holding back a retort as he sized up my bridesmaid dress. I figured the fact that he'd had to stand around and sniff Pollycock Powder for half the afternoon was punishment enough. I'd been so absorbed in my work that I hadn't noticed the smell worsening, but now that I'd been slurped back to the real world and all its glorious details, my stomach churned.

The climb to the second floor was a breath of fresh air for my nostrils. I took my time slipping into a cute white and navy blue dress that felt a bit like a sailor costume. I slid my feet into basic white tennis shoes to round out the outfit and putzed in the bathroom, fiddling with some makeup, until I could hear the lurching sound of a boiling potion below.

I returned downstairs to find Gus had put out the fire beneath the potion and left it to simmer on its own. The two men were staring at the cauldron impatiently as I stepped in front of it. I topped off the Scent Stripper with a few dried and candied violet petals to give it a sweet, floral aftertaste, and bottled it up for Ranger X.

He barely looked at it before he tipped the vial to his lips and swallowed its contents in one gulp.

"You trust your wife," Gus said, sounding impressed. "I don't know that I'd have drunk that without a dummy test first."

I scrunched up my face. "You saw me make it. It felt right."

"*You* know that, but I don't," Gus pointed out. "We're the ones who have to trust your feelings."

I acquiesced his point with a nod and waited impatiently as X returned the vial to the table. His face gave nothing away.

"So?" I prompted.

"It tasted good," he said. "How long does it take to work?"

"Four minutes," I said. "By the time we reach the prison, you'll be clear."

Gus shook his head, his cane thumps growing more agitated with each one. "I don't know why you keep paying that imbecile weekly visits."

"We need to find out information," I said. "From both of them."

"There's got to be another way." Gus's watery eyes stared at me from his wrinkled face. "You're playing right into your father's hands. This is all a game to him."

"He almost died," I said. "But he didn't. Which means his contract still stands, and if there's any hope of us breaking it, we have to keep trying. Whatever it takes."

Gus disagreed with a swish of his head. He picked up the broom and began sweeping. The place was already spotless.

"I'm by her side at all times," X said gently. "Nothing will happen. He's locked up for the foreseeable future. He assaulted the Master of Magic. Nearly killed our Mixologist. There's not a soul on earth who wants to see this man alive outside of his minions."

"Is that right?" Gus asked. "There's nobody else you can think of who might have a vested interest in him?"

The unsaid name hung heavy in the air. *Liam.* Over the past few months, my opinion of the man had vacillated between good and evil a hundred times over. As soon as he'd make a move to help us, we seemed to take two steps back in our fight against The Faction. Even when I trusted his information, that trust wasn't implicit. Not anymore.

"Let's go," I said quietly to Ranger X. "It's time."

Chapter 5

We journeyed to the prison, a secure, mostly-underground facility tucked back from the general public. The worse the offense, the deeper into the earth the cell. My father's location was so deep it bordered the earth's core.

We made the trek through security. It went quickly, both because Ranger X was a recognizable face and because we'd become regulars over the last few weeks. The visits with my father were never productive, but I had to hold out hope. It was all I had.

The elevator came to a screeching stop on a dirt floor that spanned the lowest level of the prison. The mud and soil had compacted to form damp, mostly even ground beneath our feet. Invisible drips of water seeped from behind thick walls while the soft hum of intense magic buzzed in the air around us. To most, it would look like a rough system of tunnels and caves, but I knew better.

There was nothing basic about this prison.

A group of the greatest minds on The Isle and beyond had collaborated to make this place impenetrable. Escape by oneself was impossible. The only way for someone to break free from prison was with the help of an insider. The prison's greatest weakness was also its most dangerous strength.

Rangers stood posted at various intervals. They neither smiled nor acknowledged us as we passed, trained in a rigorous program that dictated they not interact with any visitors, nor with the other guards. There was a chill of intimidation in the air that had tendrils of guilt slithering down my spine despite the fact I'd done nothing wrong.

"I should have left the Pollycock Powder on you," I said as we neared my father's cell. "It might've been a form of torture."

Ranger X gave a smile, but he didn't speak. We were too close. The stress was palpable in the air. He hated these visits as much, if not more than, I did. But I couldn't give them up; in a way, I needed them. Craved them. I was addicted to seeing the man who'd brought so much harm to this world. I might never find the reasons behind the *why*, but I had to try.

"Good afternoon." My father's voice sounded from behind the thick bars glimmering with magic. "I'd invite you to stay for lunch, but we don't have flexibility on our mealtimes here."

I turned the last corner and came face to face with the man who shared my DNA. In a strange way, prison looked good on him. He'd recovered from the serious injuries sustained during our confrontation beneath the Hall of Masters. He was thinner than usual, but his eyes were sharp and his features relaxed. The hint of smug amusement had never quite left his lips.

"Tell me about my mother," I said. "Or we'll leave."

My line of questioning differed slightly with each visit. Sometimes I focused on his goals with The Faction. Other times, I tried to plug into our family history. Still other times I showed up and stood empty handed before him, struggling to understand how he could bring so much misery to his own kin.

"What would you like to know?" Lucian asked easily. "I've told you our history."

"Beyond that," I said. "Why was she killed?"

"You know as well as I do—"

"I do know," I said, reaching forward, flirting with the idea of grabbing the bars of the cage to emphasize my point, but knowing the magic hovering within them would send me sailing back against the wall. "There's more, something you're not telling me. Her death wasn't as simple as I've been told. I found the human convicted of killing her—he didn't do it."

"How can you be certain?"

If I wasn't mistaken, there was a hint of real curiosity in his question. I'd refrained from showing him the cards in my hand, knowing that he was the sort of man who took information and used it as power. But maybe, it was my only option.

"I just know," I said. "And I am beyond certain that he not only didn't kill her, but he doesn't know who did. He did the time for her murder, but the courts convicted the wrong man. She wasn't killed in a mugging. She wasn't even killed by humans. She was murdered by *your* people."

"My people are your people, Lily," he said. "If only you could see that, there wouldn't be so much friction in our relationship."

"I'm not your people. The Faction was behind my mother's death," I said. "I have a document that states my mother—the woman you claimed to have loved—was a target by The Faction."

"That's impossible."

"I have documentation to prove it."

My father shook his head. "Impossible. If anyone would be privy to that information, it would be me. And yet..."

He trailed off, his expression stony. Lucian wasn't the sort of man to show any emotion, so it was difficult to say if he was agitated, genuinely curious, or possibly upset. Or maybe he truly didn't care.

"You don't have to believe me," I said. "But I have a legal document from someone close to you. It has The Faction's markings on it along with my mother's name. The words **TARGET ELIMINATED** are stamped across the top. Sound familiar?"

Lucian watched me through lidded eyes.

"Since you're not inclined to talk, that'll be all for today," I said. "Think about it. I'll return next week to see if you're ready to talk."

"Bring the document."

I stepped back, crossed my arms over my chest. "Not until you annul our contract."

"You know I can't do that."

"Then you'll never know what happened to the woman you loved," I said. "In a way, it's cruel. The very society you've sworn to protect... is the one who ruined your life."

I spun on a heel and hurried down the corridor, around the first corner, tears blurring my eyes as I moved. I had no clue if I was moving in the right direction, and a gentle touch from Ranger X on my elbow told me I wasn't.

X guided me with a tender hand until we reached the janky-looking elevator that appeared to be a cage made from elephant ribs. The designers of the prison hadn't gone out of their way to provide extra comforts in the system.

"You rattled him." Ranger X tugged me to his side as we stepped into the elevator. It began ascending without a command. "The information surprised him. I was wondering when you were going to let him know about Sam."

"He doesn't deserve to know the truth," I said bitterly. "He doesn't deserve to have loved her."

"But he did, and I'm glad for it." Ranger X pulled me fiercely against his chest. "If he's done nothing but awful things for this world, I'm still glad he lived. Without him, there'd be no you."

I shuddered. "Is that supposed to be comforting?"

"It is to me." He pressed his lips against my temple, held me close. "Let's go home."

"No, we have one more visit." I felt shaky, but we had more to do. "Did you get us passes?"

Ranger X nodded as the elevator clanked to its final destination. We exited onto the main level. The specific cart we'd been in was one that went only to the maximum-security cells. We shifted down the hallway and into another elevator. We rode silently until it deposited us at the lower-security cells.

This time we landed seven floors down. The vampire hunter who'd just about killed Poppy in Olympia was being kept on a much friendlier wing. Here, the guards nodded to passersby, and the floors were a clean laminate with deep beige walls along the sides. Everything was earth colored and drab, a sort of soul-sucking monotony to every inch.

As we exited the elevator, I came to a dead stop. "Poppy?"

Poppy was waiting for the cart. Her lips were pursed and she clutched a bag to her chest. She was wearing a pink shade of lipstick I'd never seen on her before, and her usual flowery clothes had been replaced by a demure black dress.

"Lily?" She gaped at me. "X? What are you doing here?"

"Questioning the man who tried to kill you," I said. "He still hasn't admitted the name of the person who ordered the hit against you."

"Because he doesn't know!" Poppy's outburst came swift and sure. "I mean, I came here to ask him the same thing myself."

I stepped from the elevator and felt Ranger X do the same behind me. "How often do you come here?"

"Not often," Poppy said, clearing her throat as she looked me in the eye. "But I'm the one he almost killed. Don't you think I have a right to know why I was his target?"

"Yes, but—"

"Not to mention, the two of you have enough on your plates without worrying about me." Poppy's eyes flashed. "I'm not sitting around until you investigate for me. If there was one vamp hunter after me, there will be more. I'm sick of having to be protected."

I swallowed my response and waited. It seemed she wasn't done.

"I know what you're thinking," Poppy continued, "and you can just say it. I'm a burden to you guys. I know it, you know it—it doesn't hurt my feelings. But don't judge me because I want to take the initiative to help myself."

With that, Poppy huffed by us and stormed into the elevator. She stared at the ceiling until the doors closed and the magical pulley carted her up to the main level.

"Is it just me, or was she acting strange?" I turned to X. "Poppy isn't usually so frazzled. Or upset. Or whatever that was."

"You know me," X said. "Emotions aren't my strong suit."

I let the odd interaction with Poppy slip to the back of my mind as we tramped down the hall toward the vampire hunter. What my normally-bubbly cousin had said was true—if there had been one hunter with a target on Poppy's back, there would be more. And contrary to Poppy's outburst, her safety was not low on my priority list. I planned to dig until I reached the truth.

"Good afternoon," I said briskly, wasting no time as I stepped in front of the vampire hunter's cell. "Are you ready to talk?"

Unlike my father, prison didn't look good on him. He looked gaunt and weak, his hair long and scraggly. His eyes had taken on a wild look, enhanced by the deep purple shadows beneath.

"I've told you everything I know," he rasped. "I don't know what more I can say."

"You expect me to believe your story?" I asked. "You went to an elite vampire hunter school on the mainland. The location switches every three years, so it's impossible for me to verify. You can't name any of your colleagues except by code words, nor can you give me the identity of your boss."

"That's right."

"I suppose it doesn't matter even if I believe your nonsense," I said. "There's no helpful information there, which means I'm not satisfied."

"I told you. I get my jobs delivered to me. I don't know who hires me, only that I get half the payment up front and half after I deliver proof my job is done. It's for their own protection. In case I get caught and captured. Like this."

The frustration rolling off of him seemed real. I doubted truly guilty parties would battle their case so convincingly, but the truth was, he was a vampire hunter. He'd tried to kill my cousin. And if he hadn't fallen in love with her, he would have succeeded.

"Look, I know you care for Poppy," I said. "But it doesn't matter. You'll never be together because of what you each are. The best way to help her, to show you care for her, is to help me stop additional attacks."

"I would if I could!" He flew to his feet, dancing dangerously close to the bars. As he neared the touching point, he flinched, trained to keep back from the magic holding him captive. "The organization is smart. Like the illegal spell-dealers or magic buyers in The Void. People need to remain anonymous to stay alive. It's Criminal 101."

The hunter's mention of The Void, a reference to the magical black market where dark spells were bought and sold and traded, alarmed me. It was a murky sort of place frequented by murderers, high level thieves, and other unsavory types.

"Fine," I said. "See you next week."

"She cares about me, too," he called after me as I turned from the cell. "Of all people, you should know better, Ms. Locke. Even the two most opposite people in the world can make something work. Ask your fiancé."

I kept my shoulders level and my gaze straight ahead, but as the elevator clanked to a stop and we climbed inside, I glanced toward X. "Is he right?"

Ranger X shrugged. "He could be."

"What do you think?"

X dragged his hand across the five o'clock shadow forming over his chin. In his multiple showers earlier in the day, he'd obviously not had time to shave while trying to scrub his skin free of the Pollycock Powder.

"He might not be lying," X said finally.

"About Poppy?"

"I don't think he's lying about that," he said. "And I don't think he's lying about his story, either."

I expelled a breath. "My gut tells me his story is true, too. But it doesn't help with anything. Who put the hit out on Poppy?"

"If he really is a hunter for hire, he might not know that answer." X met my gaze. "It's not ideal, but it might be the truth."

"But there must be more! We can't be facing a dead end. I refuse to sit around and wait until another attack is ordered on her."

"We don't have to sit around and wait, but maybe we're asking the wrong questions. There might be a different way to go about this."

I crooked an eyebrow as the elevator reached the top level. "Which is?"

Ranger X escorted me outside before he answered, taking the time to nod at his colleagues and other familiar faces along the way. Once we reached sunlight, he turned down a gravel path that led back toward the bungalow.

"You won't like it." Ranger X started his explanation in low tones. "If we work out a tracking system and a few other logistics, we could stage a breakout."

"Let him go?" I gaped. "Absolutely not. Even if he's not lying, even if he does care about Poppy, it's too big of a risk."

"I didn't say it wouldn't be risky."

"Poppy could end up dead."

"That could be the end result if we do nothing," Ranger X said, apology hanging in his eyes as he studied me. "We could stage Poppy's death. Let the hunter go, have him submit proof—fake proof—that he killed Poppy and collect his money."

"You want to set a trap." My stomach roiled, sick with the possibility of it going completely, utterly wrong. "I don't know; that's awfully dangerous."

"We can work to make it as straightforward as possible, but like anything, there will always be a risk. I'm not asking you to commit, or even bring this up to Poppy. Just think about it."

I nodded, but I already knew my answer. There was no way anything of the sort was happening. But even as I made the quick decision, I knew there was more to the story. If we successfully completed a mission like the one X had described, we might lose the vampire hunter, but we might catch the mastermind behind it all. And in the meantime, we'd have Poppy hidden, knowing she was safe.

There was a lot to ponder, but I didn't have the chance to express all my warring thoughts because a voice from behind us loudly shouted for Ranger X. On instinct, Ranger X reached for my hand and clasped it in his. We turned to face the newcomer together.

"What is it?" Ranger X carefully watched the man dressed in Ranger attire come to a rigid stop before him. "Why haven't you Commed?"

"It's..." The Ranger hesitated, his face taut with worry. I recognized him as a guard at the prison. "It's too sensitive for the system."

Ranger X's grip on my fingers grew tighter. "You can speak in front of her."

"There's been a murder," the guard said softly. "Ranger L is dead."

THERE WAS A LONE MINUTE of silence that followed the news.

A hundred thousand questions threatened to burst from my lips. How? When? Where? Why? How could a Ranger end up dead? They were some of the toughest men and women on this island and beyond. Was he absolutely certain Ranger L had died?

It was fortunate that I was stunned into speechlessness because the last question was a stupid one. Of course this guard was sure. Otherwise, he wouldn't have left his post to personally track down the head of the Ranger program.

If Ranger X had questions, he didn't show it either. He didn't bother with many words as he studied the guard, and said firmly, "Details."

"He was found on Main Street," the Ranger said. "Ranger N was doing his standard rounds when he Commed in an emergency code to Elle. She told him you were here, so he Commed the prison's private line and got me. He didn't want to spread panic over the main Ranger channel."

Ranger X gave a distinct nod of his head. "Lily—"

"I'm coming with you," I interrupted, before he could finish. "Don't try to tell me otherwise."

Ranger X stiffened, reluctant.

"I'll stay out of your way," I promised. "I won't go near the crime scene, but I'm coming with you."

Ranger X must have decided it wasn't worth arguing over because he gave a succinct nod. His hand had slipped from mine during the announcement, and as he set off following the prison guard, I found myself jogging to keep up.

Once we reached Main Street, it was apparent that something was wrong. Very, very wrong. The first Ranger on the scene had roped off the offending block and was doing his best to keep looky-loos outside of the perimeter.

Under normal circumstances, Main Street was a carnival and a shopping district all in one. It wasn't unusual to find families strolling through the streets at night, waving to familiar store owners and merchants. Street performers flocked to the area with their silver painted faces and balloon twirling tricks. It was a notoriously happy place most days. Not today.

This afternoon, the scene looked eerie, like something out of a film. From somewhere, the smell of sugary sweet cotton candy mixed with death. The tinkling music from an ice cream stand provided a creepy backdrop to the wails of a woman clearly on the verge of hysteria.

Next to the crying woman, a man painted the color of metal, who usually pretended to be a statue, reached a hand out and touched her shoulder. Behind her, the balloon man tried to stifle the animals he'd folded and enchanted with sound effects. In his haste, he dropped one, and a balloon wiener dog let out a howl to join the woman's mournful cries. Another bystander stepped on it, and the pop as the balloon exploded sent the crowd careening into silence.

Ranger X scanned the scene quickly, raised his wrist to his lips, and spoke softly. I imagined he was alerting the rest of the guards to the tragedy, but I was too focused on the hysterical woman and the white sheet draped across a sizeable figure on the ground to listen closely.

"Lily," Ranger X said. "Stay back. We can't have you closer than this—I'm sorry."

I nodded. His command was just fine by me. My stomach was already roiling, and I hadn't even seen the dead body. I generally preferred to interact with the living. This was not my usual territory.

Instead, I edged toward the woman in hysterics. The people initially comforting her backed away some as I approached, so I took the opportunity to extend an arm and let her grab ahold.

"Are you okay?" I asked her. "Did you know this man?"

"He was my boyfriend!" The woman's lip trembled. "I-I loved him! How is he dead? Who did this? What happened?"

"Come on, let's sit down. Let's get you some privacy."

I gently encouraged her to come along with me to a small shop just outside the bounds of the crime scene tape. I elbowed the door open as she clung to my arm, breathing a sigh of relief when we stepped inside. Fortunately, the shopkeeper had left it unlocked in his haste to evacuate.

"There, take a seat." I pulled a chair from the first table I could find and ushered her to sit.

Once she was situated, I moved into the doorway and scanned the crowd for Ranger X. I found him, made eye contact to let him know I was fine. He gave a brief nod to acknowledge my location before returning to his duties next to the body.

"I know I'm a stranger to you," I said, turning to face the woman. "But I'm engaged to Ranger X. My name is Lily Locke, and I was with X when he was notified about your boyfriend. I'm so sorry..."

"Melissa," she filled in with a huge sniff. "I know who you are."

I gave her a sad smile. "I'm sorry we're not meeting under better circumstances. I can't imagine what you're going through. I worry about X every day he has a shift. This is my worst fear."

"You can't imagine!" Melissa's voice came out snappish. "How could you? Your Ranger is out there, alive. *My* Ranger is dead! Shot!"

"Shot? With what?" I asked. Guns weren't a big part of island life. They usually weren't necessary with the amount of magic we had at our fingertips. If someone wanted a person dead, there were easier—and less messy—ways than to use a gun.

"I don't know, I wasn't there." Melissa calmed slightly. She seemed to teeter over peaks and valleys in her emotions, going from angry to scared to frustrated to heart wrenchingly sad. "I mean, I was there, but the whole reason we swung by Main Street was so I could use the restroom."

"So, you didn't see what happened?"

She shook her head. "I was..." She hesitated, squinted toward the windows, and then pointed. "There. The public restrooms. I came out, and he was on the ground. People were shouting."

"Melissa, can you take me a step back and explain everything that led up to your boyfriend's death?"

She gave me a curious look, holding an arm against her nose to prevent it from running. I reached behind her and grabbed a napkin from the counter. We were in a confectionary shop adorned with light pink and baby blue colors, and glass cases displaying perfectly manicured truffles flecked with edible gold and silver shavings.

Melissa took several deep breaths. She was a smallish, pretty woman, her hair a deep brown color that brought out a spattering of freckles across her cheeks. Her eyes were a bright shade of green that offset her darker features, red-rimmed from the onslaught of tears.

"You're not a Ranger," she said finally, "so why are you interviewing me?"

"No, I'm not. But I am trying to help," I said. "I'm sure the Rangers will question you later. I just don't want you to forget anything that might help us catch your boyfriend's murderer. If there was one."

"Don't be ridiculous," she snapped. "He didn't kill himself!"

"Of course not. I'm sorry."

Melissa studied my face, gave a shuddering breath before nodding. "Ranger L and I..." She hesitated. "I suppose we can use his real name now that he's... gone."

I bit my lip, my heart aching for her. I could see the loss in her eyes, the energy draining from her as truth set in that her loved one was not coming back.

"Landon," she said. "We'd talked about getting married, you know. That's why he told me his name."

"I understand."

"We were just out for a walk. He worked a bit this morning but took an early release," she said. "I work at the tea shop just around the corner and had the entire day off."

"You work for Harpin?"

She nodded, and I bit my lip to hide my dismay.

"It's okay, you can say it." She gave a dry laugh. "I am new to the island, so I didn't know the sort of fellow he was before I took a job with him. Just a few hours a week stocking stuff. I'm looking for a full-time gig, but I needed something to tide me over."

"Where are you from?"

"Wicked. The Sixth Borough of New York," she clarified. "I sold specialty broomsticks there, but obviously they're illegal here, so I needed a career change."

"I saw Ranger L at HQ this morning when I was there checking on a situation," I said. "He was just leaving for the day. Did he come straight to your place?"

"Yes. Well, our place. We live together on the northeast corner of The Isle. We had brunch together before deciding to go for a walk."

"How long have you been dating?"

"We met when I was on vacation here. Almost exactly a year ago," she said wistfully, her green eyes staring into the distance as if remembering the exact moment. "We kept in touch, visited one another, and despite the fact I lived in Wicked, we decided we wanted to be in a relationship. We did the exclusive, long-distance thing for about six months. Then we decided we wanted to take things further."

"Were you happy to move here?"

She spread her arms wide, her eyes tearing up as she cracked a smile. "Of course! It's paradise, what's not to love? Sure, I gave up a job there, but it was just a job—dead end and all that. Ranger L—Landon—had a real career. He *was* the job, you know?"

"Oh, I know." I patted her leg, gave a sympathetic smile. "I'm not sure it's possible to be a Ranger and not dedicate your life to the job."

"I knew that if I posed the option for him to move to Wicked instead, he would choose the job over me. I couldn't bear to lose him, which is why I didn't even whisper the words out loud. I knew I'd have to move here, or we wouldn't last."

"So, you moved here, when?"

"About four months ago," she said. "And things have been going well. Better than well, actually. They've been perfect. Magical. What other sort of gooey superlatives would you like me to give? We were in love, Miss Locke. It doesn't get any better than that."

I glanced down at my fingers and twisted my engagement ring. Looking back at her, I shook my head. "No, it doesn't. I'm so sorry for your loss."

"It's not your fault."

"No, but still." I hesitated, trying not to imagine what it would be like to be in Melissa's shoes. "Maybe it's best if we keep going through the events of the day. You and Landon had brunch, decided to go for a walk," I prompted. "Then what?"

"We were thinking of hitting the beach in the afternoon. Obviously, we didn't get that far," Melissa said. "We were strolling on Main Street when I mentioned... I think I said something about wanting a coffee."

I waited for her to continue. She frowned as she searched her memories.

"I think I said I wanted a coffee but had to use the restroom first," she confirmed. "So, I gave him a little peck on the cheek..."

Melissa froze suddenly, her back stiffening as she stared into nothingness again.

"That's the last thing I did," she said. "I gave him a little peck. I mean, I'm glad we weren't fighting or something, but still. It was so routine. I didn't stop to think about it. I don't even know that I looked at him. I'm not sure if he smiled at me, or... if he kissed me back... or anything at all. I didn't even think. And that was the last time I saw him."

"He knew you loved him."

"I sure hope so." Melissa's voice dropped to a whisper as she spun a ring around her pointer finger and cleared her throat. "Anyway, I heard a commotion while I was in the restroom, but I just assumed it was a street artist performing or something. It's really hard to pick cries of terror apart from shouts of joy when you're in an echoing bathroom stall."

I nodded along as she spoke.

"I came out into the sunlight, and I remember feeling disoriented." She glanced over her shoulder, then back toward me. "I didn't realize anything had happened at first, and when I did, it still didn't hit me that it was Landon on the ground. I swear, I looked at him without recognizing him for almost a minute."

"You were in shock."

"To say the least." More tears leaked onto her cheeks. "It looked... the side of his head looked like it had melted. I don't know what happened."

"You said before that he was shot?"

"Yes, magically. He was in the middle of a crowd of people. I have no idea how nobody saw anything."

"Maybe someone did see something," I said. "The Rangers will be turning over every stone, I guarantee it. I'm sure they're out there now cordoning off witnesses and getting testimonies. They'll need to talk to you, too."

She nodded, exhausted. "I figured."

"Melissa, if I can guarantee you one thing," I said, leaning forward and waiting until she met my gaze, "it's that this case is going to be their biggest priority. The Rangers are a family. I can guarantee they're feeling this loss almost as much as you are. Ranger X will feel like he's lost a brother."

The tears came then, shoulder-racking sobs from Melissa, and all I could do was prop her up and let her cry. Even as she rested against me, however, my mind wandered down a snaking alley of possibilities and questions. How had someone killed a Ranger in the center of a packed crowd? What sort of spell or weapon had they used? And what if Landon was only the first victim?

If all Rangers were a target, then X could be next.

Chapter 6

The door to the confectionary burst open. I glanced up, expecting to see X coming to find me and Melissa. Instead, Zin stood in the doorway, her eyes on Melissa.

"I'm so sorry, Melissa," Zin murmured. "I came as soon as the news broke."

"T-thank you."

"Lily, this is yours." Zin quickly shoved the blanket I'd received from The Quilter into my arms before kneeling in front of Melissa. "I hate to dive right into things, but—"

"I know," Melissa interrupted. "You're just doing your job. It's fine—I'll do whatever I can to help."

Zin nodded solemnly. "Did you see anyone you recognized this afternoon? I understand you were walking with Ranger L when everything happened."

"I was in the restroom." Melissa coughed, shivered, and regrouped. "Before that, we'd been walking, but I don't—I'm trying to remember who I might have seen. We were just having a stroll like any couple. I wasn't paying attention, really."

"Anyone familiar?" Zin asked. "Friend, colleague, someone you haven't seen for a while, or someone who you might be close with?"

"We said hi to Ranger H on Main Street," Melissa said. "Then I ran into a girl, a regular at the tea shop—Brenda something or other. We talked for a second. And Arnie, the owner of the hot chocolate stand, stopped us to ask about our weekend plans. But none of that was unusual."

"Thank you, Melissa," Zin said. "We just need to know whatever you can remember."

"How is any of this important?"

"We're not sure what's important yet, so we need to cover our bases. Lily, maybe you can give us some space? I'm going to finish up with the interview and then get Melissa home as soon as possible."

"Of course." I squeezed Melissa's shoulder. "Let me know if there's anything I can do to help."

Melissa rested her hand on mine, a few tears sliding down her cheeks as she gave me a grateful smile before I slipped away. When I closed the door to the shop behind me, I found the ambiance outside had grown even more somber. The crowd had shifted and some new faces were visible over the crime scene tape. I could hear one person being sick off in the distance.

An infusion of Rangers had crashed onto the scene as well, swarming Main Street. The dirt road in front of the shops was scuffed with dust as work boots stomped around the perimeter. Rangers everywhere kept folks back, questioned witnesses, and examined every inch around the crime scene.

Ranger X was surrounded by his colleagues. All faces were stony, lips drawn into thin lines, eyes downcast. When X saw me, he excused himself and stepped away from the crowd.

When he reached my side, he stopped. We watched one another carefully, trying to decide where to begin.

"Melissa's inside," I said finally. "She's devastated. Obviously."

Ranger X jerked his head in a nod, but his movements were so slow they barely qualified as such. "Thank you for stepping in to help. Zin's assigned to her care now."

We broke into silence again as X ran a hand through his hair. He seemed bigger than usual next to me. The black suit he wore from head to toe was too dark against his white shirt suddenly, his eyes too sad, his movements too robotic.

"I'm so sorry," I said, feeling my eyes tear up again. "I know how awful this must be for you. I can't imagine."

Ranger X's gaze turned toward me, and while his face was stoic, his eyes were tender. "We have work to do."

I sniffed, wiped a hand across my eyes. "Sorry."

"Don't apologize." X pulled me gruffly against him and planted a kiss on my forehead. "We'll find who did this."

"What can I do to help?"

Ranger X's hands slid up to my shoulders where he squeezed, pulled me back just far enough to look me in the eyes. "I need you to go home."

"Why? I know I'm not a Ranger, but I could help. With Zin and Melissa, or paperwork, or something."

He gave a brief shake of his head, looked behind him and checked for eyes on us. There were several, so he took my arm and pulled me between the confectionary and the little bookshop next door. Once we were tucked in shadows, he lowered his voice until I could barely make out his words.

"There's one thing I've kept from you about Ranger L," X said carefully. His dark eyes searched mine expectantly. "He was looking into a private case on the side of his regular duties. Something... somewhat personal."

I frowned. "For who?"

"Me."

I digested the information. "Do you think that's what got him killed?"

"I'd hate if it was, but I have to entertain that as a possibility."

"What did you ask him to do?"

Ranger X blew out a breath, his rugged features looking tired and worn as shadows flicked over him despite the sunny day. "He was looking into your mother's history."

The world seemed to shift beneath my feet. "My mom? But..." I trailed off. "You gave him the file from Liam."

"I didn't give Ranger L anything, but I did ask him to look into Delilah." Ranger X's gaze met mine. "I'm sorry I didn't tell you sooner, but I would have let you know the second he found something."

"You're talking about the paperwork Liam gave us," I repeated, still trying to comprehend. "That claimed my mother was an assassin. A target terminated by The Faction."

Ranger X nodded. "I looked into it myself and found nothing, but I didn't have enough time to dedicate to it. I worried I missed something. I trusted Ranger L; I'm positive he kept the information quiet."

I couldn't figure out how to react. A part of me felt betrayed by Ranger X's secrecy. This was my *mother* we were talking about. A woman who had been killed soon after my birth. But another part of me was desperate to know if Ranger L had uncovered anything about her.

"I need to ask a favor of you," Ranger X said. He kept his voice low and soft, but firm. "Go home, stay there for the night. Make sure Gus doesn't leave."

"But—" I started.

"Please."

"What about you?"

Ranger X bit his lip and scratched at the stubble on his jaw. "I won't be home tonight. I... it might be awhile."

"I figured as much."

"We have a crew diving into the investigation this afternoon that will continue through the night. I'm going to stay with them, and I'll check in with you when the morning shift comes on."

I bit back the rest of the words hovering on the edge of my lips and simply bowed my head in agreement. The crowds were growing larger by the second, pressing in on us. Media swarmed at the outskirts, and the buzz of conversation grew to a dull roar.

Before I could think, my hands reached upward of their own accord to grasp at Ranger X's shirt. My fingers twisted in the fabric as I pulled him close. "Be careful," I whispered against his ear. "I love you."

"I love you, too," he murmured, his hand pressed against my hair. "Call me if anything comes up."

I stepped back and watched as Ranger X threaded his way through the crowd, back to the crime scene. Then I glanced over my shoulder to where Zin and Melissa sat with their heads bowed together. Everyone was partnering off and sliding into their designated roles. I felt more out of place than ever.

Shifting my new blanket higher on my shoulders, I turned away from the masses of people and pressed through the wall-to-wall line-up of Rangers all dressed in black. I fought my way to the back of the crowd, busting out my elbows when I reached the layers of media vultures crushing toward the caution tape.

When I finally broke free, I found myself at the bottom of Main Street. I was as far south as the dusty road went before it trailed off into something that could only generously be called a path.

I followed the twists and wound my way around the bottom half of The Isle until I reached the Lower Bridge. My head swam, filled to the brim with thoughts and questions that wouldn't see answers for days, maybe weeks, if ever.

And while I'd promised Ranger X that I would go home and stay put for the night, my brain was already working in overdrive, trying to figure out a way to contribute from the sidelines. I felt helpless.

Fortunately, I'd only promised Ranger X that I'd stay put overnight. Which left tomorrow wide open, and if I played my cards right, I could get cracking at dawn. I was so lost in thought that as I stepped foot on the Lower Bridge, I didn't see the woman in the center of the path, her creaky old knees crossed as she sat happily on the rickety wooden panels.

"Two gifts in one day!" The woman grinned, looking up at me. "I think that must be a record."

On impulse, I stepped to the side as my heart raced.

"You startled me," I said. "What are you doing here?"

The Quilter, as she called herself, wore new attire this afternoon. Her outfit could give Hettie's a run for its money. She wore a knitted skirt with holes as large as my fist draped carelessly over a pair of neon yellow leggings. On top, she had on a chunky pink sweater with tassels dripping from the bottom halfway down to her thighs. On her head was a bright orange scarf wrapped in a bow that flopped down to her ears.

"I knew that blanket would come in useful." The Quilter eyed the gift I had draped over my shoulders. "I'm glad to see you appreciate it. You know, it takes some people a while to warm up to me, believe it or not."

"I do appreciate it, but I don't know how it works or what it does," I admitted. "If anything at all. And I'm sorry to cut this conversation short, but I have to keep moving."

"Don't let me hold you up." The Quilter scrambled nimbly to her feet. "I'll give you your gift and be on my way."

"That's really not necessary. I already have one blanket from you."

"Well, I don't have an option, and neither do you," she said blandly. "Take it, please."

My gaze was drawn toward something in The Quilter's arms. There, yet another blanket had appeared—this one almost miraculously. The gift caught me by surprise.

My heart lurched as I took in the pastel yellow shade, a color so pure that a single glance at it made me think of a giggling child.

The texture looked soft enough to have been fashioned with clouds, sweeter than the most expensive cashmere money could buy. My breathing sped up, my fingers longed to stroke the fabric. I knew, deep down, that it belonged to me. The gift was already mine.

Until I realized with horror that the very gift I so desperately wanted was a baby blanket. No matter how long I stared, no matter how hard I tried to keep from reaching for it, I knew there was a part of me that desired it more than anything. Yet I couldn't keep it. There was no way.

Reality finally kicked in, and I shook my head, my heart thudding in my chest.

"I don't want it." I backed away, waved my hands at her. "Please, take it away."

"It's not a matter of want," The Quilter said patiently. "I'm never wrong. This is meant for you."

"You're mistaken." I took a step to the side, as far away as I could get while entrapped on the narrow bridge.

The Quilter swished closer to me. She extended her arms, placing the blanket mere inches from my nose. Without thinking, my hand stretched forward, my fingers dragging across the gentle fabric. Someone sighed—maybe me. But that didn't stop the terror from piling in my throat.

"I said *no.*" I pushed the blanket further into her arms, trying not to shake the old woman off balance. I side-stepped The Quilter and made a move to pass her, but she was faster.

"It's yours!" she insisted. "My gifts can't be refused, nor can I give them to anyone else. You can't fight fate."

"I can too. I'm telling you I don't want it."

"You might not want it." The Quilter was annoyingly pleasant as she argued with me. "But mark my words, you'll need it."

"No!" I said, and the exasperation leaked out. "Please, don't give me any more gifts."

Without looking back, I picked up the pace until I neared a jog. I cleared the other side of the bridge and cautiously glanced over my shoulder, relieved to find The Quilter standing where I'd left her. She looked incredibly content as she ran her fingers gently over the blanket and hummed to herself.

I continued my journey home. By the time I reached the bungalow, it felt like I'd run a marathon. I was breathing heavily as I swept through the door and tossed the first blanket on a chair by the fireplace.

"You sound like you're dyin'," Gus said from where he sat at the long table in the center of the storeroom. "Who's chasing you?"

"Have you heard of The Quilter?"

Gus didn't look up, but his eyebrow raised. "She gave you a gift?"

"She did, then tried to give me a second. I refused."

Gus snorted a laugh. "Good luck with that."

"What's that supposed to mean?" I snapped. "If I don't want a gift, I shouldn't have to take it. It's my choice."

"Your loss." Gus said. "If you want my advice, don't think of it as a gift, think of it as a blessing."

"Since when did you turn all soft and gooey and *woo-woo*?" I grumbled, inching closer to the table. "I liked crusty old Gus better."

"I'm as hostile as ever." Gus peered at me, giving me a look that meant he was serious. "But when that woman gives you something, you'll need it. Mark my words."

"She said the same exact thing, but I don't believe it. I don't *want* to need it."

Gus sat back, crossed his arms over his chest. "Look, I don't know what she tried to give you. Frankly, I don't want to know. I'm not interested in any of your personal drama."

"I know. You've made that plenty clear."

"Good. Then I'll leave you with one last thought on The Quilter. Her gift *might not be* what it appears on the outside. It might not even be meant for you. Or maybe it's not what you assume it's for. You could merely be a conduit to the gift's final destination."

"What sort of nonsense is that?"

"Think about it," he said. "That's all I've got to say on the matter."

"A Ranger died today." The words came out suddenly. They just fell out of me, floated into space like they were too much to keep inside.

Silence descended over the room, and this time all the sarcasm drained out of Gus's voice, leaving behind something I could only describe as reverence. "Were you there when it happened?"

"I didn't see it. Ranger X and I were just leaving the prison when we got the news. We arrived at the crime scene shortly after, and I met the dead Ranger's girlfriend."

"Melissa," Gus said, in understanding. As usual, he was three steps ahead of me.

I swallowed before responding. "I sat next to her and all I could think about was—"

"Don't say it," Gus said. "It's not you. It's not Ranger X on the ground. He's fine, and so are you."

My hands gripped the table before us. "I know, but they're both Rangers. It could've been X just as easily as it was Landon."

"But it *wasn't*," Gus pointed out again. He turned his attention back to the various herbs and spices and potion ingredients on the table before him. "Don't play the what-if game because it's not going to get you anywhere."

"If something did happen to him, where would that leave me?" I pressed, not willing to give up so easily. "How could I go on?"

Gus smacked a knife against the table, slicing a heart of palm in half. "I'm guessing you want comforting words and mumbo jumbo. You want me to tell you that it's never gonna happen to X."

"Not exactly."

"You've come to the wrong guy for sympathy. It wasn't Ranger X who died, and I know you don't want to hear it, but if it had been him, you would've figured out a way to go on."

I crossed my arms over my chest. Gus looked up at me unapologetically.

"You didn't come to me for comfort," he said softly. "If you wanted that, you would've gone to your Aunt Mimsey. You only come to me when you want the hard truth."

I let go of the table and felt my fingers form fists. "Actually, I came to you because I promised Ranger X I'd come straight home and stay here for the rest of the night."

"You didn't have to talk to me though," Gus said. "We work in silence just fine. So, if you want my help, then tell me what you're asking. Otherwise, I'd prefer we go back to that silence thing I love so much. I've got a potion due by midnight if you want to fill your orders for tomorrow, so I suggest you let me get to it unless you want to fall behind."

Gus was logical and infuriating, and both of those traits made me feel like banging my head against the wall, but I knew he had a point. I hadn't come to him for sympathy, but I did need to talk.

"Who would've done something like that?" I mused, slinking into a chair opposite Gus. His lack of eye contact and busy hands made it easier to hold a difficult conversation. "Who goes after a Ranger in a public place, in the middle of a sunny day, while his girlfriend steps away to use the restroom? And why? What message were they trying to send?"

"I assure you every single Ranger is asking themselves that very thing."

"I know, but it just doesn't make sense. If someone was trying to make a statement, it wasn't very clear."

"It could get clear real fast if the killer's not caught," Gus said, "which is why I'm sure Ranger X and everyone else will be working all through the night. And so will I. As soon as I'm done with this, we've got another to get started on. Ranger X put in a request for a potion that's due by eight a.m."

I narrowed my eyes at Gus. "You know he just wants you to babysit me. He doesn't need the potion."

"I know," Gus said with a thin smile. "But since you're imprisoned here with me anyway, I propose we don't sulk all night. Go upstairs, shower, and when you've got your head on straight, we'll get ahead on tomorrow's orders because I imagine once your prison sentence comes up at dawn, you'll be flying out those doors."

I couldn't help but smile.

"I'll shower later," I said, grabbing a seat at the table. "You've got me until daybreak. Where should I start?"

Chapter 7

G us and I worked hard through the night. We kept ourselves busy as the fire roared high, continuing to tinker with potions and charms and spells until the flames burned themselves down to red hot embers.

By the time graying wood cracked and smoked above the orange glow, the storeroom table sat littered with dried chamomile, newt's tail, and the freshest hair plucked from a unicorn's tail (free range and cage free) this side of the equator. Over the mess of ingredients, Gus had perched six golden stands, each rising to eye level.

Each stand bore an individual flame in varying colors: yellow, green, blue, orange, red and purple. Above the fires sat vials and cauldrons of all shapes and sizes, filled with potions of all different shades and tints. Each mixture varied in density and smell and boiling point. They all gurgled and burped happily in the cozy little bungalow as the sky settled into darkness around us.

Sometime after the moon began its descent, I curled up on the couch, the lingering warmth from the fire licking at my feet, and drifted to sleep with the smell of lavender, lemon verbena and smoky wood drifting over me. A light soundtrack of potions bubbling worked in symphony with Gus as he tottered about the storeroom, clinking stir sticks against vials and scraping his chair forward and back, forward and back.

I slept fitfully, waking and drifting off as often as Gus shuffled between the cauldrons. I couldn't shake the nightmares of the white sheet draped over the fallen Ranger, or the somber expression on everyone's face as they stood around and realized what had happened.

Worst of all were the cries of Melissa and the anguish in her eyes. They woke me over and over again.

I rose shortly after the sun and wiped sleep from my eyes as I perked up and glanced around the storeroom. Magically, Gus looked as grumpy as ever, sitting in the same spot as when I'd fallen asleep, carefully bottling the last of the potions.

"Store isn't opening till noon today," he said gruffly. "Sign's out front. I'll handle the first few hours, but we'll need you around to close up shop late this afternoon."

I took that as my cue to get a move on. I ran upstairs, jumped in the shower, and made quick work of getting dressed. By the time I skidded back to the table, I had a plan for the day.

But my plan fizzled as a very obvious realization hit me.

"Crap," I said to Gus, rolling up the sleeves to my knitted sweater as I stopped in the storeroom. "I'm not a Ranger."

Gus glanced over at me. "How hard did you hit your head in the shower?"

"No, I mean, I was planning to try and help the Rangers find out who killed Landon today," I said. "But I don't have any right to go around asking questions of the victim's loved ones. Nor do I have any insider information as to what really happened."

"That's never stopped you before. Don't you have a cousin who's a Ranger? What about your fiancé?"

"Right. Thanks," I gasped breathlessly. "See you."

I wasn't sure, but I thought there was a good chance I'd gotten a smile out of Gus as I raced out the door. I didn't have time to check, however, because my brain was whirling in an attempt to figure out the best way to donate my time to the case. I might not be a Ranger, but I wasn't completely useless.

I immediately dismissed Gus's suggestion of going to Ranger X. He would be busy enough as the head of the program. He was in charge, and he'd likely be in high demand organizing folks, sharing instructions, and piecing together the information filtering back to him. The last thing he needed was a nosy fiancé begging for scraps of information.

Instead, I turned my attention to Zin. There was a chance I could get her to help me, but she wouldn't do it out of the kindness of her heart. If I wanted Zin's assistance, I needed to bring something to the table.

My feet carried me over the sandy beach in front of the bungalow as I turned north and headed toward The Forest. The morning had dawned cooler than I'd expected, and I was grateful I'd layered an over-sized knit sweater on top of my tank top.

As I headed north of the bungalow, I chose to take winding roads through the western half of The Isle instead of the main drag. Even so, my stealthy route didn't fool the one woman I was trying to avoid.

"It doesn't pay to hide from me, you know." The Quilter's voice rang out over the dewy grass. "Good morning, Lily."

I whirled around and found her leaning against a sunflower stalk that was nearly two stories high and as thick as my thigh. It was on the border of The Twist, the labyrinth outside of my grandmother's house that deterred unwelcome visitors.

"I see you like your gift," she said. "I'm quite pleased with that one. Not to toot my own horn, or anything."

I glanced back at her warily. "What gift are you talking about?"

"Where do you think you got that sweater?" She giggled, and it sounded like a young girl's laugh. It was jarring coming from a woman who had frizzy gray hair and a sunflower dress that buttoned down to her ankles. "I know *you* didn't make it. No offense."

I glanced down at my attire. "You didn't give this to me. I have a self-populating closet. And, no offense to *you*, but quilting and knitting are not the same thing."

"I'm a woman of many talents." She laughed again, her eyes crinkling. "I'm just glad you found it. What's important is that you've realized there's a need for my gifts."

"You tricked me." My voice came out accusatory. "I wouldn't exactly say I've accepted your gifts."

I considered tugging off the sweater and throwing it back to her, but I refrained for two reasons. The first, because it was actually quite cold, and the sweater was the only thing keeping me from turning around and running back to change clothes. Time was of the essence this morning. The second reason was that it really was comfortable.

"You'll come around, don't worry," she encouraged. "When the time is right, you'll know."

"Where is it?" I glanced behind me first, then toward The Quilter as I scanned her from head to toe. "If you're trying to trick me into taking that baby blanket, it won't work. I won't accept it. I'll bury it or throw it in the lake. I'm sorry if I sound rude, but I cannot accept that gift. It's nothing to do with you, I promise. It's me."

"Well, not exactly," she corrected. "It *is* me a little bit, seeing as I'm the one giving you the gift, but I can see you're not ready for it. No worries. I will be back, and next time, I suggest you don't refuse."

I blinked, and she was gone. The only clue to her disappearance was the slight wavering of the sunflower petals a good ten feet above my head.

Trying not to panic, I pushed all thoughts of The Quilter out of my head as I hurried into The Forest and prayed that Elle had worked her magic and had an opening waiting for me. Fortunately, she did. There was a reason the Rangers had kept her around for centuries.

"Good morning, sunshine." Elle smiled politely as I approached the front desk. "I should let you know, we've banned all flower deliveries until after you're good and married."

I groaned. "I don't blame you."

Elle laughed, but it didn't reach her eyes. Despite her show of bravado, she was feeling the ache of the lost Ranger as well.

"I'm sorry," she said eventually. "I-I'm not myself this morning. It's difficult."

"I understand. I wish there was more I could do to help."

Elle's lips quirked up in a flimsy attempt for a smile. "Am I right to assume that's the reason you're here?"

"You wouldn't be wrong."

"You know none of this can be on the record." Elle quickly scanned the lobby to make sure we were alone. In the hush of the early morning hour, and considering the events of the previous evening, Ranger HQ was eerily quiet.

"I don't mean to put you in a tough spot," I murmured, "so if you're uncomfortable with my asking, feel free to tell me to leave. I swear I won't be offended."

Elle bit her lip, somehow not smudging the perfect red lipstick that decorated her face.

I sensed there was an opening for me to plead my case, so I took it. "I'm just here because, well... yesterday, I sat with Melissa. I saw how hard this was for the Rangers. And what's more, the island is in jeopardy. If someone can get away with murder on Main Street, what's next?"

Elle simply watched me.

"I promise not to interfere with anything." I paused. "Frankly, I can't even tell you why I feel compelled to be here asking for your help. All the Rangers are much smarter than me and they're already on the case."

"Because you care," Elle said, "and you know what it's like. If you promise to keep this information quiet and leave my name out of it, then I'll do what I can to help you. And you must promise not to upset Ranger L's loved ones."

"That's the last thing I want to do."

"If I were to suggest a theoretical place to start digging," Elle said lightly, "I would gently push you toward his personal side."

I frowned. "I was under the impression he was well liked. Ranger X always had good things to say about L's work. He trusted him."

"Ranger L was a good man," she said. "That's why the Rangers will be focusing on his work obligations. The rumor is that he was involved in something top secret, possibly even a favor to Ranger X."

She watched my face carefully, and I tried my best not to give away anything. I knew people wondered how much Ranger X shared with me about his work life and how much he kept private. In truth, I wasn't exactly sure.

I *did* know there was a world, an entire universe, of Ranger X that existed beneath the man I knew and loved. There was a giant part of him that I would never be allowed to know, and that was something I had needed to understand before we agreed to an eternity together.

"I don't pry into X's business," I said in explanation to Elle, then gave her a quick smile. "Er—not usually. This is an exception."

She gave a dainty laugh. "Well, as I mentioned, I think you'd do the most help by examining L's private life. Frankly, most Rangers are men. They focus on the facts more than the emotions, and a woman's touch is sometimes just what it takes to see a thread of discord and tug on it."

I listened, nodded.

"It sounds like you have already met Melissa," she continued. "I'd suggest another visit to her once she's had some time to rest. See if she's remembered anything else helpful. Maybe a quick visit to Landon's family in the meantime to get a feel for their thoughts on Melissa. See what Melissa thinks of his family. Did Landon have friends? A partner? A side job?"

Elle had obviously picked up a lot in her time at Ranger headquarters, and she was a wealth of tips and information.

"I just need two addresses, please," I said. "One for Landon's family, and one for Melissa."

She pursed her lips. "I imagine you've worked out a way to introduce yourself so that they'll let you through the door?"

"I'm working on that part," I admitted. "By the way, any chance you can help me out with Zin's location?"

Elle's fingers were already tapping away. "I thought you might be going that route, and as a matter of fact, today's your lucky day. Ranger Z is over on Main Street, canvassing door-to-door in an effort to dig up any leads from the shop owners. It's a lot of time and effort, but all it takes is one tip... something someone didn't even know they saw..."

Elle sighed, and the sound was filled with exhaustion. I'd never seen her look tired before, but this morning she seemed to be wilting.

"I know it's a long shot," I said, "but I'll do everything I can to help. I promise."

"I know you will, Lily," she said, giving me a flickering smile. "But just remember, he's already gone. Take care of yourself, okay? Please... be safe."

Chapter 8

I swung back over the Lower Bridge, treading carefully as I crossed. I couldn't shake the eerie sensation that The Quilter seemed to know me better than I knew myself. I picked at the sweater, still unable to take it off despite my growing frustration with her.

The piece of clothing was annoyingly perfect. It was soft and fit gently over my shoulders and hung loose around the waist. I genuinely liked it, which only made my frustration burn stronger.

If, as Gus had said, The Quilter's gifts were always needed, then what did the baby blanket mean? I supposed maybe it was a gift for someone else, and it was my job to get it to them. Or there was the possibility that I'd entirely misinterpreted the meaning of the gift and it wasn't for a child at all.

Still, I couldn't get over the feeling that it meant something for me. Between my impending wedding with Ranger X and the magically bound contract with my father, there was too much risk to assume it meant anything other than the obvious—which I was trying everything in my power to avoid.

"Good morning," a voice chirped. "Where are you off to so early?"

Poppy strode next to me dressed in a bright orange skirt with a thin white tank top, her summery look completed with a huge floppy hat.

"You look like you saw a ghost," she said when I gave her a startled blink of surprise. "Who were you expecting to see?"

"Not you." I raised an eyebrow. "You aren't usually out and about at this hour."

"Some days I am," she said cryptically. "Anyway, where are you off to? Need some company?"

"Actually—"

Poppy's eyes glinted as she looked at me. "Up to no good? I like it."

"You can't tell anyone."

"Fine."

I narrowed my eyes at her so she knew I was serious. When I got a scrunched-up face in return, I sighed. "I was going to ask some questions this morning. I assume you heard about Ranger L?"

Poppy's face immediately fell. "Yes. I wasn't working, but I heard the emergency Comm go through when they asked for all hands on deck. It's just awful."

"Have you heard any chatter about what might be happening? Who would have done something like this, or why?"

She shook her head. "I'm not exactly in the loop. Zin would know better, but she's not sharing. And I'm sure she's busy. Those guys are barely going to eat or sleep until they catch the killer."

"Yeah, I figured. That's why I'm trying to help."

Poppy considered. "If you want my opinion, it's a bad idea to get involved."

"Maybe. But the longer the killer is allowed to roam free, the more dangerous it is for everyone."

"I can see I won't change your mind." Poppy shrugged. "So, I guess I'll help you. Why don't we start with Ranger H? I just left him with a drink."

"What?"

"Ranger L's partner," she said impatiently. "You really have to up your research if you want to play detective. This is basic level stuff, girlfriend."

I crooked an eyebrow. "Or maybe my plan was to find you this whole time."

"Machiavellian," she whispered. "I love it. Let's go—he's at The Black Cat."

The Black Cat was a bar and restaurant that had long since forgotten about the restaurant half of its name. It was located along the eastern edge of the island. I hadn't heard of the place, let alone stepped foot inside, and I soon discovered why.

The bar itself was actually a cave roughly carved into the side of a rock wall by some magical explosive that hadn't involved finesse. In order to even see the entrance, I had to shimmy down a chunky flight of stairs that were basically jagged rocks someone had piled up with a hefty bit of Moving Magic. More than half of them wobbled, and one lost half its girth the moment I put my full weight on it.

"That's part of the appeal to this place," Poppy explained at the look of horror on my face. "It's pretty dangerous to even get inside. Then again, if you're coming to The Black Cat, you're probably not all that worried about getting out alive."

I was sweating, crawling on my butt and holding onto the sides of the rock wall while concentrating with every last ounce of strength. "How are people supposed to climb these stairs if they've had a pint too much to drink?"

"They're not," she said simply.

"How many calls do the Rangers get each year to come and collect a body at The Black Cat?"

Poppy went silent, and I was sincerely worried that she'd begun counting on her fingers and toes.

"Don't answer that," I muttered. "Are we almost there?"

"Just slide down this last part," Poppy encouraged. "There's a little jump at the bottom, and the third board on the deck is loose."

"How does this place pass any inspections?" I grumbled as the third board moaned under my heel when a tiny centimeter of my shoe landed on it.

"Because the inspectors are too afraid to come down here," Poppy said. "It only took Barty Knucklebaum, the inspector two decades ago, to die. Since then, the rest have just passed this place with flying colors."

"Ah," I said.

By the time Poppy gestured to what appeared to be a door, I was suffering from extreme fatigue. It was no wonder people needed a drink when they arrived.

I gritted my teeth as Poppy pushed the door open and ducked into the cave. I followed her, my head brushing against the ceiling even after bending low. Arriving safely inside was truly a feat of athletic ability.

The Black Cat's ambiance fit its name well. Mostly, it was all black. The whole *cat* part of the name didn't seem to have any bearing on the place at all except that it looked like a whole lot of bad luck heaped into one spot.

Everything was made from stone, or at least what I could see of it. A long bar sat along the right wall with a grizzled, one-eyed bartender standing behind it. His good eye swiveled toward us. He took us in with a huff. We clearly didn't belong. I *hoped* we didn't belong.

I followed Poppy through the bar, ignoring the squelches and squishes that sounded as I lifted my feet off the ground. I gave up trying to watch where I stepped because it was better to just not know what was down there.

I could feel eyes sizing us up, but I couldn't make out any one particular patron. My eyes hadn't entirely transitioned to the near blackness—the only light was a single torch flickering behind a hunk of rock on the counter that I assumed acted as some sort of a cash register.

Despite her rainbow style and frolicking pace, Poppy moved through the bar like she was in charge of it. I did more of a slinky sort of thing and hoped the eyes shifting behind hooded cloaks and shadowy tables were drawn to Poppy's orange skirt and not my stupid knitted sweater.

"Hey," Poppy said softly. "I have a friend here who wants to talk to you. Lily?"

I was completely unprepared for the introduction. My sandal stuck at that moment in something gunky on the floor, jolting me backward as I reached a hand toward the figure sitting on a bar stool. Calling it a seat would be too generous a word, seeing as the stools before the counter looked like naturally appearing stalagmites rising from the ground. The one in front of me had a point on top that would make sitting a very uncomfortable experience.

"I'm so sorry to show up like this," I said, my voice echoing around the dim cavern. I felt like I was on stage and someone had wired me with a mic. "Especially during this difficult time."

Ranger H looked to me, his eyes bleary. He'd obviously been at the bar for a few hours, and the smoking blue drink before him was clearly not his first. As I watched, he crooked a finger, and a bottle of alcohol floated across the room and poured itself into his glass.

"I understand you were partners with Ranger L?" I asked. "Actually, I should take a step back. My name is Lily Locke, and I'm here—"

"I know who you are." The Ranger's voice was low and smoky, steadier than I'd expected from the glassy look in his eyes. "Let me guess, you're just trying to help?"

"Actually, yes."

"Forget it," he said. "If a whole team of Rangers can't find out what happened, neither can you."

"I'm well aware the probability of me turning over useful information is very low, but—"

"Snap out of it," Poppy said, her voice soft, but firm. "I know this is awful for you, H. But it's awful for everyone else, too. We all lost a brother last night. Yes, you were closer to him than us, but we're all feeling the pain. Nobody minds you sitting this one out—we all support it. But hell, don't get upset because someone is trying to assist."

Ranger H wobbled a bit, leaned his arm forward on the bar, and studied me more intently. "What do you want from me?"

"I'm just asking a few questions, looking into Ranger L's personal life," I said. "You can trust that I'll keep everything I find quiet, aside from sharing relevant information with the appropriate authorities."

"Why should I trust you?"

"Because I've had secrets dragged through the media before," I retorted. "I hate it more than anyone. If you've ever picked up a copy of *The Wicked Weekly*, you'd know that."

Ranger H swirled his glass. "L was involved in a tough case. Everyone expects that's what did him in."

"I heard about that," I said vaguely. "But I figure the Rangers are more adept to cover that aspect. I'm more interested in his relationships. Who was he close with? Did he have enemies? What was his family like, his girlfriend, his private life?"

"In case you haven't heard," H said roughly, "we were colleagues, not lovers. I didn't ask about his personal life, and he didn't ask about mine."

"You can't tell me that two people who were so close, who spent so much time together and trusted one another with their lives, weren't a little bit in tune with each other." I leaned one elbow on the huge stone slab and waved off the approaching bartender as he extended a glass toward me. "If I have a bad day at home, sometimes it trails in to work."

"We're not allowed to bring personal lives onto the job." Ranger H raised his eyebrows. "I thought you'd know that."

"Tell me about his girlfriend."

"Melissa? She's..." H shrugged. "Fine. He seemed happy when they first got together. He was ecstatic when she let him know she'd be moving to The Isle. Did I hang out with her? No, not all that much."

"Are you in a relationship?"

Ranger H made a low noise of disapproval in his throat. "What does that matter?"

"I'm just wondering if he held back talking to you. Maybe he worried you'd be jealous about his having a relationship while you were single."

"I wasn't jealous."

I'd hit a roadblock with that line of questioning, so I turned toward another avenue. "His family. Did he ever talk about them?"

"He's got one sister and two parents," H said sarcastically. "That makes a family, and it's all I know."

"Is he close with them? Did he see them often?"

"More than most of us," Ranger H said, and finally, I'd reached a fissure in his exterior armor. "They did Sunday dinners together."

"He was doing them right up until he died?"

"Standing commitment," H said, probably parroting what L had told him. "And I only know that because knowing one another's schedules is part of the job. You've come to the wrong guy if you want to pry into his personal life."

"What other sorts of commitments did he have?"

"Why am I talking to her?" H glanced at Poppy. "Remind me."

Most Rangers were familiar with Poppy, probably trusted her more than someone they'd never met, like me. She worked dispatch for Ranger HQ in between shifts at Mimsey and Trinket's supply store.

"Because she's trying to help your drunk rear end," Poppy said. "The Rangers gave you the night to wallow, but guess what? It's morning. Snap out of it and get with the program. Landon needs your help."

"Now he's Landon, huh?" H shook his head. "His work has ended."

The words slid across the smooth silence in the room and had a sobering effect on the bar as a whole. The sentiment definitely rattled H's cage. He bowed his head, lost for words.

"I think he was involved in something," H finally said, his voice on the brink of cracking. "Something that was either a private mission for someone big, or an off-the-record gig."

"What makes you say that?" I shifted in my seat. "Who is someone big?"

Ranger H stifled a caustic laugh. "I'm surprised you haven't heard more about this mission, considering the only person who might have given it to L—and got his vow of silence—would be X."

I swallowed. "Why do you say that?"

"Contrary to what I said about our personal lives, we did discuss the job. Every aspect of it." Ranger H dragged his hand over his jaw. It looked dark and bruised in the torchlight. "We told one another everything: no secret too big, none too small. We had to trust each other with our lives. He trusted me with his..."

"It's not your fault," I said. "Nobody blames you for what happened."

"It doesn't matter what anyone else thinks; it matters what I think."

"What makes you believe you could have helped him?"

"I knew he was into something; I just figured it was for X. So, I didn't press as hard as I should have. Maybe if I had..."

"If he said it was private," Poppy said, "it was private. That is part of being a Ranger and trusting your colleagues or partners. If he had orders from X—or anyone—that were meant to be quiet, he was doing his job by keeping quiet."

"A partnership goes beyond the job," he said. "If I'd been in his shoes, I would've at least given a head nod to what I was working on. I know that's not what I should be saying, but it's true. That's how much I trusted L—I would've tipped my hat, let him know I had some business for X and would fill him in when I could."

"You got none of that?" I asked. "Yet you trusted him implicitly?"

He nodded.

"Could he have been hiding something?"

"You're talking about an off the books job," he said. "Something he shouldn't have been doing—at least not on company time. Something that *wasn't* for X?"

I raised one shoulder in a shrug. "I think we need to examine the possibility."

"I bet you can confirm for me." Ranger H looked at me with darkened eyes. "I'm sure you and your sweetheart share private tips about the job."

"H..." Poppy warned. "Watch yourself."

"I'm just saying." He threw his hands up. "She's questioning me, but if X was giving orders, I didn't know anything about it. She'd know better than me."

"H!" Poppy's command was sharp. "Stop it. You're accusing the Mixologist and Ranger X's fiancée of things when all she's trying to do is help your partner."

A flicker of remorse passed over Ranger H's face, but it wasn't strong enough to prompt an apology.

"He's not wrong," I murmured. Lowering my voice even further, I glanced over my shoulders to ensure no one else was listening, but that was impossible to say in the complete blackness. "There was a mission."

Ranger H raised his glass, took a deep swig, as if that proved his point entirely. Poppy just gaped at me, and her surprise had me hoping I knew what I was doing. Otherwise, it could come back to bite me.

"But before you gloat, you should know that I had no clue about it until after his death," I said to H. "I didn't know who Ranger L was until I ran into him at HQ the morning he died. We crossed paths—that's it."

Ranger H smirked. "Right."

"I'm telling the truth. Yesterday, after L was found dead, Ranger X informed me that he'd had L looking into one particular person."

"And he told you this because you're an important part of the Ranger program," H said dryly. "And you should be involved in an investigation."

"He told me because it involved me." It was difficult to let H's caustic attitude roll off me, but I knew he was only speaking from a place of hurt. I was the easy target, and he was lashing out. "He told me only the most basic of information before he sent me home for the night, thinking I might be in danger."

The gap between Poppy's lips had grown wider and wider as my story unfolded. By the time I finished, she had to pick her jaw up from the bar.

"That's all I know," I finished. "I swear. I don't know anything more about the case or what L found—if anything. As L's partner, I figured you deserved to know, too. He was on a mission for X, and it was something very sensitive. That's why he couldn't talk to you about it."

Ranger H didn't look all that convinced by anything I'd said. "So that's why he had those weekends away?"

"I told you, I don't know anything more. I just know he was looking into something."

"The covert meetings in the woods," H said with a dry laugh. "I thought that was all stuff of fiction. I didn't know Ranger X would operate that way."

I shrugged. "I'm not sure, but I guess he thought the situation called for it."

Ranger H flicked his wrist, brushing his hand nonchalantly through the air in a wave of dismissal. "Apparently you know more than I do. I've nothing to add."

"That's not true," I said. "The rest of the Rangers need your help."

"You can't sit here and wallow forever," Poppy said. "Lily's right. This wasn't your fault. It hurts to lose a brother, a friend. But we will mourn him later, once we catch the bastard who did this to him."

I thought Poppy's pep talk was quite rousing, but it seemed to have the opposite effect on the Ranger. H slumped forward, his arms crossed in front of his face. I couldn't tell if the man had passed out in a dead faint, or if he merely wanted us gone.

After a moment, Poppy gave a disappointed shake of her head, then pushed herself away from the counter. I carefully untangled myself from the awkwardly shaped bar stools and followed her across the treacherous floor toward the front door.

My Comm started buzzing halfway across the squelchy mess, and I silenced it until we reached the sunlight. Closing the door solidly behind me, I returned the Comm and heard Ranger X's exhausted voice wash over the line.

"Lily, where are you?"

I glanced upward, saw the sunlight, the waves crashing against the shore. The tide must have risen because the water lapped over my sandals. "Outside."

"Forgot to mention," Poppy whispered, "when the tide's high, it's almost impossible to get in here."

"Right," Ranger X said. "Who are you with?"

"Poppy," I said, as she waved her hands wildly to silence me. "Sorry," I mouthed to her.

"Doing?"

I exhaled for quite some time as I prepared a fitting tale, but finally, I opted for the only story that would make sense. "I'm at The Black Cat. It's my fault, not Poppy's. We just talked to Ranger H."

"I thought I asked you to stay at home."

"You told me to wait the night out," I said. "So I did. I left at dawn."

I could hear the groan slip audibly over the Comm line. "What did H have to say?"

"Not a whole lot," I said. "He knew, or at least suspected, that you'd given Ranger L a private mission. But Landon kept all that a secret—H had no clue what it actually entailed except a few weekends away and some shady meetings in The Forest."

Silence hit the line so intently I had to tap it and clear my throat to get a response from Ranger X.

"You there?" I prompted. "Hello?"

"I'm not aware of any standing commitments Ranger L had in The Forest," Ranger X said. "Or weekends away, for that matter."

I stilled, my body frozen. "What do you mean? I thought you said the mission was private. Isn't it possible Ranger L was working the case and just hadn't told you about every detail? You did say you weren't sure what he'd found, if anything."

"That's true," Ranger X agreed. "And while it could be related to the mission, he was supposed to keep me apprised of his general movements. It's protocol for him to report any extended trips—like weekends away—to me. Those were his instructions."

"So, what does that mean?"

"Either he hadn't yet apprised me of an aspect of the case he was following," Ranger X said. "Or he was involved with something—or someone—he didn't want us to know about."

My blood chilled. "Someone who might have gotten him killed."

I could tell by the hitched breath from Poppy, and the quiet on the other end, that I'd said aloud what we'd all been thinking.

"Do me a favor," Ranger X said, clearing his throat. "Be careful. I don't love the idea of you hanging out at The Black Cat."

"I know, but I have Poppy with me."

"Strangely enough, that makes me feel better," Ranger X said, "but be careful not to step on the third board from the bottom, don't get washed away by high tide, and definitely don't drink anything in that place."

"Aye-aye, Captain." I glanced out at the water, watching as Lake Superior wrapped around the island in a tight little hug. The waves at my feet were chilly and cool. They kept my mind churning and sharpened my senses. "Speaking of the lake, I think Ranger H might need a good dip in it this morning to clear his head."

"He's suffering," X said. "We agreed to give him the night to mourn."

"Well," I said, squinting into the distance as the sun crept higher, burning the pinks and oranges away. "It's dawn."

Chapter 9

"Be careful on the stairs," Poppy said. "And scrape your shoes before you climb up. If you have gunk on the bottom of your sandals, they'll stick to the steps and you'll lose your footing. That's how you slip and die."

At Poppy's dire warning, I shut up and focused on climbing the janky stone staircase that could barely be called any such thing. By the time we surfaced, I was feeling like we'd been dragged through a dumpster and left for dead.

"Well, I've gotta run!" Poppy brushed her hands against her hips, her orange skirt swishing in the breeze. "Good luck."

"But—"

I barely had time to suck in a breath and call after my cousin before she was gone. I was left staring after her, the words dying on my lips.

"Okay, then," I muttered. "See you later."

I glanced over my shoulder to see if Ranger H had followed us out and needed help, but I imagined he wouldn't be moving anywhere on his own soon. The Rangers would collect him when the time was right, and I didn't feel like being around when that happened.

I headed northwest toward Main Street, and once I reached the carefully manicured shops that kicked off the start of the festive strip, I slotted myself in with the crowds and tried to blend in as I studied each shop I passed.

Despite the colorful sheen of Main Street that never let up, something was different today. Just a little bit off. A breath in the air, a lull in conversation, a hush over the dusty dirt path. The balloon animals didn't make sounds and the street performers had lost a touch of exuberance. The memory of yesterday was still fresh in everyone's mind.

However, there were a few children and families that moved about with unabashed excitement for the day, slurping at ice cream cones and laughing at the enchanted fireworks shot into the sky by a shop on the north side of town. It was easy to tell who'd witnessed the tragedy yesterday, and whose lives had gone on without a clue, save for a blip in the newspaper.

I blew an errant strand of hair out of my face as a door to a kitschy gift store swung open and Zin bounced down the front steps. I was on her before she could catch her breath.

"I need your help," I said. "Please. Half an hour."

"I'm on the clock, I'm sorry."

Zin's face was drawn, her skin paler than usual. There were bags under her eyes so heavy I could practically feel the weight of them. Even her hair, normally a glossy black, looked stringy and unkempt as she irritatedly shoved a strand of hair behind her ear.

"This has something to do with the job," I said. "Please? I know you don't want to be on canvassing duty."

Zin glanced behind her, then crossed her arms. Her eyes were bloodshot. "I'll do whatever I have to in order to help find the killer. We're a team. We all contribute equally, just in different ways."

"I didn't mean you weren't contributing," I said. "I'm sorry—that came out wrong. All I was trying to say is that I need a favor, and it's related to the case."

"How related?" Zin's eyebrows cinched together.

"I have the addresses of Ranger L's family and his girlfriend."

"I already talked to Melissa," Zin said, but curiosity beamed from her eyes. "How'd you get those addresses, anyway?"

"Sources," I said. "Anyway, I don't have a way in to actually talk to the family members. Will you come with me? We can question them about Ranger L's life. Together."

"I can't," Zin said. "I have orders."

I raised my wrist. "Comm your boss."

"He's a frightening man on a good day," Zin said. "He told me what to do, so I'm doing it."

"Please. I'll owe you," I said. "Have you found anything here that's helpful?"

Zin's silence was all it took for me to pounce on my next opening.

"You'll be back here in an hour, tops," I said. "If you have to clear it with X, go ahead. Tell him you're babysitting me."

Zin's eyes brightened at the idea. She raised her wrist to her mouth and took a step away, but not so far that I couldn't hear every word she said. I soon realized that'd been on purpose.

"Good morning, sir," Zin said into the Comm. "I have your fiancée here claiming she has the addresses and the go-ahead to pound on some doors today. She wants to ask a few questions to Ranger L's family and seems intent on going alone. Would you like me to accompany her?"

Zin waited a beat.

"Yes, sir, canvassing Main Street." Another pause, and then, "No, sir. I've got nothing yet."

I clapped and grinned when Zin turned around after disconnecting. "Did he give you permission?"

"He said not to let his meddling soon-to-be-wife out of my sight," she said. "I have one hour. I can't believe your harebrained plan worked."

"It's not harebrained," I said. "It's effective."

"We have every single Ranger on the case," Zin said. "No offense, but that's a lot of trained man power. You're one untrained woman. How is this going to help anything?"

I sniffed and lifted my chin higher. "I might be one untrained woman, but I'm an untrained woman who might have discovered that Ranger L was working on something unrelated to the job."

Zin's mouth dropped open. "What?"

"Stay with me, grasshopper," I said, throwing my arm around Zin's shoulder. "I'll teach you how to come up with harebrained schemes if you're lucky."

We began the trek north through Main Street as I pulled out the address to Ranger L's family home and handed it over to Zin. However, when I looked up, I realized we were standing just across from the confectionary where I'd comforted Melissa the previous afternoon.

"Where was he shot from?" I asked abruptly. "And what was it specifically that killed Landon?"

Zin bit her lip.

"I told you a bit of my news," I said. "I expect you to keep it quiet. I'll do the same with yours."

Zin rolled her eyes, but she turned around and faced away from the chocolatier. "He was hit somewhere over there. Trajectory looks like it came from the tree line just behind Main Street, but it was a long-range instrument."

"Why?" I asked. "It's so...bizarre. In a world of magic, someone using an instrument of death similar to the humans?"

"There was nothing similar except the style of shooting," Zin said. "The killer loaded their gun—a magical sort of rifle—with a spell purchased from The Void."

I shuddered, thinking any spell purchased from the black market couldn't be good, especially not one that'd been intended to kill a person as strong as a Ranger.

"It's called a Mind Melter," Zin said, forcing back a wince at the very mention of it. "A small ball of magic erupts from the gun, travels through the air, and expands when it hits its target. It's meant for headshots. It kills within seconds and is a favorite of assassins."

My back straightened at the word. "Assassins?"

"Contract killers, hitmen, that sort of thing."

"Why would an assassin choose this technique?"

Zin sighed. "This spell comes from deep within The Void. It's expensive. Big money means it's completely anonymous. Unlike human guns, there are no shell casings, no matching bullets—nothing. The spell hits the target's head and immediately spreads, seeps into their brain, and boils them alive from the inside out. It's awful."

I shuddered. "Poor guy."

"The biggest question," Zin said, "is why an assassin would be after a Ranger. And was he really the only target? Was it personal? Or will there be more?"

We reached the house belonging to Ranger L's parents in silence. There wasn't much to say. Rehashing what little information we had only led to more anxiety.

"I'm trying to get a feel for L's personal life," I told Zin as we reached the front steps. "If he was working something off the books, I'm guessing it was for a friend. A favor. Or he was in trouble and needed money, assurances of safety, or something of the sort. There's a fissure somewhere in L's private life, and we've just got to find it. I'm sure of it."

Zin raised her fist and rapped against the door several times. It was pulled open by a woman with a healthy mixture of gray and brown hair pulled back in a ponytail. She was petite, just shorter than me and just taller than Zin, and looked shriveled, frail as she leaned against the doorframe.

"Yes?" she asked, clutching a tissue in her hand. "Can I help you?"

"I'm sorry to bother you during this time," Zin said, "but I'm Ranger Z, and this is the Mixologist, Lily Locke. We were wondering if we could speak with you for a few minutes."

The woman sniffed, eyed us. Zin retrieved her badge and held it out for the woman to examine, which she did carefully. Once she approved its authenticity, she raised her head and gave a sad smile.

"I was the mother of a Ranger for many years," she said in explanation. "Old habits die hard."

Her eyes teared, and my heart cracked at her obvious anguish.

"We are so sorry," I said. "I'm engaged to a Ranger, and my cousin is a Ranger, and... I can't imagine being in your shoes."

"Well, you might be someday. It's the nature of the job, isn't it?" She looked at us, her expression blank, as if she hadn't realized what she'd said. Then understanding flooded her eyes, and she shook her head. "I'm sorry, that was so rude of me. I'm just—I've been out of it since we heard the news about Landon yesterday evening. Come in, come in."

Landon Smith's mother, Retta Smith, led us through a dimly lit entryway and into a living room. It had the cozy, lived in feeling of a house that had seen children born and raised, that bore scars on the walls from toys and errant toddler magic screeching out of control.

The scent of spiced apples came from the kitchen, and I wondered if Retta baked to ease her stress, or if she'd been flooded with food and gifts after word of her son's death had spread.

"I talked briefly with the Rangers yesterday," Retta began, sitting on the armchair along one side of a cold fireplace and gesturing for us to take the couch. "I mean, I'm not sure what more there is to say, really. I was close with my son, but he kept his work private."

"I understand," I said, "but we're not actually here to talk about work."

"I thought the Rangers said they thought he might have been targeted because of a job he was on," she said. "Some sort of high-risk mission, or a disgruntled criminal he helped put away maybe. There's nobody I can think of who would have wanted to see Landon dead from his personal life."

"Tell us a little about your family," I said. "We're just trying to paint an accurate picture of your son's life—nothing more than that. The better we know who he was, who he loved and how he acted, how he existed in the world, the better the chance we'll have of finding the person who did this to him."

"Well, his father is right here." Retta gestured toward the kitchen. "Arthur Smith. We've been married forty-two years."

Footsteps creaked from beyond the wall. There was a familiarity in her gaze, dripping with sweetness, as she glanced up at Arthur when he appeared in the doorway. It was a level of comfort that most couples desired in a marriage.

Retta offered a quick introduction between us and Arthur, but Landon's dad chose to remain standing while his wife continued. "Landon has a sister, our daughter, Liddy. She's upstairs—she's twenty-one and took her brother's death very hard. As I said, we were close. All of us."

"Was there anyone you can think of who might have had a reason to target your son?" I asked. "Anyone. Anything. Nothing is too small to be relevant."

"They already asked us these questions." Arthur looked at his wife, but he was speaking at us. "They really don't know anything, do they?"

"We're doing everything we can," Zin said. "We don't share every lead we get because we don't want to get your hopes up if it's a false alarm."

"How would it get my hopes up?" Retta swiveled to face Zin. "My son isn't coming back. Of course I want his murderer found, but I've already heard the worst news a mother can hear. Anything short of you telling me he's coming back won't make much of a difference at this point."

Zin looked down at her hands, her black-painted nails twisted over her lap.

"We all feel the loss of your son, Mrs. Smith," I said carefully. "The job your son did every day was a noble one that protected us all, and we have all lost him. We understand you are in pain, but please. Anything."

Arthur rolled his eyes to the ceiling as if he didn't believe a word we said.

"Mr. Smith," I said. "Can you think of anything that might be helpful?"

"This is a waste of time. Get out there and do your jobs," he mumbled before turning back into the kitchen. "And no, I have no answers to your questions."

"He's just upset," Retta said with an apologetic flicker of a smile. "And we did get some of these questions when they visited us yesterday. Truthfully, I can't think of what else you want us to say."

"How about his girlfriend?" I asked. "Do you like Melissa?"

Mrs. Smith blinked. "Yes, of course. You don't think she had anything to do with this, do you? She was devastated. She spent the night here, as a matter of fact, and just went home this morning to get some rest. Poor thing moved to this island for my son and has no family here."

"You didn't think their relationship went too fast, or that she was bad for him in any way?"

"Gosh, no," she said, clapping one hand against the other in exclamation. "I was wishing they'd get married and have children. If you haven't guessed, we're very family oriented. I've loved nothing more than being a mother and having babies, and I hoped..." She paused, eyes tearing. "I hoped he'd experience the same joys."

"I'm sorry," I said again. "Had his behavior changed recently?"

Mrs. Smith started to answer, then stopped. "I was going to say no, but as a matter of fact, he did seem to have more work obligations lately. He missed three out of our last four Sunday meals. Thank God he made it to the one this past week. I got to see him one last time."

"Did he say anything about the nature of this work that was taking more of his time?"

"Just that it was confidential," she said. "But I did notice that last week when he came to dinner, he had scratches on his arms. Leaves in his hair. It was a bit odd. Usually he cleans up before he comes over here, but I suspect he was in a rush and didn't want to make us wait to eat. He was always very respectful."

"Did Melissa come to these family dinners?"

"Usually," Mrs. Smith said. "Once in a while she had to work, but that wasn't often the case. I think Landon explained in no uncertain terms how important it was for us to have family time together." She gave a light laugh. "I don't want to paint a picture that we're overbearing parents, but I do believe it's important to put time on the calendar. I'm sure you know what it's like having a Ranger in the family."

"I haven't seen my own for dinner in quite some time," I admitted. "But he's doing important work, especially today. Zin has been canvassing the neighborhood all night. I know it won't bring your son back, but hopefully it will give you some closure."

"Do you really think it might have been an attack stemming from his personal life?" Mrs. Smith asked. "I just can't think of anyone who would want him dead who actually knew him. Maybe one of the crazies he dealt with in his career."

"Did he ever have a stalker, anyone who came to the house?" I asked. "What made you say that?"

"Oh, just some of the stories he'd tell us about old arrests. Nothing confidential," she said quickly. "And no, nothing affected his life so much that I saw it. If it affected him personally at all, he hid it well. Except..."

"Except?"

"Well, now that I'm looking back, he was a little grouchier over the last month or two." Mrs. Smith pouted her lips in thought. "I legitimately hadn't thought about it once except for a night two weeks ago when he just didn't show up for dinner, nor did he cancel. I knew he'd been stressed at work, so I didn't say anything about it to him at the time. Though I did tell his father he didn't have to take out his frustration on us."

"That points back to his work," I said. "The Rangers are covering his current cases and if there's something related, they'll find it. Do you mind if we have a quick word with Landon's sister?"

"She's really not in any state," Mrs. Smith said. "But I suppose the choice is hers."

Mrs. Smith led us upstairs. We passed over a staircase outfitted with decades old carpet, an odd shade of green shag that had probably hidden a lot of flaws, spills, and other messes over the years of raising small children. We climbed behind her, leaning on the creaky wooden railing. I admired a spattering of family portraits along the wall.

In the majority of photos, Landon's face shone down on us. He'd been a smiley kid and had grown into a handsome man. He had landed a few inches shorter than me, but his body was incredibly compact and muscular. He must have been close in height to Melissa.

According to the portraits, Landon and his sister, Liddy, looked alike. They both had dark hair and brown eyes and infectious smiles that lit up the hallway. Mrs. Smith barely seemed to glance at the walls; she'd probably walked by these photos too many times to count and barely noticed them anymore.

Retta knocked on the door to her daughter's room. A second door across the hall was snugly closed, and a third and fourth stood open on the other side of the small upstairs landing. The third room was a bathroom, the fourth the master bedroom. I suspected the room behind the second door was Landon's, a space Retta seemed to be carefully ignoring.

"Honey," she called through the first door. "We've got a couple of people who worked with Landon here to speak with you. Do you want to open up?"

"No!"

Retta turned toward us, her eyes filled with sorrow. She shrugged, as if to say, *I told you so*.

"May I?" I asked.

When she nodded, I stepped forward and rested a hand against the wood, then my forehead. I could almost feel the sadness radiating from inside of the room.

"My name is Lily Locke," I said softly. "I'm engaged to Ranger X. And from the moment I heard about what happened to your brother, I couldn't stop thinking about what I'd be feeling if it were me instead of you mourning the loss of a loved one."

I waited a beat, listened. There was a slight break in sobs.

"I know I'm in no place to ask you questions, or to tell you how you should feel, but I've had a pit in my stomach since we heard about Landon. I'm not a Ranger, nor am I law enforcement or media of any kind. I just want to help because that's what I would want from a friend if our positions were reversed."

After a minute of silence, I stepped back from the door. I'd said all I could, and I still hadn't gotten a response. Maybe I hadn't appealed to her. Maybe I really didn't get it. Maybe my what-if scenarios came off as haughty and unfair to her. I hoped to never be in her position to know and truly understand.

"Thanks for your time," I whispered to Retta. "If your daughter changes her mind, she can find me at the Mixologist's bungalow, any time, day or night. Even just to talk."

Retta nodded and started down the stairs. Zin followed. I gave one last look at the door, then I followed, too.

"Wait," came a whisper from behind me. "I'll talk. To you. Just you."

I turned, found the dark-haired sibling of Landon standing puffy-faced and red-cheeked in the doorway to her bedroom. I nodded and gestured for Zin and Retta to continue downstairs while I spun around and joined Liddy in a room that looked as if it hadn't aged since her teenage years.

The walls were a light pink, the pillows on her bed fluffy and frilly. A cute little desk sat pressed against one corner with a chandelier for a light and a notepad that hovered in mid-air just underneath the tip of a levitating pen.

"I will be moving out soon," she said as if explaining the state of her room. "No sense redoing it."

"I'm so sorry for your loss," I said. "Thank you for taking the time to talk with me."

"How are you helping in ways that the other Rangers can't?"

Despite her tear-streaked face, Liddy was direct and to the point.

"Your brother taught you well," I said with a smile. "It's a good question. I don't have a good answer because I might find nothing. But I'm focusing on your brother's personal life. It seems to me that everyone liked him, so I'm coming up against dead ends. But it wasn't an accident that someone killed Landon, and there's a fissure somewhere. We just have to keep pressing until we find it."

She nodded, looked satisfied. "What do you think of his girlfriend?"

"I thought I was supposed to ask the questions," I joked lightly. "I've only met Melissa once. Yesterday. It obviously wasn't an optimal time to get to know her. What do you think about her?"

"I don't like her."

I stood straighter, hands clasped in my lap as I tried not to show my surprise. "Really?"

"I know my mom probably told you she was great, but she just really wanted to see my brother married." Liddy shrugged, sat on her bed and toyed listlessly with the pale-yellow comforter. "I think deep down, she thought that maybe if Landon got married and had kids, he'd reconsider his career."

"Your mother didn't like his career?"

"She was proud of him, but she worried. I'm sure you understand."

I acknowledged her point with a quick smile. "What about Melissa didn't you like?"

"She's got..." Liddy hesitated, her hands coming up before her face to emphasize her point. "She's got these crazy eyes. I just don't trust her."

"Crazy eyes?"

"It's nothing I can put my finger on. I know I probably sound delusional, but whatever. I've never liked her, and I didn't make that a secret. I'd told my parents before, but they said I was just jealous he was spending more time with her than with us."

"That's not true?"

"Come on," she said. "I'm a twenty-one year old female. I don't hang with my brother all that much anymore. Of course that's not why. My mom just didn't want to see any flaws in Melissa."

"I asked Landon's partner in the Ranger program; he said she seemed to make your brother happy."

"She did at first, but lately, he's been *cran-ky.*" Liddy drew out the word in true little-sister form. "He missed three Sunday dinners recently. He kept saying it was because of the job, but I don't know. He loved his job. Even if he had a tough assignment, he always seemed invigorated by it. Never... I don't know. Depressed. Bothered. I think there was something going on, but I'm not sure if it was with Melissa or something else. I don't think it was the job."

"Do you think..." I hesitated, struggled with how to phrase my next thought.

"Do I think Melissa would have killed my brother?" Liddy channeled the same concentration her brother had probably needed on the force as she met my gaze. "I don't have a good answer to that. I don't know her well enough. But I would like to think she didn't."

I nodded in agreement, but noted Liddy's statements as something to follow up on later. While it seemed impossible that Melissa had killed Ranger L herself, there was the chance she had hired an assassin to do the job. But even that seemed highly unlikely. There were so many easier and cheaper ways to have someone killed than to go through the effort of finding an assassin, vetting them, and forking over a huge sum of money.

Not to mention, Melissa had seemed truly distraught when I'd sat with her in the chocolate shop yesterday. It just didn't make sense. And what motivation did she have to kill her boyfriend? If the relationship hadn't been going well, she could have just moved home to Wicked and never seen Landon again.

"I'm not saying she had anything to do with it," Liddy said, seeing my hesitation. "I'm just being honest. I don't think their relationship was all it looked to be on the outside. My mom was blind to it, the other Rangers don't really care—it seems like they mostly have dude talk, not any sort of feelings talk—but I'm his sister. I know things."

"I know, and I believe you," I said. "Is there anything else you can think of that might help me paint a better picture of your brother? Unfortunately, I didn't know him well. He seemed like a great man."

"He was." Liddy's lip finally trembled, her concentration waning. "He is. I don't know. I don't know why anyone would have wanted him dead."

"Is there a chance he'd have gotten involved in something off the books?"

"You mean, something illegal?"

"Not necessarily," I said. "Maybe looking into something in the gray areas of the law—a favor for a friend, something for a quick infusion of cash. Did he ever say anything that might insinuate he had extra work?"

She shook her head. "My brother wouldn't have done any of that. I swear it. He was the most honest man I know."

"Thanks for sharing everything," I said. "Truly. I appreciate it. And I'll keep you posted if we find anything."

"Unless..." Liddy's neck snapped upward as she met my gaze. "He wouldn't have done anything off the record unless someone he knew and loved was in danger."

I couldn't help wondering if Liddy had just hit upon some sort of a breakthrough. "Someone like you, or your parents..."

"Or Melissa," she whispered.

I thanked Liddy for her time, let myself downstairs, and collected Zin from where she'd been making awkward small talk with Arthur in the kitchen. Retta had taken to resting on the couch in the living room.

"Come on," I said to Zin. "I want to talk to Melissa again."

She looked at her watch, shook her head. "My hour's up, and I'm not babysitting you any longer. I have to get back to Main Street and keep canvassing."

"But—"

"It's Melissa!" Zin prompted. "Just go visit her as a friend. You don't need me—what's the worst that can happen, she doesn't let you inside?"

"Right," I agreed, watching as Zin turned and strode back toward Main Street, leaving me to examine Melissa's address alone.

Something Liddy said had clicked in my mind. Had Melissa been in trouble? She did work for Harpin—a man I hadn't trusted since the day I stepped foot on The Isle. Was it possible he'd dragged the poor girl into something dangerous, and her boyfriend had tried to stop it?

Whatever the answer, I planned to find out.

Chapter 10

The house that belonged to Landon and Melissa was a cute little A-frame tucked off a side street in a quaint residential section of The Isle. It was near the river that cut the island in two, just west of Main Street.

I stopped outside of it and studied the neat little yard that had overgrown a bit in the past few days. A white picket fence lined the perimeter, a few posts in need of repair. Weeds poked through the grass and a lovingly planted garden sprouted a few tomatoes that were beginning to rot on the vine.

It was sad to think that Landon would never fashion a Clipper spell to mow the lawn again, nor would he get the latest Weed Whacker potion I'd created to tidy up the grass. He and Melissa would never argue about whose turn it was to tend the garden or sweep the front walkway.

With a heavy heart, I walked through the gate and made my way up the path to the front door. As I knocked, my heart lurched, and I preemptively felt sorry for the prying questions that needed asking.

Melissa called a warning through the front door, asking me to wait for a minute. I stood impatiently, shifting my weight from one foot to the next and scanning the neighborhood for any sign of activity. But if the rest of the people living on this quiet little cul-de-sac knew anything about what had happened, it wasn't obvious on the outside.

"Sorry," Melissa said, tugging a pink bathrobe tighter to her body as she opened the door. "I wasn't expecting company."

"I didn't exactly call in advance," I admitted. "Do you mind if I come inside for a moment? I wanted to check on you, see how you were doing."

"I'm fine," she said, her nose stuffed and puffy. Her eyes were bloodshot, and she looked as if she'd spent hours sobbing. "I stayed the night with Landon's family."

"I heard," I said. "I visited them this morning to pay my respects."

Melissa narrowed her eyes at me.

"And to ask them a few questions," I said. "It's just... I want to help."

Melissa opened the door the rest of the way. It wasn't exactly an invitation, but I took it to be one when she shuffled her fluffy pink slippers toward the living room and gestured for me to follow.

Melissa and Landon's living room was significantly more modern than the Smith's. A black leather couch spanned one wall while a funky red chair sat propped before the bookshelf. A series of bright, multicolored lights ran along the wall, and through the living room I could see an open kitchen, dining area, and a cute little backyard adorned with fairy lights.

"What do you want to know?" Melissa ran a tissue across her nose then shoved it into her pocket, which was overflowing with them. "I imagine you didn't come here just to check on me."

"I do care about checking on you," I said. "I'm sorry if I—"

"I'd rather you not apologize. Just ask what you came to ask." Melissa's gaze landed on me, and through her bloodshot eyes, there was a look of determination. "I want to know who took him away from me. If I can help you do that, I will."

I gave a careful nod. "At the moment, I'm mostly trying to get a feel for Ranger L's personal life. Obviously, you were a huge part of it—the biggest part. I understand he was a family man, loved his parents and his sister—" I watched carefully for a reaction from Melissa, but I didn't get one—"and his colleagues."

"He and his sister were a little..." Melissa cocked her head to the side. "I don't want to speak ill of her."

I waited as she gathered her thoughts.

"It's just... I always told Landon he was strangely close with his sister." Melissa shrugged, not seeming particularly bothered by it. "They spent a good amount of time together. I mean, I'm all for family, but they were both grown adults."

"Why was it weird to you?"

"She just seemed a little possessive. I mean, they were siblings. Siblings are meant to grow apart a little as they age. Do you have any sisters or brothers?"

"No."

"Well..." Melissa shrugged again as if that answered everything. "I have a younger sister. I love her dearly, but when Landon asked me to move in with him, I didn't stay home because of her."

"Did Landon stay back on The Isle because of Liddy?"

She hesitated. "I didn't force him to make that choice. Like I said, he was all about his career. He wasn't leaving this place. And now, I guess he won't have to. Born and buried."

Melissa raised a tissue to her eyes and wiped wet streaks from her cheeks. The tears came silently as she spoke.

"Anyway, I don't think his sister had anything to do with his death," she continued. "I mean, I hope not. You just asked about relationships and that one came to mind."

"Anything is helpful," I said. "I did talk to Liddy. She didn't know of anyone who wanted Landon gone either."

"What'd she say about me?"

"Not much," I said, but at Melissa's gaze, I scrunched up my face. "Fine, I'll admit—she's not a huge fan."

"At least you're honest." Melissa's lips twitched into a sad smile. "People are lying to me enough these days. It's a relief to hear the truth."

"What do you mean? Who's lying to you?"

"All the people coming to me with advice. I've heard it all, and Landon's barely cold. 'You'll be okay; time heals all; you're strong enough to get through this.'" Again, her shoulders moved in a tired effort. "It's all bullshit. Sorry for the language, but honestly, I was going to marry him. I don't know how I'm supposed to just move on."

"I guess I won't beat around the bush, then. Liddy said one other thing that caught me a little off guard. She said there was no way Landon would have gotten himself involved in anything dangerous enough to get himself killed outside of his job—nothing illegal or sketchy, at least, without a good reason."

Melissa had already proved smart, and she understood without me spelling it out. "You think I got myself into trouble and that's what got Landon killed."

I pressed my hands together, then separated them, keeping my face blank. "I'm open to suggestions."

"No," she said. "I'm new here. How would I have enemies?"

"I didn't say they had to be from around here."

"It sounds like you're accusing me." Melissa's fingers clenched tighter around the tissue. "I thought you were trying to help me get closure. If you're not, I think it's time for you to go."

"It's Harpin," I said. "The man makes my skin crawl."

"Harpin?" Melissa looked genuinely surprised. "My employer?"

"You said you work at his tea shop?" When Melissa nodded, I continued. "Since we're going the honest route, I wouldn't feel right holding out on you. I clash with the guy. We haven't gotten along since I stepped foot on this island. If he got you into anything, I just want you to know that we can help."

"I appreciate your concern, but no, thanks." Melissa stood, shoved her used tissue in her pocket, and some more spilled over the side. "I mean, sure, he's a bit of a creep—but you and I both know that. We're women. We have our radars. Harpin knows...er, knew I was dating Landon. He wouldn't have tried anything."

I raised my hands in submission. "I didn't mean to accuse. Like I said—"

"You're trying to help, so you said," Melissa parroted. "I appreciate it, but I don't have any more information for you. I loved Landon. Neither of us had gotten into any trouble so far as I knew."

"Is there anyone else you can think of who might have had ill will toward you or Landon?"

"No," she said shortly. "I told you that already."

"Did you see anyone yesterday? I know you mentioned greeting Ranger H in passing, along with a few vendors and an old friend," I said. "Is there anyone else that caught your eye? Familiar or strange, suspicious?"

She shook her head. "I didn't know I was supposed to be watching. I was focused on my boyfriend and our conversation."

"I understand, really. I was just hoping..."

"Don't you think I'm hoping too?" Melissa threw her hands in the air and sent tissues flying from the pockets of her bathrobe and scattering across the coffee table between us. "I've gone over it in my mind a hundred thousand times. I watch the scene play out when I try to sleep. When I blink. When I stand in the shower. I can't stop replaying it, and yet, I can't remember. I can't *freaking* remember."

A part of my brain was working, telling me to calm the poor girl down, to reassure her that everything would be okay. But my eyes were drawn to the coffee table where, along with the tissues, an envelope had fallen out of Melissa's pocket.

The parcel was small and white, completely ordinary, save for the name scrawled across the front. Melissa caught me staring. I felt her eyes drilling holes into my head as she realized what had happened, but I was too frozen to move.

"Liam," I whispered. "You know him?"

Melissa snapped forward, yanking at the envelope and shoving it into her pocket. "What's it to you? Is there only one Liam in the world?"

I narrowed my eyes at her. "It's a small island."

"It's none of your business."

"It might be if it's related to your boyfriend's death."

"It's not! And you're not a Ranger, so just leave me alone. They've left me alone, so why can't you?"

I thrust myself to my feet. "Is that a letter to him? I told you, we can help you, Melissa. He's dangerous."

"I don't need your help." Her voice turned into a hiss as she leaned forward. "And if you don't leave this alone..."

"Are you scared?"

She opened her mouth to respond, but she held back. Her hand raised to her lips and she bit down on her knuckle. Her fingers trembled. "I—I can't, Lily."

My mind was whirling. I'd just been ready to start depositing trust back into Liam's jar, a container he'd shattered thoroughly when I'd found him in cahoots with my father. Liam still claimed to be a double agent, that he had never really worked for my father in any real sort of way. My father was convinced they were thick as thieves. I didn't know the right answer.

But the timing of Liam's name popping up couldn't be a coincidence. After all, it was Liam who'd given the file to me and Ranger X as an engagement gift of sorts. The very file that had possibly gotten Landon killed.

I cursed. "What'd he do? Say?"

"I saw him." Melissa's eyes widened in fear. "The day Landon died. Behind the restrooms. I didn't think much of it. I knew he'd been working with Landon on a case. They'd met a few times."

I frowned. While strange, none of the information I'd gathered so far was quite clicking. My brain was firing away, but each thought felt just a hair too elusive to grasp, like a lightning bug just out of reach. What had Liam wanted with Ranger L? Was it related to my mother's case, or was it something else entirely?

"What does the letter say?" I asked. "It's for him if his name is on it."

"I don't know." She sniffed. "I found it in Landon's things."

"Why didn't you turn it in?"

"I wasn't sure it was relevant," she snapped. "I mean, I'm not trying to hide it, but it might be dangerous. I was planning to get rid of it."

"Did you read it?"

"No." She hesitated, read my expression. "Fine, yes. I did."

"What did it say?"

Melissa tossed the envelope down on the coffee table. Tissues scattered, blown away by the swirl of air as she stormed past me. "I need a glass of water. Can I get you something?"

"No, I'm fine." I eased back into a seat, my fingers toying with the edge of the envelope, grateful for a moment alone with it.

I considered the handsome mystery man who danced on the edges of my trust as I slid my thumb under the edge of the envelope. *What is he up to?* I mused, feeling a shake in my finger as I pulled the paper free. After all this time, a part of me still desperately wanted to believe in the good in Liam. I'd seen it. I hadn't imagined it; I couldn't have.

Inside the note, in chicken-scratch handwriting, were a few simple words, their meaning clear.

Liam,

Leave her out of it.

L

I swallowed. It was easy to see why Melissa might have wanted the note kept quiet. If Liam—or whoever was behind Landon's murder—found out that Melissa knew his name, it could put a target on her back.

"What did you get yourself into, Landon?" I asked quietly. "Who did this to you?"

The sound of glassware came clanking from the kitchen as I lowered my head to my hands and massaged the stress out of my temples. My mind felt stuffed. Too much information without anything connecting it. Liam. Harpin. Melissa and Landon. Liddy and the Smiths. Ranger H in the dreary bar. The puzzle pieces just didn't fit together.

The scream sounded first. Then a crash of glass, a thump, a shriek. The slamming of a door along with what I imagined were noises of thrashing.

"Melissa!" I leapt to my feet, the letter falling from my fingertips. I dashed into the hallway, stopping to grab a pillow from the couch along the way. It wasn't an ideal weapon, but my travel belt had only healing potions, and there wasn't a handy bat sitting around. I crept down the hall.

"Melissa, are you there?" I called. "Answer me!"

When there was no answer, I dropped the pillow and picked up my pace. The house had fallen silent. I careened around the corner and came to a stop in the kitchen.

Glassware lay shattered on the floor, a pitcher of water overturned on the counter. It slopped over the edge with an eerie *drip, drip, drip.* The puddle spread as my brain kicked into gear. I hurried toward the back door. It had been flung open and left that way by the intruder.

Bursting into the backyard, I scanned the horizon in every direction but couldn't see a thing. A row of hedges lined the back of the yard as a low privacy fence. There was an apple tree heavy with red fruit that gave a rustle and then fell silent when I looked at it. Beyond Melissa's lawn ran the river that split the island in half. On both sides were neighboring houses.

Melissa had disappeared, along with whoever had taken her.

As I raised the Comm to my lips and called for X, one name rested on my lips.

Liam.

Chapter 11

"Let me get this straight. You were sitting here talking with Melissa," Ranger X said, surveying Melissa's living room. He gestured toward the couch. "She got up to go to the kitchen and left you alone."

"She wanted a glass of water," I said. "As evidenced by the busted glassware and pool of liquid all over the floor."

"Then, you heard sounds of a struggle. You raced after them...with a pillow..."

"I didn't have a ton of options."

Ranger X glanced at the bookshelf behind me that housed a series of bookends, trophies, and other heavy objects. Along with a lamp next to it that would also have worked as a defensive tactic.

"I was rushed," I said. "I wasn't thinking straight. I ran to the kitchen, but she wasn't there. The back door was open, so I went outside. When I couldn't find them, I Commed you right away."

"Then?"

"Then I looked around, hoping for a glimpse of whoever took Melissa. A trail or something. I mean, it's like they just disappeared. Then you showed up."

Ranger X muttered more to himself than me. "How could they have just disappeared?"

"I'm not sure how it happened or where they went," I said, "but in case you're not aware, we live in a magical world."

"Lily."

"Sorry," I said. "I'm upset."

Ranger X put his hand on my shoulder, squeezed. "I know, and I hate having to do this to you, but it's my job. We'll get you out of here in a few minutes."

An hour had passed after Melissa had gone. I'd recounted my story innumerable times to the mess of Rangers who had appeared at Landon's house. A few of the tiny details I reserved, thinking I'd share them more privately with X later. Like the note, and the name that had been on the envelope.

I wasn't planning on keeping the envelope a secret, but I needed to think. To converse with X somewhere else, somewhere without extra sets of ears and eyes laser focused on us.

"What can I do to help?" I asked tiredly. "If possible, I'd like to see you tonight."

"Lily..." Ranger X hesitated.

It was easy to see he wanted to say no. To claim he had to work. And truthfully, he probably did have to work. But the bags under his eyes were now bruises, and the exhaustion was scrawled across his face. He would burn himself out if he didn't take a breather, so I stood my ground.

"Please," I said. "A few hours."

He gave a nod. "Eight o'clock. I'll have until midnight."

"It's not enough," I said. "You need sleep."

"It's the best I can do."

"I'll take it." I shivered, my arms coming up to hold myself. "I miss you."

Ranger X glanced over my shoulder. Seas of men in black plagued the apartment. But something snapped in him, and he pulled me roughly to him. "I'll see you tonight, sweetheart. I love you."

I nodded, repeated the phrase back, and pulled away. "I have to get back to the bungalow."

After I signed out of the newest crime scene, I pointed my shoes toward the Lower Bridge. But I had one stop before I headed home.

I burst through the doors of the tea shop. "What do you know about Ranger L? Melissa?"

The horrible excuse for a wizard looked up from his place at the far end of the room. The shop was long and narrow, like a shrunken airport carrier but dark and damp and filled floor to ceiling with shelves. On the shelves were jars of teas. Some had contents as innocent as mint leaf. Others were topped off with powder of crushed dragon skulls. Dangerous, bordering on illegal, and very expensive.

"Lily," Harpin said in an oily voice. "What can I do for you?"

"Melissa," I said. "I know she works here. Where is she?"

Harpin tucked a strand of long, greasy hair behind his ear. "She doesn't work until next week. How should I know? She hasn't missed a shift."

I sized him up, looking for any evidence that he'd been in a tussle lately. The letter had said Liam's name on it, but I couldn't shake Melissa's connection to Harpin. I didn't trust him as far as I could throw him. And arm strength wasn't my forte.

"If I find out that you were involved," I said, raising a finger and letting the threat hang in the air.

Harpin merely smiled. He clapped his hands, faced his palms outward. In dismay, I noted a smoky substance appearing from the walls of his shop, sweeping upward in creepy, steamy spires.

I spun on a heel before his fog stole my breath and clogged my throat. I wasn't sure if Harpin was shaken or offended, but he wanted me gone. Fortunately for him, I didn't want to be around a second longer than I needed.

"Lily," he called after me. "You're looking in the wrong place."

"You'd better hope so."

"When will you grow to trust me?"

I burst into the sunlight, stopped, and turned to face him. "Never."

"Always trusting the wrong person," he said. "It'll be your downfall. If you knew better, you'd trust The Quilter. Me."

"What about my father?" I asked. "Should I trust him, too?"

Harpin's lips drew into a thin line. "I don't know what you're talking about."

"Right."

"I'd look at those closest to you. I take it from your accusations that Melissa is gone?" He paused for an answer, but I didn't give him one. "Well, how did the kidnapper know you'd be at her house? Who's watching you? I can guarantee it's not me."

As much as I distrusted Harpin, he had a point. And the thought followed me all the way home as chills crept down my spine, and I wondered.

Who was watching?

"YOU'RE BACK JUST IN time." Gus looked up from the center of the storeroom. "I need you to finish this elixir now."

A wash of familiar mustiness and the warmth of the colored vials surrounding us on the shelves gave me the pinch of calmness that I so desperately needed after a frustrating visit to Harpin's shop.

"Elixir?" I peered closer at the order sheet. "We didn't have an order for any elixirs last night, and the store hasn't been opened yet this morning. Who needs it?"

Gus raised his eyebrow. "Special order."

"From?"

He sighed. "People are scared, Lily. A Ranger was shot—Mind Melted, no less—in the center of Main Street. Do you remember how people flocked here demanding protective spells when they thought there was a corrupt Ranger in the program?"

I exhaled a huge breath. "It wasn't all that long ago."

"Well, this is going to be just as bad. If not worse."

"What did you tell everyone who came by?"

"I thought it best we just make one huge batch of an Energy Elixir."

I frowned. "How's an energy boost potion supposed to help keep people protected?"

Gus's nose hairs twitched with amusement. "I might have whispered to Kirby Berknuckle that this new blend of energy elixir is so good it just about gives a man superpowers. Extra strength, all that goodness."

I rolled my eyes. "They'd have more luck drinking a Caffeine Cup. An Energy Elixir is about as strong as a cup of chai."

"Exactly." Gus shrugged his shoulders. "No unfortunate side effects from people misfiring spells."

"Except for the side effect of people thinking they're invincible."

"I can't help stupid."

I shook my head, peered into the potion. "This isn't a new blend."

"It is too." Gus viciously chopped up some mint leaf and dumped it in the potion. "This time it'll be green instead of purple."

"Oh, golly gee."

"Hey," Gus said sharply. "I didn't lie to Kirby. I told him we had a new mix of Energy Elixir that gives people a burst of energy. I can't help it if he's spreading rumors about it turning people into demigods."

I bit my lip, trying to hide a smile.

"Unless you'd like to spend your next three days fashioning Spell Shields, Purple Pansies, and Fire Flakes, then I suggest you get your rear end into the chair and finish up the Mix. The base potion is brewed, and the ingredients are prepped. Just needs your magic touch."

As usual, Gus was smarter than anyone gave him credit for. His quick thinking had saved me from spending the next seventy-two hours creating throwaway potions that'd do no good protecting the islanders from whichever killer had Mind Melted a Ranger. It would've been a waste of mine and Gus's time, and nothing more.

By the time we finished the Elixir, the store had opened, and true to Gus's prediction, we were flooded with customers. Gus had once again thought ahead. He'd called Mimsey over from the supply shop, and the two had put together a kitschy sign that blinked and shimmered with magical enhancements. Mimsey had ordered a Light Bright potion to spritz on the cardboard to make the entire sign so luminescent it was hard to look straight at it.

The sign advertised "All New Energy Elixir! Get your dose of protection now. Limited time only!".

The line of customers snaked along the side of the building and down the beach, staring at the sign as if it alone would save them from the murderer on The Isle.

"I wish there was more I could do," I told Mimsey as she huffed outside and stepped up beside me at the bar for Magic & Mixology to help package Elixirs. It was selling just as fast as we made it. "Is it ethical to be promising protection from an energy boost?"

"That's what the fine print is for," Mimsey said with a chuckle. At my distraught expression, she cleared her throat. "Come on, dear, what you're selling today—what people are buying, what they *want* to buy—is comfort. It's the least you can do for your people."

I looked out at the islanders crowding into my space. *My people.* In a sense, they were the only family I had. And the first rule of family was to be there for one another, no matter what.

My glance out at the people crowding the bungalow told me people were anxious. Twitchy limbs, shifty eyes, nervous tics. Mothers, fathers, children, teens all thinking the same thing: if a

Ranger—the highest trained individuals of all of us—could be killed, then who would be next?

"Not a single person out there believes they can save themselves from whoever murdered Ranger L," Mimsey said in a sad whisper. "But how can a husband not want to protect his wife, or a mother her children? They need to do something, to feel useful. You and I both know this from experience, yes?"

I swallowed, nodded, and then called inside to Gus. "Let's add a few cinnamon sticks to the batch. Anise and orange peels from three oranges."

He looked up from his perch, confused. "That's not in any book I've ever read."

"I know," I said, a hint of a smile. "But let's add a little holiday cheer to the mix."

"Spirit boosters," Gus said, a hint of surprise. "Give people a sense of optimism with their new boost of energy."

"Exactly. In hopes they'll use this new energy for good."

Gus's hands busied themselves with the jar of candied oranges, and I took it as a sign that he approved. Beside me, Mimsey's cheeks turned pink and her lips quirked up in the tiniest of smiles. It was all the encouragement I needed.

"Just a few more minutes," I called to the crowd. "And you'll all have your new and improved Elixir. It won't turn you into a demigod, but I think you'll like it."

By the time the crowd had been served their vials of Elixir and the Flare Flashers on Mimsey's sign out front had died down, the sun had long since set. Mimsey tiredly dragged her collapsed sign inside while Gus set to work tidying the storeroom after a frenzied day brewing Elixirs in every spare cauldron.

As I closed up the register and dragged my own weary feet inside, I found myself hoping that the Elixir wouldn't be a letdown, that the customers would find themselves waking in the morning with a cheery bounce to their step.

"You did good," Mimsey said. "Word is already traveling around The Isle about your Elixir. Go get some rest."

I nodded. "Take Gus home with you. I've got cleanup tonight. I need to wind down, anyway."

I let Gus and Mimsey have a few minutes alone in the storeroom, listened to them argue. Gus wanted to stay and get a start on brewing the next day's potions. He'd be here until the wee hours of the morning if I let him, cleaning, scrubbing, chopping, prepping.

I was just about to step into the storeroom and intervene when someone else did it for me. The front door to the bungalow opened, and the heavy, familiar footsteps warned me of Ranger X's presence.

I hurried into the storeroom and found Mimsey and Gus looking up in surprise.

"Sorry to startle you," X said, looking exhausted as he swept a hand through his hair, which went from disheveled to chaotic. "I thought Lily was expecting me."

I glanced at the clock, saw it was just a few minutes past eight. Right on time, as he'd promised.

"Oh," Mimsey said in understanding. Then, "*Oh*."

Without further delay, she pinched Gus's upper arm.

He grunted. "What's that for?"

"Come on," she said. "I think it's time we get out of here. You can come back at the crack of dawn if you'd like, but you're not getting anything else done tonight."

Gus's eyes raked over me, Ranger X, and finally Mimsey. "I'll be back," he said finally. "Good night."

We waited for Mimsey and Gus to disappear. I stood in the doorway, watching their feet leave soft imprints in the sand, Gus's large and angry looking, Mimsey's small and dainty. When I couldn't hear a whisper of their muted conversation, I retreated inside and closed the door behind me.

X had made his way deeper into the storeroom where he stood with his arms folded over his chest and stared into the fireplace. He looked gorgeous as usual, but somehow more ruffled. His white shirt was open at the neck and he had draped his suit jacket over one chair. He was in the process of rolling up his sleeves over a set of tanned arms when he turned to face me.

He'd showered and shaved since I'd last seen him, but it hadn't washed away the tension from his forehead or the stress in his eyes. The faint smell of his woodsy shampoo filtered across the room to me, mixing with a touch of sharp cologne, minty breath, all against the backdrop of cozily burning wood in the fireplace.

I made my way to him but hesitated. "Thanks for coming by."

"Of course," he said. "I hope you know—I wouldn't ever... I don't forget about you, Lily. Even if I'm absorbed on a case. You will always take first priority, but sometimes—"

"I understand. I know you're busy during times like this. How could I ask you to relax and enjoy your evening with everything you have weighing on your mind?"

Ranger X gave me a soft smile, one that turned his face from harried and stressed to that beautiful hint of brightness that I'd fallen in love with. "I can always enjoy my time with you. I might be a bit scattered, but that doesn't stop me from loving you. If anything, cases like this make me appreciate every moment just a little bit more."

"I think—" I swallowed. "There's something I'd like to talk to you about."

"Is it urgent?"

I shrugged. "It's important, unless... you have something more pressing?"

"As a matter of fact, I do." Ranger X stepped toward me. "Can I take you upstairs?"

I saw the desperation in his eyes, the need for escape. The utter sorrow behind all of it, and still a need to be close and warm and secure with someone he loved. My worries about Liam had waited this long; they could wait for one hour more.

I took his hand, let him pull me upstairs. We reached my bedroom where the moonlight glinted off the ghostly white pillows and a soft comforter spread over a fat, familiar mattress.

Ranger X drew me to him, kissed me, held me. I could taste his desire, feel his passion as he pressed against me. His body molded against mine as his lips feasted, his fingers intertwining in my hair.

He let out a groan, delved deeper. I sank against him, let myself be carried away by the wave of sheer helpless love. The sort of love that left tears drying on my cheeks to imagine life without him, to feel a pit in my stomach at the whisper of losing him. The sense of soaring completeness when we joined together, collapsed onto the bed, and forgot about all the desolation, the death, the sorrow in the world in favor of the one thing that could conquer it all: Love.

Chapter 12

"So, what was it that you needed to talk to me about?"

We moved downstairs after an hour spent wrapped around one another in bed. I shuffled over to the coffee pot, grabbed two mugs, and filled them both. I didn't particularly need the caffeine this late, but I wouldn't be surprised to learn that X's rest for the evening had ended the second we'd climbed out of bed.

He'd changed into a clean set of clothes, courtesy of my Self-Populating closet, and was fastening the buttons on his sleeves as I shuffled back with our mugs. I wore a robe cinched tight around my waist and fluffy slippers on my feet. The warmth from the fire kept me toasty and filled the room with comfort. As I glanced outside into the chilly darkness, I found myself wishing that X could stay here forever.

"Right," I said, handing over his coffee. "Well, there was one thing I didn't tell you from before. At Melissa's."

Ranger X's gaze narrowed as he looked at me. "Something you forgot and remembered later?"

"Sure," I said unconvincingly.

When X's gaze narrowed further, I shrugged.

"What do you want me to say?" I pressed. "I didn't think it was fitting to share this news with you in front of all your buddies."

"My buddies." Ranger X's voice had gone from soft and loving to hard and businesslike in seconds. "You mean the other Rangers. My colleagues."

"Those would be the ones."

"What is it?"

"Better if I show you," I muttered.

I pulled the note from my pocket and handed it wordlessly to Ranger X. "This fell out of Melissa's robe just before she went into the kitchen."

Ranger X's face went stony as he read the name on the outside of the letter. When he flicked it opened, his jaw tightened further. "You've had this all day?"

"Since I left Melissa's," I said, trying desperately to keep my chin high. "It's the reason I made sure you were available to come over tonight. I knew you needed to see this."

"You didn't think I needed to see it hours ago?" Ranger X looked out the window, tapped the card against his open palm. "And here, I thought you wanted me to come over to spend time together for personal reasons. Not to discuss the case."

"Look, I know you're tired. Exhausted. Heartbroken. But please don't take it out on me. Maybe I made a mistake keeping this from the Rangers at the scene of the crime, but I didn't do it out of spite. I did it because I was worried."

"About?"

"Gee, I don't know. Someone's killing Rangers. I don't know who to trust."

"You can't think it was an inside job. Even if you don't know the Rangers, you should trust me."

"I do trust you! But who else has the ability to kill a Ranger?"

"How about the man whose name is on this very card?" Ranger X held it up, his eyes darkening. "Or your father, the man you insist on visiting over and over again, despite the fact that he'll never cooperate with us. He will never change."

Ranger X's words smarted, stung. I knew he hadn't slept and was lashing out in frustration. The Rangers had no clue who had kidnapped Melissa or murdered Landon, and it was weighing on him. But my feelings weren't bulletproof, and his jarring tone had shaken me to the very core.

"I love you, X, but I don't think I can have this conversation right now," I said. "I think we're both stressed and need some time to cool down."

"Maybe."

I stared at him. "Why are you upset with me? I did the best I could."

"You should have been honest. We need to lead by example, Lily. And you not trusting the other Rangers—when you're engaged to me—what does that say to The Isle? To the islanders, to the other Rangers? Am I supposed to tell them that you forgot to give me a key piece of evidence because it slipped your mind?"

"I didn't think it was that big of a deal," I said. "You keep things from me when you feel it's important, and I don't question your judgment."

"It's my job. I have to keep things separate."

"Is the investigation into my mother's life and death your *job*?" I snapped. "Was it essential for you to keep that little mission from me? Why was it your decision to share that information with Ranger L without consulting me? That was not Ranger business, X, and you can't pretend it was. That was my file as much as yours. It was ours. So, excuse me if I kept something secret from you for a few hours because I thought it might help for you to hear the information first, alone, before I broke the news in front of a crowd."

Ranger X looked at me, complexity scrawled across his face. There was uncertainty, love, anger, sorrow—all mixed in his deep brown eyes. His mouth twitched, and he looked ready to say something. Eventually, he just shook his head, words eluding him.

"I have to go," he said.

I glanced at the clock. It was barely nine thirty, and he'd promised me until midnight.

Ranger X followed my gaze. "Sorry," he said gruffly.

I followed him to the door. "Will you keep me posted on what you find?"

He swallowed, scuffed a shoe against the floor. "When I can."

"I love you."

"I love you," he said, but the sentiment was a trail into darkness, and by the time it finished, he was long gone.

I shivered, watched the blackness of the lake as it lapped against the bone-white sand, but there was nothing for me to see. I closed the door, locked it, and prepared for a long night alone.

I CURLED MY MUG OF hot cocoa closer, stared deeply into the top of the chocolatey beverage, and inhaled the sweet steam as it rose up in delicate twists. The marshmallows spattered across the top looked like a gooey galaxy, and I watched them drift and float about aimlessly, as if my beverage held the cosmic answers to the universe.

I raised the cup to my lips and took a sip. No sooner did the glass touch my mouth than a loud *rap* sounded on the door. It startled me, sent hot cocoa flying down the front of my robe, practically burning my chin as I cursed under my breath.

"Must clean up this filthy mess,
So I don't need to get undressed.
Stains and drips, a chocolate spill,
Disappear now, it most certainly will."

Like magic, the chocolate vanished. Apparently, I was a little too overzealous with my cleaning curse because even the hot chocolate inside the mug completely disappeared. The mug was spotless, save for a few dehydrated marshmallows stuck to the ceramic at the bottom.

Grumbling, I stood and made my way to the door. "Who is it?" I peeked out and saw nothing. Nobody.

My heart began to race. "Who's there? Answer me. Rangers are on the way here."

Only the sound of grunting filtered through the door.

"Show yourself!" I demanded. "I'm armed!"

"If you got that lower peephole like I've been telling you for ages," a familiar voice growled as a face popped into view of the peephole, "you wouldn't be threatening someone who's here to help you."

"Chuck?" I pulled the door open, and the small gnome tipped forward, losing his balance on top of the porch chair he'd dragged over. "What are you doing here?"

I caught Chuck as he fell forward, and together we sort of collapsed into an awkward pile in the doorway. The chair tipped and clattered behind him. I tried my best to play it cool as I stood up, brushed myself off, and moved the chair back to its rightful position. Meanwhile, Chuck regained his footing and swiped at imaginary dust on his outfit, looking fully disgruntled by the time I returned inside and locked the door behind me.

"Want some hot chocolate?" I asked. "I was just about to make some when you arrived."

"Actually..." Chuck thought about it. "Yes."

"Good. What brings you around?"

"I'm here begging you to drop all charges against my girlfriend."

I stilled. "You have a girlfriend?"

He scowled. "Why's that the most surprising part of what I just said?"

"I just..." I hesitated, treading carefully. "Is she a gnome?"

"Yes. Mary Swetin." Chuck's eyes went all dreamy and his lashes fluttered over his squashed-tomato nose and burnt-red cheeks. "She's a real catch. Just like me."

Chuck wasn't exactly a looker, at least in the human community, but I was beginning to think he was a bit of a ladies' man in the gnome community. He'd gotten a lot of attention lately for his work in the Grove of Gnomes, and apparently, his local heroism had helped him out in the dating division, as well.

"Congratulations, Chuck," I said. "I really mean it. There's nothing better than falling in love."

He shrugged, looked bashful. "Yeah, it's a pretty sweet deal, and we're really meant to be together. Star crossed lovers. Soul mates. Bonnie and Clyde. The whole shebang."

"Really?" I studied him. "I don't know that you want to—"

"Do we have a deal?" Chuck pressed. "I'll be your informant if you agree to drop all charges against Mary. She really is a sweet girl, the sweetest. You just have to get to know her. This one misstep doesn't define her; just a little veer down the path of criminal life. We've all been there, haven't we, Mixy?"

"Mixy?"

"I was trying out a new nickname." Chuck wrinkled his nose. "You know, Mixologist, Mixy—doesn't work?"

I wrinkled my nose right back. "Lily is just fine."

"Yes, sir, Miss Locke." Chuck bobbed his head obediently, then stuck out a hand full of what appeared to be chubby sausages. "Do we have a deal?"

"I don't know what I'm shaking on," I said. "I need more information first. What did this soulmate of yours do?"

"It's about that girl. The missing one."

Chuck's nonchalant phrase had me startled, and I turned away to prepare the hot chocolate ingredients in hopes he wouldn't notice. I added a few spoonfuls of marshmallows to each cup.

"Don't be stingy," Chuck said. "I don't drink hot chocolate a lot. More 'mallows."

I dumped a few more into Chuck's cup, too distracted to realize I'd mounded the marshmallows right over the lip of the mug so some of them spilled onto the floor.

Chuck dove for the beverage and moved it carefully to the table. He took a moment of silence to survey his lost comrades, the marsh-mallows that had hit the floor. I grabbed the entire jar of sweets, put it on the table, and watched as Chuck promptly dumped it out with a huge grin on his face and began munching on them one by one.

"Now we're talking," Chuck said. "Er, are we? You didn't agree to the deal."

"The missing girl," I said. "Who are you talking about?"

"The dead Ranger's girl. Melissa, I think. You haven't heard about her?"

"No, I have. I wanted to be sure that's who you meant," I said. "Fine. You have a deal. I'll do whatever I can to help get Mary out of trouble in exchange for information on Melissa. But it has to be good information. Nothing helpful, and my promise is null and void."

"Oh, it's great information," Chuck said. "I don't take my girl-friend's fate lightly, and I can't handle thinking about her being stuck in jail. I don't think conjugal visits fit my style."

"Ew, Chuck. Can we focus?"

"Sure," he said, and then stuck out his hand solemnly. "Promise me you'll use whatever means necessary—including sexual favors to your almost-husband—to free my girlfriend."

I shook his hand, careful to head to the sink and scrub each fin-ger clean after our deal was solidified. Returning to the table, I pulled my hot chocolate closer, noticed a few missing marshmallows from the top and a spoon in Chuck's hand—suspiciously full of the can-dy—and cupped my shaking fingers around its warmth.

"Time to spill," I said. "What do you know about Melissa?"

"I think we need to start with Mary," he corrected. "Because that's how we ran into Melissa. Literally."

"When does your story start?"

"The day she disappeared."

"Today?"

"Today, yeah. Long day." Chuck glanced at the clock, then at the fire. "Whew. It's been a whirlwind, this life of crime."

"What time did you see Melissa?"

"This afternoon at her house—don't know the exact minute, but you were there too. You should know when it was."

"I was at Melissa's house when you were there?"

"Well, technically, Mary was in her yard. In the apple tree, specifically."

I thought back to my frantic rush to the backyard, the beautiful apple tree and the slight rustle of leaves I'd heard. "That was your girlfriend hiding in the tree?"

"So, you did see her?"

"No, er—not Mary. Did she see Melissa get kidnapped?"

"That's what I'm so confused about," Chuck said. "I was there, too, so I can coordinate—what's the word I'm looking for?"

"Corroborate?"

"Yeah, that," Chuck said. "I can corroborate Mary's story. She thought it was weird that Melissa rushed out of the house screaming, making this huge racket. Glass shattering, door cracking open, things breaking—when it was just her alone out there."

"Alone?" I said slowly. "No, that's not possible. She was taken from her own house by force. There were signs of a struggle."

"See, I honestly thought you was chasing her," Chuck said, raising an eyebrow. "Melissa comes out making this huge racket, and then not a minute later, the next thing we see is you standing in the doorway huffing and puffing like you was after the poor thing. I just about showed up here tonight to say, 'I know what you did, Lily Locke', but then I got to thinking. Maybe I can blackmail you."

"Blackmail me how?"

"I won't tell anyone what you did if you free my girl. That's the real deal."

I leaned forward, rested my head in my hands. I considered Chuck's story, and Mary's, and tried to let it sink into my brain, but nothing was clicking.

"Remind me why Mary was there?" I asked, for lack of something else to say.

Chuck grumbled something indiscernible.

"What?"

"I said," he repeated angrily, "that she was borrowing some apples. Melissa's got one of the crunchiest apple trees on the island. I mean, she didn't plant it; it was there before her. That's why I'm all like, 'Is it really hers?' Shouldn't it be community property?"

I squinted. "You're worried that Mary is going to be prosecuted for pilfering a few apples?"

Chuck sucked in a deep breath. "Well, yeah."

I molded my best serious expression. "I will take care of any charges brought against her. Promise."

Chuck wiped several very-real beads of sweat from his forehead, though whether they were from nerves or from the rate at which he had downed his hot chocolate, it was impossible to say.

"But I don't understand what you're trying to tell me about Melissa," I said. "Are you sure there was nobody holding her captive? A knife to her throat, someone keeping her at spellpoint? Something?"

"I'm positive," Chuck said. "I had all that adrenaline coursing through my body. It was just racing through, flooded, you know. I remember everything like it was slow motion."

"That doesn't make sense," I said. "It sounded like she was being kidnapped."

"Now that I think about it," Chuck said. "I can see that. But from where I was standing, it looked like she was being chased."

"By me."

"Well, yeah. Unless there was someone in the house."

I debated for a moment. "You didn't see anyone between the time Melissa rushed out and my appearance in the doorway?"

Chuck shook his head. "Neither did Mary, and she had the best vantage point. She was up in the apple tree the whole time. In fact, I thought you saw her; you looked right at her."

"I guess I was distracted," I said, wondering what else I had missed.

I knew for a fact I hadn't missed another person in the house. There had been nobody in the kitchen when I'd rushed to Melissa's aid. I'd just assumed Melissa had been taken by someone who'd snuck in the back door. But if what Chuck said was true, then Melissa might not have been kidnapped at all.

My mind raced. Had she faked her own kidnapping, thinking that Liam was coming after her, that she wasn't safe in her own home? Or was the truth far stranger than what I could have ever imagined? Had Melissa been involved from the beginning?

"Well, I guess I'll be going then," Chuck said. "Anything else?"

I stood, releasing my hot chocolate mug from unsteady fingers. "Did you see which direction she went?"

Chuck nodded. "She ran north out of her yard. Stopped screaming once she went through the hedges, ducked over that little stream there. Then she disappeared into the woods near the river that splits the island in half. No clue where she was headed, but she didn't want to be found. And she wasn't... looking around all frantic or anything. She had a route, you know? She knew exactly where she was headed."

On that note, I walked Chuck to the door and considered all he'd told me. I thanked him, sent him home with a leftover bag of marshmallows, and promised to follow up on Mary's narrow avoidance of jail time in exchange for Chuck's new status as my CI.

I raised my wrist and Commed Ranger X. He didn't answer, which had my heart racing even faster than before. I left a quick message explaining I needed to talk to him about an update possibly relevant to the case.

For three hours, I waited up. I sat in bed with a spellbook propped on my lap, reading the same paragraph over and over again, and still, I had no clue how to make Lemon Littles. Finally, I slid under the covers, glanced at my silent Comm, and let myself drift into a fitful sleep.

Chapter 13

I woke to find zero messages on my Comm. Not so much as a missed peep from Ranger X. Rolling over in bed, I pulled the covers up to my chin and pondered what that might mean, hoping against all hope it wasn't an ominous sign.

Ranger X and I hadn't exactly parted on the best terms, but it hadn't been entirely awful. We had still said we loved one another. And I doubted that Ranger X would completely ignore me just because he was frustrated with me—especially not if I had information regarding the case.

Which could only mean one of two things.

Either there'd been a huge breakthrough in the case and X was busy... or my fiancé was in trouble.

I threw on the first outfit I could find, jean shorts and a tank top, shoved my arms into a cardigan to combat the surely cool morning breeze, and raced downstairs. I didn't stop to say hello to Gus, nor did I bother to look at the coffee machine.

"Where're you off to?" Gus asked. "There's a mug for you on the table."

"No time," I gasped.

"It's a travel mug," Gus said. "I sensed you might be on the run today. When should I open the shop?"

I considered for the briefest of seconds, shook my head. "I don't care."

"But—"

"I'll be in touch as soon as I can," I said. "I think Ranger X is in trouble. He's not answering his Comm."

"Go."

I grabbed the mug, gulped back a sip of the piping hot liquid, and propelled myself through the front door. I slammed it shut, then raced across the beach. My shoes sank into the sand, spitting up a trail as I jogged north toward Ranger X's home.

His home, really, was a glorified cabin in the woods. Before he'd met me, he hadn't had visitors, which was horribly apparent by the streamlined barrenness of his place. It was nice enough with all the necessary amenities, but it could at best be described as a clean and efficient place to sleep and change clothes. I wouldn't call it luxurious by a long stretch.

Before we'd gotten engaged, he'd given me a key to his front door, along with the open invitation to use it anytime. I intended to use it today.

Fingers shaking, I slipped the key into the lock and twisted. It took me a minute or two to get it open; I'd barely ever used his key. We spent most of our time out and about or at the bungalow, and when I came by X's cabin, he was usually home and ready for me.

"X?" I asked, coming to a stop in the entryway. "Are you..."

I trailed off at the sight of X sitting at his kitchen table. He had one hand looped around a coffee mug that looked untouched, steam swirling beneath his chin, and the other arm leaned against the table. There was a tiredness to him that hadn't been there the night before, a resigned weariness as he looked up at me when I entered the room.

He didn't seem surprised to see me which wasn't shocking, seeing as I'd rattled the key in the lock for over a minute. We watched one another carefully for a moment before I broke the silence.

"I was worried when you didn't answer your Comm," I murmured. "I know we left things a little... unresolved, but I just had to know you were safe."

Ranger X didn't immediately respond. It seemed as if he hadn't heard what I'd said, but that was impossible. Raising his coffee mug to his lips, he took a sip—not appearing to care the liquid was scorching hot. I waited impatiently as he raised his gaze and met mine.

"We made an arrest," he said finally. "We found Landon's murderer."

My throat constricted, my gut twisted as I waited for the name. "Who is he?"

"She," Ranger X said on an exhale. "She is in prison."

"But—"

"Melissa wasn't kidnapped," Ranger X said. "She staged it. Upon thorough investigation of her home, we found enough information on Mind Melters to secure necessary warrants. A search of her work locker—"

"At Harpin's tea shop?"

Ranger X nodded. "Inside the locker were Residuals from a Mind Melter. We called in the Reserve, Detective Dani DeMarco of the Sixth Precinct—who confirmed the findings for us early this morning. We found Melissa holed up in the woods."

"I don't understand. What motivation does she have to kill her boyfriend?"

"She's still denying any involvement," X said. "But with the Residuals, we have a solid case against her. Enough to make an arrest."

"But—"

"Her only alibi was that she used the restroom—and we can't find one other person who saw her in there. She claims it was empty, but... it's Main Street. People are always around."

"You don't think she might be telling the truth?" I asked. "That someone might be framing her?"

"I don't know the answer." He shook his head. "All the evidence is stacking up against Melissa, but something isn't right. Why fake a kidnapping?"

I shook my head. "I don't have an answer to that."

"You said you had something to tell me?" Ranger X pinched his forehead. "I'm sorry to have worried you. It was a busy night."

"I can see that. And, uh, my thing isn't exactly important anymore," I said. "But I suppose it doesn't hurt to tell you. I had a visit from Chuck last night."

"The gnome?"

"The one and only. As it turns out, his girlfriend was stealing apples from Melissa's tree while I was at her house. During the time of Melissa's supposed kidnapping."

Ranger X's eyes lit up. "And?"

"And he thought I was the one chasing her out of the house," I said. "Chuck said both he and Mary, his girlfriend, saw Melissa run outside of her own accord—screaming, breaking glass, making a ruckus. I was the next person they saw. Chuck showed up trying to blackmail me, thinking I had something to do with her disappearance."

Ranger X didn't look surprised, just disappointed. "Damn."

I raised my own coffee mug to my lips and took a sip. It tasted sour. "So," I said. "What comes next?"

"She'll be put on trial," Ranger X said. "If proven guilty, she'll spend the rest of her life in prison."

"I see." I swallowed. "And what about us?"

"What do you mean?" Ranger X shot me a confused glance. "Oh, last night. I'm sorry—it's been a long few hours. I'm sorry if I overreacted. I know you only wanted to help."

I raised my shoulder in acceptance of his apology and inched closer. He pulled me onto his lap and wrapped his arms around me, pressing a kiss to my neck that sent shivers down my spine.

"Can we please forget about it?" he whispered in my ear.

I wrapped my arms around his neck. "I think that's a very good idea."

Chapter 14

The next two days passed quickly. The first was a day reserved for Ranger L. The Isle as a whole shut down for the funeral, and the turnout for islanders to pay respects to Landon was overwhelming. Not a soul missed it—except for the notoriously absent person who should have been seated in the front row with the family.

Melissa was deep within the confines of The Isle's prison. Probably on a similar level of maximum security as my father. Short of trying to wipe out an entire population of people, a la my father, Melissa had committed one of the worst offenses in the islanders' eyes, and she'd pay dearly for it.

The day after the funeral, I woke with Ranger X beside me in bed for the first time in several days. With the case mostly wrapped up, X had finally taken a full night off work after nearly 'round the clock duty since the murder.

Following a leisurely morning relaxing in bed, we finally pulled ourselves free of the tangled sheets and made our way downstairs. As I brewed coffee, I cast a glance over my shoulder at X. "I don't mean to bring up the case already," I said carefully, "but what are the chances I could get in for a visit to prison? I just want to talk to Melissa."

Ranger X looked handsome in a quarter zip gray sweater, soft as butter, as he sat at the table in the middle of the storeroom staring at a plate of food. "I don't know. I can't get you in there myself—there's a ban on visitors to her cell, and I can't afford to risk people thinking

I'm showing you favoritism on this one. We have to do everything by the book. Maybe once the trial is complete."

"I figured you'd say that," I said. "I just... I want to understand. Maybe if I could talk to her..."

"We're all thinking that." Ranger X's jaw went tight. "We all wonder why, but the truth is, she's not talking. I'm sorry, I don't see that changing for anyone—even you. She killed the man she claimed to love. I am not sure there is any explanation that would make this better."

"Maybe that's true." I pulled the coffee cups off the table and set one in front of X. "At least it's over now, and Landon's family can have closure. Not that it helps all that much in easing the pain they must be feeling."

Ranger X leaned toward me and pressed a kiss to the edge of my mouth. "Try not to worry."

"I'm not worried," I said. "I just wish I understood. There are still some things that don't quite make sense. The letter with Liam's name on it... Ranger L's visits into The Forest and weekends away. I don't know how that's explained by Melissa's arrest."

Ranger X raised his shoulders and lowered them. "We've got our work cut out for us in piecing together the details to the case. With any luck, Melissa will try to strike a deal and start talking. If not, we might never know. Sometimes, the worst criminals aren't meant to be understood."

"I suppose you're right."

We finished our breakfasts and coffee, lingering over a shared doughnut for dessert, before Ranger X stood to leave.

"I have to go into the office for a bit," Ranger X said, apology in his eyes. "As you said, we don't exactly have this case tied up in a bow. And I'm not risking Melissa going free on a technicality."

I kissed his cheek. "I understand. See you tonight?"

He turned my peck into a full-on smooch, leaving me fluttery and happy inside. I waited until he'd disappeared down the path in front of the bungalow before closing the door behind me and turning to face the storeroom.

I had the entire day in front of me. Ranger X was at work, and I'd instructed Gus to take time off to be with Mimsey. He'd been reluctant to do so, but a nudge from Mimsey had been all the convincing he'd needed. With the capture of Melissa, the island was in a noticeably more celebratory mood, and the requests for Energy Elixers and protective spells had slowed to a drizzle.

Humming, I began rearranging the vials on the shelves. I'd been meaning to do a thorough reorganization of the storeroom for quite some time, but one disaster after the next had made that impossible. I'd just unloaded a very expired bottle of spider legs from the back of a dusty old shelf when a noise from somewhere near the fireplace startled me, and I whipped around, losing the jar in the process.

The glass shattered on the ground, just before the feet of an unfamiliar man standing in front of the hearth. A glance toward the front door told me it remained closed and locked.

"How'd you get in here?" I asked. "And who are you?"

The man smiled. He stood taller and thinner than Ranger X and was quite handsome in a sleek, polished sort of way. His hair was dark, but his eyes were a startling blue, and he wore a dressy suit that was obviously expensive.

"Good morning, Lily," he said in a deep voice. It was easy to listen to him talk. He spoke with slow, measured speech and sounded inherently calm. "I'm not here to hurt you; much the opposite. I've come to check on you."

"Me? Why?" I glanced once again at the door. "How'd you get in here? And *who* are you?"

"Call me Banks," he said with a smile that lit up his features. "How did I get in here? That's a story for later. If, of course, you agree to come with me."

"With you? Where?"

"I have something I'd like to show you."

"I'm sorry, but I'm not going anywhere with you."

Banks stepped closer, gave me another smile. "I think you might change your mind once I explain—after all, we're about to be family."

"What is that supposed to mean?"

"You see, Ms. Locke—" Banks paused, extended his hand toward me. "You're engaged to marry my brother."

IT TOOK HALF AN HOUR before Banks was able to thoroughly convince me of his identity. Eventually, he'd offered enough proof to satisfy most of my doubts, and when he'd extended his hand a second time and asked me to come with him to talk, I took it.

"Where are we?" I asked, after a light popping sound and a twist in my gut deposited us at a gazebo shielded in every direction by tall pines. "And what sort of magic was that?"

Banks's eyes flicked toward me as he began walking. "We're on the mainland. New England, ever been?"

I followed him from the gazebo and found that we'd arrived on the doorstep of a neat little town that looked as if it belonged in a movie set somewhere. Old homes in red brick and stately white, handsome browns and noble blues stood tall on either side of us.

The leaves were just starting to change colors for fall, painting the horizon a brilliant portrait of bright red and sunburst yellow and brilliant orange. There was a crispness to the air that smelled of apples and cinnamon, roasted squash and pumpkin pie. I shivered under my sweater, ready to be inside one of these old homes, warming by a fire.

I shook my head. "I grew up on the mainland, but I didn't get much travelling done."

Banks nodded but didn't look surprised. "I'm sorry to have appeared the way I did this morning. I hadn't meant to startle you."

"What *did* you expect to do? Usually, people appearing in my living room aren't a good sign."

He gave a low laugh. "No, I imagine not. But I didn't want to be seen, and I didn't know another way to reach you. And," he continued quickly, "I needed you to trust me. I figured you'd need to see me in the flesh to believe it."

I scanned him over, knowing he was probably right. After he had managed to convince me through a series of rigorous questions involving X's real name, history, and other things only a family member would know about him, I'd then taken a closer look at the man who'd claimed to be X's brother.

They did look alike, in a way. The dark hair, the intelligent eyes. While they were different in stature, there was something in the way they moved, the way they spoke that—despite many years without communication—made it obvious they shared a genetic pool.

"And the sort of magic that allows you to pop places you want?" I asked. "What's that all about?"

"I think we should get inside before we discuss magic." Banks raised an eyebrow. "I'll tell you whatever you want to know over a drink."

"You still haven't explained how you found me... or why."

"Brotherhood is a two-way street in my book," Banks said. "I know Cannon has been keeping an eye on us for years. Just because he thinks ties are cut... doesn't mean we *wanted* things that way."

"He cut ties?"

"I imagine he told you what happened between us."

"He accidentally hurt you with his magic," I said. "Badly."

"That was a long time ago," Banks said. "A part of me thinks he's been spending his whole life dedicated to the Ranger program in an attempt to make up for what happened between us. It wasn't his fault, though. He was young and inexperienced. My parents didn't know how strong their son's magic was, so it went unchecked for too long. I don't hold a grudge."

"Have you tried to talk to him?"

"We did, early on," he said. "Eventually, we gave up. Figured he'd come back when he was ready. But that didn't mean we'd forgotten about him. I know he checks on us, and the reverse is also true."

"How do I fit into all this?"

"When I heard he was getting married, I thought maybe it was time to repair old bonds." Banks gave me a side-eyed glance. "That's where you come in."

"You think I can convince him to... reconnect?"

"I don't know. Can you?"

I was still pondering the influx of information when Banks stopped in front of one of the oldest-looking houses on the street. He made his way down a narrow path, his feet crunching over leaves as we passed flower gardens that had begun to brown.

Banks let us both inside and kicked off his shoes while I followed suit. He led me through a small entryway where my suspicions that the house was an old home were confirmed by the strange nooks and crannies and built-ins that made absolutely no sense in a charming sort of way.

We reached the living area complete with a crackling fire, just as I'd hoped for when chilled to the bone outside. To either side, floor-to-ceiling bookshelves had been crammed full with worn paperbacks and several sturdy looking hardcovers. A detour and closer inspection of the shelves told me that one side covered all non-magical related reading—James Patterson, adventure novels, and an old set of Encyclopedias that pre-dated the internet.

To the right of the fire was everything magical. Witchcraft, spell books, potion making do-it-yourself tutorials. I ran a finger over several of the books, wondered again what it would have been like to grow up in a family that split their time between the human world and the magical one. Would I have turned out to be a better Mixologist if I'd learned about my magic from a young age?

I made my way into the kitchen a step behind Banks. It was a warm space with earthy tones on the walls.

Banks reached for two mugs from the cabinet. "Can I offer you something to drink?"

"I'm fine, thanks."

"You're cold." His gaze landed on me. "Tea?"

"That would be lovely."

Banks moved quickly through the kitchen, putting on the kettle and preparing two mugs while I stood by and surveyed his movements, startled to see how similar some of Banks's mannerisms were to Ranger X's.

When the water was boiled and the tea was good and steeped, Banks handed me a glass mug and nodded toward a different door than the one from which we'd entered. It led to an enclosed four-season porch with a beautiful view of a forest beyond a small backyard, the tops of the trees fiery with fall-colored foliage.

I cupped my hands around the mug and raised it to my lips. "So, am I allowed to ask about magic now? I'm not familiar with the sort of spell you used to get us here."

"I'm a Spellbinder."

"I've never met a Spellbinder," I said. "What does that mean? What sort of magic is it?"

"Tell me about Mixology," Banks said, ignoring my question. "How does it work?"

I considered. "Well, it's difficult to explain, I suppose. I mean, the basic concept is that I blend potions and other concoctions together.

I use a variety of ingredients and the help of my assistant, along with a spellbook that's been passed down through generations of Mixologists. A lot of it is studying, learning what mixes well with what, and testing."

"But..." Banks prompted. "There's more."

"There is," I said carefully. "There's an element to Mixology that I'll never be able to explain, no matter how hard I try. It's just a part of who I am. Some pieces of it are unteachable. It's either in your blood, or it's not."

Banks gave a knowing nod. "Spellbinding is much the same. Simply put, I fashion spells. On a very... shall we say, high-caliber level. My services are not inexpensive."

"How is Spellbinding different than just writing my own spell?"

"Most witches, wizards, sorcerers, and the like can create their own spells without too much trouble. However, it is considered a relatively dangerous practice. Spells can be finicky, interact with one another in strange ways, and without proper training, it's rare to be able to concoct a truly powerful spell. Spellbinding is a specific trade meant to create the most difficult or dangerous of spells."

"No wonder. My own spells aren't exactly perfect," I said dryly. "I tried to write a simple cleaning spell the other day, and my hot chocolate disappeared with it."

"As long as you're not hurting yourself or blowing anything up, you're doing pretty good."

"I don't write my own spells often—if I need something big, I usually make a potion for it."

"Two different paths to the same outcome," he said. "That's the beauty of this thing we call magic. If you're truly interested, it's probably easier to show you what I do rather than try to explain it. Do you remember the cleaning spell you came up with that backfired?"

I felt the back of my neck redden. "I'd really rather not share. It's quite embarrassing."

"Like I said, if you didn't hurt anyone, you're doing better than most people who've tried to write spells. My mother worked as an emergency nurse in a magical hospital and..." He blew out an exaggerated breath. "The stories we've heard from misguided spells would set your hair on fire."

"Fine," I agreed.

I took a deep breath and repeated the spell I'd used when Chuck had startled me at the door. By the time I finished, Banks was nodding.

"Nothing to be ashamed of," he said. "But there's room for improvement."

"I figured as much."

"First, I would add a timing clause. It gives you control of when the spell fires, instead of just going on command. Second, I'd recommend you isolate the mess instead of leaving the terms vague."

I considered his advice, but it was about as clear as the swamp in the Grove of Gnomes.

"Spellbinding is a form of magic that weaves words together. Words, as I'm sure you know, are powerful things. Sometimes we mean exactly as we say, other times, we don't. Spells work the same—we have to be very careful, exceedingly cautious, to think of all possible interpretations of a spell. Otherwise drastic, and sometimes devastating, consequences can occur."

"No pressure."

"The wrong inflection on the word 'wound' can mean several very different things," Banks explained. "The word 'read' can be past or present tense, and if we don't know the words we're speaking before we say them aloud, it can have interesting consequences."

"I'm beginning to think I'm quite glad I didn't blow up from my dinky little cleaning spell."

Banks gave a thin smile. "I'm very cautious, probably on the tail end of too cautious. It's just, between my years of studies and my mother's stories, I've seen too many spells go wrong to take it lightly."

"I understand. I'd feel the same way about having someone drink a potion I wasn't confident I'd made correctly."

"The upside to this—believe me, there is one," Banks said happily, "is that when it's right, it's right. It's a beautiful thing. A harmony in the world of magic, a feeling—and you'll know once you've achieved it. You just know."

"I understand."

"To demonstrate, let's take your spell."

Banks stood and moved to the kitchen. When he returned, he had a glass of steaming hot cocoa with him. The second he reached the porch, he turned the mug upside down and let half of the chocolatey liquid splash all over a furry white rug. When I gasped, he smiled.

"Now," Banks said slowly, watching as hot chocolate seeped into the beautiful white fabric. "Let's work on isolating the mess first, then adding a timer clause. I'm thinking, something like this."

He hesitated, drew in a breath. I was torn between watching the hot chocolate spoil the rug and keeping an eye on Banks's face, which had gone slack with concentration. He closed his eyes, his lashes flickering as his forehead pinched in thought.

When his eyes opened, he smiled.

"This mess that's made,
Will be cleaned and fade.
Only that which shouldn't be,
will disappear on a count of three."

Banks pointed to me.

"One," I said, uncertain. My voice grew stronger as he pointed a second time at me. "Two," I said, then fixed my eyes on the mess. "Three."

Seconds later, the hot chocolate that had stained the rug slowly began to fade. Behind, it left only a sparkling area—cleaner than before Banks had dumped hot chocolate all over everything.

"Voila," Banks said, tipping his mug slightly, so I could see the rest of his hot chocolate contents safely where they belonged. "Only the mess disappeared. You had control over the spell. We cleaned and vanished the mess."

"And how did you know to do that?"

"It's like..." He thought on it again. "Weaving, knitting, any of those things, except with words. There are basic patterns to follow, and then a million variations on those patterns. You must first learn the basic patterns that everyone else has learned for centuries, and once you've mastered those, you begin to feel your own way through the nuances, the rest of it, until you're making up your own patterns."

"Just like Mixology," I said. "There are templates passed down in the book, but often, the best potions take a bit of tweaking to make them just right."

The sound of the doorbell out front interrupted Banks's response. He stood, collected the three mugs we'd brought with us onto the porch, and excused himself to greet the visitor. I sat back in my seat, arms wrapped around my legs, and waited.

Banks returned shortly with a large box in his arms. He gave me a strange sort of smile, then extended it toward me. "This is for you."

I blinked. "Is this some sort of a joke?"

"I wondered the same thing."

My blood ran cold. "Who knows I'm here? Even I don't know where I am. Did you see who delivered the box? Did he say anything?"

"She," Banks corrected. "Older lady, sort of frizzy hair. Bright orange dress with a pink scarf around her head. I asked her to come inside, but she was gone before I shut the door."

I closed my eyes. "I really don't want to open it."

"That's fine." Banks set the box down with a shrug. "Though I thought it might be urgent, seeing as it's a bit odd she went to the trouble of tracking you down here."

I leaned forward, my fingers playing over the edge of the parcel. While I didn't particularly want to open the package at all, Banks had a point. Why had The Quilter stopped by now with a gift? Of all times?

With a sudden burst of hope, I glanced up at Banks. "Are you married? Expecting a baby?"

"No."

I heaved a huge sigh. "I was really hoping she'd meant for me to give this to you."

"You don't sound thrilled with my answer."

"The Quilter has been trying to give me a gift recently that I just don't want. I keep hoping that it's actually for someone else."

"The Quilter?" Banks's ears perked up. "You've met her?"

"You did, too," I said. "That was probably her outside. She's been after me for days."

Banks politely sat back in his chair and let silence take over, but his gaze was fixed keenly on my fingers as I tussled with the parcel. When I peeled back the top layer, my heart sank.

On top of the package was a most unwelcome gift.

There, wrapped in a gorgeous bow, was the softest, most beautiful baby blanket I'd ever seen. And it was mine.

"LILY, ARE YOU OKAY?" Banks's voice shook me out of my daze. "Is that what you expected?"

"Unfortunately." I removed the blanket and set it on my lap, fingering the cloth. "Do you need this by any chance? Or know anyone else who could use it?"

When Banks didn't respond, I looked up to find his gaze fixed on the box. I followed his line of sight to find that the package wasn't empty. There, tucked into the bottom of the box, was the first gift The Quilter had given me.

"Oh, that," I said. "I knew about that one. It's not as upsetting as this."

"Is that a Muse? I've only heard of them—never seen one for myself."

"A muse?"

"Do you mind if I..." Banks trailed off, gestured toward the package. "I'm sorry to pry, but—wow. These are amazingly rare."

"I've no clue." I shrugged. "Feel free to take a look. I've not been able to figure out if it's supposed to do anything."

Leaning forward, Banks removed the blanket from the cardboard box and held it reverently in his hands. "Yes," he breathed. "This is it. A Muse, a very powerful one at that."

"But—if that's a Muse," I hesitated, looking at the gift on his lap. "Then what is this?"

Banks's eyes again glanced at the yellow blanket. "Um, I've no clue. A baby blanket?"

"You don't—it's not some magical thing?"

He shrugged. "I just recognized the Muse. I can't tell you about the one you're holding. Sorry."

"What does a Muse blanket do?"

"A Muse is a form of magic that can't be replicated by most of us. It's a supernatural power granted to very few. I know of three people who've had the gift, only two are alive."

"Is one of them The Quilter?"

"Yes."

I studied the fabric in Banks's hands. "I had no clue it was so valuable. How did you recognize it?"

"Valuable?" His eyebrows shot up. "It's priceless. You can't sell something like this. It can only be given away, and often then, the only person who can prompt the change in ownership of a Muse item is the creator. If it falls into someone else's hands, at best, it won't work."

"At worst?"

He gave a non-committal shrug. "You asked how I recognized it. Well, I've studied all types of magic, and I recognized the Muse from my schooling. Do you see the slight shimmer here? The magic is woven into the strands of the blanket."

I looked closer and, sure enough, flecks of silver so tiny they might've been bits of crushed starlight appeared soaked into the fabric. "I hadn't noticed that before."

"You wouldn't—not unless you're looking for it. The Muse magic has been engrained into this very blanket, made just for you—for a purpose. The Quilter needs you to have this, and apparently, it's quite urgent."

"How do I figure out how to use it?"

"That's the beauty of it," he said. "You don't need to figure anything out. Just keep it close. Use it when you like. Don't be afraid of it. Muse magic will guide you in the appropriate direction."

"Guide me how?"

"I don't know the answer to that, as it's different for each person," Banks said. "But you'll know. Put it on, go ahead."

"But—"

"It's yours," Banks encouraged. "It won't hurt you. It's here to protect you."

"I—later," I said. "I'll look into it later. More importantly, are you sure—absolutely positive—that you don't recognize this one?"

Banks took the blanket from my hands and examined it, a hint of skepticism in his eyes. "I'm sorry," he said finally. "I can't determine if it's magical at all."

"Well, then why did The Quilter give it to me? Why was it so *urgent* that she needed to track me down at your house?"

"I don't know, Lily. Is something wrong?" Banks watched me carefully. "You seem quite upset."

I ran a hand over my forehead, frustrated that The Quilter hadn't listened to my wishes. All I'd asked was for her to keep her gifts to herself. I shook my head.

"I'm sorry," I said quietly. "I didn't mean to take any of this out on you. I'm just—I'm dealing with something stressful."

"Is there something I can help you with?"

"I need a spell." I blurted the words out suddenly, and for a moment—it felt like they hadn't even come from me. I didn't remember thinking them, or saying them. As I rested a hand on the Muse blanket, it felt suddenly warm, and I wondered...

"Is it working?" Banks asked. "Did you feel something?"

"I don't know." I shook my head. "That was weird. I was just thinking that I needed a spell, and it was like the words just popped out of my head without my having a say."

"I might be able to help you with a spell."

"Not this one," I said wearily. "It's complicated and personal, and I can't let Cannon know about it."

"I can only help if you ask."

"I can't ask you to do something of this magnitude."

"You can ask," he pointed out. "And I can always say no."

I hesitated, scratched at my arm. My nerves were ramped up to an all-time maximum. "I need a spell that guarantees I won't get pregnant. No matter what."

Banks shifted, but he did a good job of masking any surprise at my request. "There are ways to prevent that without magic. Ways that are far more reversible than a spell."

"I know, and I understand that," I said. "But this is a very special circumstance. I've already chosen not to have children, and I just need to make it final."

"Final?" A hint of curiosity crept into Banks's voice. "I take it you have discussed this with your fiancé?"

"I've expressed my wishes to Ranger X, but he doesn't know I'm looking for a spell—I doubt he'd agree to it. But I promise you, Banks—I wouldn't be asking you if it wasn't crucially important."

Banks thoughtfully glanced down at the yellow baby blanket, giving me time to rid myself of the tears threatening to fall before he looked back to me.

"I see," he said simply. "I'm sorry."

I bit my lip, stifled a sob. "Me too."

"You'll understand that I can't give you an answer yet," he said. "I need time to think, and I suggest you do the same. Maybe the Muse blanket can help with your decision."

Unless the Muse blanket could somehow rid this earth of my father or dissolve our iron clad contract, I didn't see how it could help. I sincerely doubted it had the power to do any such thing.

"Thank you for considering it," I murmured. "And please, don't say anything to Cannon. Not yet. I need to talk to him first."

"Of course," he said. "This is between us. It seems... maybe it is time for me to get you home."

"I think that's a good idea," I said, my voice raspy. "I think—"

My Comm buzzed, startling me back to the world of The Isle. I glanced at the name on it, then looked up at Banks,

"It's your brother," I said. "I should get going. I'll Comm him once I'm back on The Isle."

"Of course." Banks stood. "Lily, it was great to meet you. I hope you'll consider my proposition."

I'd forgotten all about the reason Banks had introduced himself to me in the first place. I'd been so caught up in his lessons on Spellbinding, on the sudden appearance of The Quilter in a place she didn't belong, and on the request I'd found myself asking of Banks. "I'll talk to X. Er, Cannon," I said. "What should I say?"

"You'll know better than me." Banks gave a tight smile. "It's been years since I've spoken to him. If you could just let him know... we'd like him back."

I nodded, silencing my Comm as it interrupted with a second buzz. When it sounded for the third time, I gestured to my wrist as an explanation to Banks and stepped into the kitchen to answer it.

"Lily, where are you?" Ranger X asked. "I've been trying to get ahold of you."

"A meeting," I said. "What's wrong?"

"There's been a breakout," Ranger X said, his words urgent. "The vampire hunter who attacked Poppy is missing."

I tried to swallow, but my throat was dry. "What? How is that possible?"

"I'm not sure," Ranger X said. "But that's not all."

"Well?" I demanded, my mind racing toward the worst-case scenario. "What else?"

"Poppy's missing," Ranger X said. "Or, she didn't show up for work this morning. There's a chance she's not missing at all and is gone of her own free will, but with the disappearance of her attacker, we need to assume the worst."

I froze. "She's gone. He's got her."

"Lily, breathe. We don't know that," X said. "But I think you should get back here. Just in case Poppy tries to contact you. Where did you say you were?"

"I'll be back soon," I said. "Do you know how the hunter got away?"

Ranger X sighed over the line. "I'm afraid he had help. Escape from our prison cells is virtually impossible without inside assistance. Especially for someone like a vamp hunter with limited magical capabilities. I'm wondering if it's possible that Poppy helped him escape?"

"He tried to kill her!" I cried, but it rang a little hollow. I shook my head, suddenly sick to my stomach. "I'll meet you at the bungalow in twenty minutes."

Chapter 15

Banks dropped me off behind the bungalow in an outcropping of trees and greenery. Once we'd popped into place and I'd gotten my bearings, I turned to face him.

"Thank you," I said. "For everything. I'm glad I got the opportunity to meet you."

Banks bowed his head. "I'll think about your request. You do the same."

"I'll talk to X," I said. "I can't guarantee what his response will be."

Banks gave me a thin smile, though there was a twinkle in his eye when he spoke. "That's a given. He always was independent, even when he was young. But I have a feeling you might be able to change his mind."

I turned, made my way to the edge of the trees. By the time I glanced over my shoulder to wave goodbye to Banks, he was gone. I followed the sandy path up to the bungalow, thoughts of Banks and Ranger X's family slipping from my mind as thoughts of my own cousin came front and center.

What was Poppy up to? Had she been kidnapped, or was she in on the whole thing? I eased through the front door of the bungalow and found an audience waiting for me. Gus and Mimsey sat next to one another at the storeroom table while Ranger X leaned against the wall nearest me. Mimsey's face was white as a sheet, and Gus had his arm draped over Mimsey's shoulder. They weren't speaking, just waiting.

"Sorry I'm late," I said. "Any word on Poppy?"

My first look was to Mimsey, but she seemed too catatonic to respond.

"She's not saying much," Gus said in explanation. "It's a bit of a shock. Poppy was due to work dispatch at Ranger HQ this morning, but she didn't show for her shift. That all coincided with the approximate time a call originated from the prison announcing that the vamp hunter had escaped."

Ranger X turned to me. "I don't have any news yet. I do have to report to HQ, but I wanted to make sure you were okay before I did. Where did you say you'd gone?"

"I'll tell you about it later," I said. "It's not important. What are we going to do about Poppy? What can I do?"

"I've requested an update from all on-duty Rangers," X said. "They're prepping everything as we speak. We'll have everyone looking for her." He turned toward Mimsey. "We'll find your daughter."

Mimsey just nodded. She gave a sniff, wiped at her nose with a tissue.

"I'll pour over my books and see if there's some sort of potion or spell I can find that'll guide us to her," I offered. "Gus, you can help me. Mimsey you can stay put and have a cup of tea. X will let us know the moment the Rangers find anything."

Ranger X nodded and disappeared without argument, though I didn't miss the way his eyes lingered on me in question—specifically on the box in my arms—before he closed the door behind him. I wasn't sure how I'd broach the subject of his brother's meeting, but for now, Banks could wait.

"We'll find Poppy," I repeated, as much to myself as to Mimsey and Gus. "I swear it, we'll find her."

I plopped myself down at the table and dragged *The Magic of Mixology* toward me. Gus had wisely pulled it out and prepared a slew of basic ingredients that could quickly be readied for whatever potion struck my fancy. As it was, I had no clue how to find Poppy and her captor, and I was hoping for a little inspiration from the text.

Inspiration, I thought, tapping a finger against my lips. Banks's admiration of the Muse blanket popped into my head, so I pulled it from the box that sat by my side. Ignoring Gus's curious stare, I wrapped it around my shoulders, hunched over the table, and began to thumb through the ancient pages.

Some twenty minutes later, I shot to my feet. "I don't need to be here."

"What?" Gus asked. "What are you talking about?"

"Did you find her?" Mimsey asked anxiously. "Are you going after her?"

"I don't think so," I said, feeling puzzled at my own outburst. "I'm not—er, I'm not actually sure why I said any of that."

I sat back down, but the seat felt too warm. I yelped and leapt up, tugging the blanket closer as my fingers treaded carefully over the fabric.

"Oh, no," I muttered. "I think I need to go somewhere."

"Where?" Gus demanded. "What's gotten into you, Lily?"

"I'm sorry," I said. "I can't tell you. I literally can't say because I've no clue. All I know is that I need to go somewhere. I'll be back. I'm sorry."

With my unsatisfying explanation, I let myself be tugged out of the bungalow. I shifted the blanket tighter to me, wondering if this was what Banks had meant. If I was being guided by something bigger, stronger, more powerful than myself.

Whatever it was, I was desperate enough to give it a try.

"Where to now?" I asked the blanket. "Help me find Poppy."

My feet were pulled down a familiar path across The Isle. I didn't know where I was going, but the route was so familiar that I had no doubt I'd recognize the destination once I'd arrived.

Sure enough, a short walk later, I was outside of the house Mimsey and Poppy shared. It was a neat little cottage adorned with overflowing flowerbeds and cute decorations, looking like something out of a fairytale.

"What am I supposed to do here?" I asked the empty air before me. "Poppy wouldn't be at *home.*"

There was obviously no answer, seeing as I was speaking to a blanket. Still, I'd come this far, so it was worth a shot to go inside. I shrugged the blanket off and rested it over the porch railing before trying the doorknob, only to find it was locked.

A sudden chill rushed over my shoulders, sending me into shivers so violent my teeth clashed together. "Jeez," I mumbled. "I get the picture."

I wrapped the blanket once more over my shoulders and, on a sudden impulse, tried the doorknob again. There was the slightest of clicks, a sound like a bell tinkling far in the distance, and the knob twisted and let me inside.

I admired the blanket in a new light. "I guess you are more impressive than I gave you credit for. Thanks."

If I wasn't mistaken, the blanket warmed ever so slightly around my shoulders. As soon as I entered the house, I heard the whisper of muffled voices from a few rooms over.

I opened my mouth to yell for Poppy, but before I could, I tasted cotton and yarn as I found myself on the verge of swallowing a ball of lint. The blanket had inched up and shoved itself into my mouth—obviously to stifle my call.

"I guess I'll keep quiet, then," I said, once I'd pulled the blanket out of my mouth.

Creeping through the house, I followed the voices toward Poppy's bedroom. There were two voices—one male, one female. My stomach muscles clenched in anticipation. Had Poppy brought the man who'd tried to kill her into her home? Had Ranger X been right this whole time about Poppy orchestrating the vamp hunter's escape? My question was answered as I stepped into the open doorway and spotted my cousin. I gaped, unable to keep quiet any longer. "Poppy?"

Her head flicked up, swiveled to face me from where she'd been leaning over a backpack on the floor. "Lily? What are you doing here?"

"Um..." I shifted, looking over her shoulder to where the vampire hunter was standing. "Looking for you. And him. What's going on?"

"I can explain," Poppy said, nervously flicking her hair over her shoulder. "It's not what you think."

"Really? Then maybe you can help me out because I'm not sure what to think," I said. "I got a panicked call saying you were missing. Do you know your mother is sitting at my house, too shocked to even speak? We all assumed you'd been kidnapped."

Poppy's face went drawn and pale, and she could barely manage to shake her head. A whispered, "No" slipped from her lips.

For whatever reason, I didn't feel particularly in danger. I surveyed the vampire hunter carefully, but whether it was supernatural cues from the Muse blanket or just my own gut instinct, I didn't sense harm radiating from him. In fact, I felt completely calm as I met Poppy's gaze head on.

"All the Rangers are looking for you. Tell me what's going on. Please."

Again, Poppy just shook her head. Anguish filled her eyes. "I can't."

I blinked, and it dawned on me. "Your mother knows exactly where you are," I said, understanding sinking in. I rubbed my forehead. "I should have known. Mimsey's not talking because she doesn't trust herself to lie. She's covering for you, isn't she? You'd never worry your mother like this on purpose. You wouldn't put Mimsey through this after the last time you'd been taken and imprisoned, your memory wiped."

"I needed to ask her blessing." The voice was deep, rolling. It came from the vampire hunter. "It's not Poppy's fault, it's mine, too. We are in love, Miss Locke."

"You, pipe down," I said. "You're supposed to be in prison."

"He's not!" Poppy insisted. "It's all wrong. His name is Chase, and he's telling the truth. He doesn't know who hired him. He's being held on trumped-up charges with the hopes that he can lead the Rangers to someone bigger than him. Well, he can't! They can't keep him locked in there like that—he was wasting away!"

"Because he tried to kill you!"

"Well, he didn't succeed," she said stubbornly. "I've forgiven him, and I didn't press charges. You, of all people, should understand. You used Amuletto Kiss on him—you're the one who knew he loved me before anyone else."

I vividly remembered the rush of emotions as I'd stepped into the vampire hunter's body, mind, and soul. I shivered, knowing that his love for Poppy was the only truth I believed about him.

"What's next?" I asked. "You can't exactly send out save the dates and grab a gown from Wanda's Weddings—he's a wanted criminal!"

"We're going to run away," Poppy said. "We'll elope."

"Poppy, listen to yourself," I said. "You haven't known him long enough. Even if this man hadn't tried to kill you, I'd say it's too soon."

"When you know it's right, you just know."

"You're a vampire," I said. "He's a vampire hunter. This can't possibly work."

"You weren't supposed to work with Ranger X either," Poppy pointed out. "I'd say you're working just fine."

I swallowed what I was about to say next because she was right. "Fine. Maybe you could have made things work under different circumstances. That doesn't mean you can bust someone out of prison because you think they're innocent. That's not how the law works."

"What would you have done if it was Ranger X being held unjustly?"

I closed my eyes. "It's not the same, Poppy. It's... I have to turn you in. Everyone is scared. They think you're his captive."

"Then set the record straight," Poppy said. "After we leave. Give us half an hour—that's all I'm asking. Take the scenic route back to the bungalow. By the time you get there, we'll be gone and you can clear your conscience by trumpeting our news to the world."

My head was already shaking of its own accord. "I can't, Poppy. I just can't."

She shrugged. "Then do it already. I'm not going to fight you, Lily. If you feel the need to turn me in, I won't stop you."

Poppy reached for her vampire hunter boyfriend. She locked hands with him and met my gaze. I was struck by how eerily perfect the two looked together. Poppy's vibrant, flushed face flanked with blond hair matched perfectly against Chase's taller, leaner figure, his eyes a piercing blue, his hair neat and tidy—combed probably for the first time since he'd been carted to prison.

When Poppy looked at him, their gaze connected in a fiery tangle. It became clear to me that I'd wildly underestimated their feelings for one other. They were crazy-in-love. Crazy enough to break Chase out of prison and attempt a life on the run just to be together when it would make survival for Poppy difficult. After all, she needed Vamp Vites to live, and she was best friends with her mother. She'd been an Islander for life, and I couldn't picture her being happy away from home.

I hugged the Muse blanket closer to me and closed my eyes. I let the silence of the room surround me while a calmness settled on my shoulders.

When I spoke, I could hardly comprehend the words coming out of my mouth. "You have until I get to the bungalow."

"Oh, thank you, Lily," Poppy gushed, a visible rush of breath leaving her body. She moved toward me and then pulled me against her. "I knew you would understand, and I wanted to tell you. But I couldn't put that burden on your shoulders."

I stiffly accepted the hug. Logically, I wasn't happy about any of it. My brain screamed that everything I was doing was wrong. I should Comm Ranger X! Call Mimsey! Demand Poppy put the vampire hunter right back where he belonged—in prison!

But I couldn't do it. I didn't know if it was me, magic, the Muse, or some combination that told me to let them go. And despite my brain nagging at me to stop this crazy plan, my body was frozen in place. Until a flash of movement outside the window caught my eye.

"You've got to move if you're going," I warned, still in disbelief that I was helping not only Poppy, but the man who had tried to kill my cousin. "I think Zin's on her way here."

"You have to distract her!" Poppy said. "Just give us a way out. Please."

"I'm not lying to your cousin for you."

"Don't lie then," Poppy said, her eyes pleading. "Just... stand there. Two minutes. Please."

I watched as Poppy grasped for Chase's arm and squeezed. The look of desperation in her eyes was a familiar one. I'd felt it myself, too many times to count. When I'd thought Ranger X had been dead on The Forest floor from a bout of Lumiette. When I'd been forced to sign a contract with my father or face life without X. When I thought Poppy had been kidnapped for good.

"Go," I said. "Now."

Poppy nodded, tears sparkling on her cheeks. "I'll never forget this, Lily."

I tried for a smile but didn't make it. I could barely bob my head. Before I could change my mind, I turned away from the lovestruck couple and let myself out of the house. I came to a stop on the front steps face to face with my other cousin.

"There you are," Zin gasped. "I guess you heard about Poppy. Did you find anything inside? I thought I heard something, but I can't be sure. Seems stupid for that vamp hunter to bring Poppy to her own home after a kidnapping, but we've got to be thorough."

"Yeah, I thought the same thing."

"So?" Zin squinted at me. "Did you find anything in there?"

"Zin—"

At that unfortunate moment, a crack sounded from behind the house. If I could hear it, Zin's animal-like senses would've deciphered every detail of the noise.

"They're inside!" She looked wild-eyed at me. "We need to get in there. Move, Lily—what are you doing?!"

"Zin, wait!"

Before I could stop her, Zin sprinted toward the back of the house. Her hair lengthened, her stride quickened, her posture lurched forward. There was a pop as she rounded the corner, and I had no doubt that Zin had shifted into her most familiar form to track her cousin and the vampire hunter.

For Poppy's sake, I hoped she and the hunter had a solid escape plan. I most certainly wouldn't want to be hunted down by Zin in her jaguar form. She had very big teeth.

But, I thought darkly, *Poppy's new boyfriend is a hunter, too.*

Hunter against hunter.

I felt my feet being pulled toward the path that would lead me home. Apparently, the Muse wanted me to keep my promise to Poppy. A scenic route back to the bungalow, and then I could spill everything.

"DID YOU KNOW ABOUT this?" Gus turned to Mimsey. "Did you know your daughter was running away with her would-be killer?"

Mimsey's face paled. She sat looking shrunken and tiny on an over-sized armchair near the fireplace as Gus rounded on her. Ranger X stood in the doorway, having just rushed from HQ at my Comm. I leaned over the table, feeling the back of my neck burn after divulging all that had happened during my visit to Mimsey's property.

"Don't make this about Mimsey," I said to Gus. "It's about Poppy and Chase. We were dragged into it unwillingly."

"*You* let her go," Gus said. "Her mother is sitting here, worried sick about her. Can't speak."

"I knew," Mimsey croaked. "I knew all about it. She showed up with him. I was ready to kill the man on the spot, but my daughter threw herself in front of my spell. What could I do? What could I do, Gus?" Mimsey turned toward him, reached for his shirt. Her fingers clenched tightly in the fabric. "I would never hurt my daughter, and she was ready to protect him with her life. What could I do except walk away?"

Silence filled the room. Gus played with his nails, then finally looked up. "When were you going to tell me?"

"She asked for thirty minutes," Mimsey whispered. "I lost track of time. I just sat here, frozen. Wondering when, how, why, my only daughter had gotten this idea in her head that she was in love with a man who had tried to kill her."

"He didn't succeed in killing her," I pointed out, earning shocked stares from around the room. "Believe me, I don't know why I'm defending him. But I can say for certain that Poppy is in no danger from him—he loves her. Chase had the opportunity to put a stake through Poppy's heart, and he didn't. I saw it through the Amuletto Kiss potion."

"He might not hurt her," Ranger X said, his voice carefully measured. "But that doesn't change the fact he belongs in jail until his trial."

"I agree," I said. "And I made the same argument to Poppy. She said he wasn't getting a fair trial—do you know anything about that?"

"No," Ranger X said. "But I'll look into it."

"There you all are." A venomous voice hissed as the door flew open and banged against the back wall. "Are we sitting around, chatting about how this whole Poppy being missing thing was a ruse?"

I looked over at Zin, saw fury and flame in her eyes. "Zin, please. It's not like that. You didn't see them together."

"You're right, I didn't. Because they escaped." Zin turned to Ranger X. "Sir, I tracked them as far as possible, but he's a hunter. He's good; I couldn't follow them off The Isle."

"They're off-Isle?" Mimsey asked weakly. "Where...?"

"You knew, too—didn't you?" There was a tinge of hurt in Zin's voice when she looked at her aunt. "That's the only way Poppy would have left voluntarily. She wouldn't have put you through the misery of thinking she was dead."

"I didn't mean for it to get so out of control," Mimsey said. "I don't... I don't know what I expected. But not this."

"At least we know Poppy is safe," I said. "That's the most important piece."

"What about the loser boyfriend belonging in jail piece?" Zin snapped. "Huh?"

I raised my shoulders. "I don't disagree. It's up to the Rangers how to track them now. I'm certainly not protecting him."

"We wouldn't be in this situation if either of you had just reported it from the start," Zin said. "That makes you both accessories to a jail break. Mimsey, you helped to harbor a known and dangerous criminal, and Lily—"

I raised my arms. "Arrest me then. I know what I did."

Ranger X's face constricted as he glanced at Zin's outstretched finger, pointed accusingly at me.

"We will be tracking them, right, sir?" Zin asked of Ranger X. "He's a wanted criminal. We can't have people escaping from prison and letting them get away with it. That would set a dangerous precedent."

Ranger X cleared his throat. "Ranger Z, please report to HQ. Get a briefing set up on the hour. I'll cover everything then."

Zin nodded, then shot a heated look my way. "I'll see you there, sir."

The room descended into a crispy chill. Only the sound of Zin storming out of the room and slamming the door shut behind her broke the tension.

In the next moment, Gus helped Mimsey up, mumbling something about taking her home, getting her a sedative spell and something to eat. They shuffled out quickly, leaving Ranger X and I alone in the bungalow.

"I need to talk to you about something," I said. "Do you have a minute?"

Ranger X shot a curious look my way. "Is something wrong?"

"Not more so than usual," I said. "But it's important."

"What is it?"

I grabbed Ranger X's hand and dragged him over to the extra-large chair in front of the empty fireplace. He sat first, and I crawled in next to him—holding his hand tightly as I stared at my lap and wondered how to begin.

"I had a visitor this morning after you left," I said. "I'd never met him before, but he knows you."

Ranger X's gaze was measured. "Okay."

"It was your brother."

His shoulders stiffened. "Banks."

I nodded. "He wanted to talk, so I let him. I went with him to his home, and—"

"How could you go off with a stranger?"

I ignored X's frustrated tone and tried not to sound snippy with my own. "I made him prove his identity to me until I believed him. Obviously, I was right. I'm here, and I'm fine. He wanted me to talk to you about something."

"What?"

"He wants a relationship with you, Cannon," I said. "He said he's tried to contact you over the years but has given up because you've clearly cut ties."

"I have a good reason for it," X said in a low, growly voice. "And you know it as well as I do."

"Yes, but don't you think it might be time to reconsider? Before it's too late?"

"What do you mean, too late?"

"I'm just saying—Banks isn't a child anymore. He doesn't hold a grudge over what happened years ago, and he wants a relationship with you. Your parents do, too."

"Nice of him to say so," X said shortly. "Did he want anything else?"

I swallowed. The conversation wasn't exactly going the way I'd planned. "I just think... it might be worth considering—"

"I'll consider it. Is that all?"

"No," I said, scrounging up any confidence I could muster. "It's not. I asked him to create a spell for me."

"Lily, he's a Spellbinder. He only deals in incredibly powerful spells."

"Exactly," I said. "And I don't know if he'll do it yet, but you should know I asked him about it."

"What sort of spell?"

"You have to understand, there's no way around it."

"Around what?"

"My father's contract!" I burst, my throat tightening, my entire body tense with nerves, hatred for my father, fear for X's reaction when I finally came out with the truth. "I asked your brother to fashion a spell that would prevent me from ever having children. I didn't—I would've talked to you first, but I didn't have time. I couldn't have anticipated his visit."

"Is he going to make you this spell?"

"I don't know," I said. "And I wouldn't have used it without talking to you first. I just think... it's an option we need to consider."

The temperature in the room felt positively arctic. I couldn't tell if X was in shock, or if he was angry at a level I'd never witnessed before. Likelier, he was torn between the two.

"I don't know what to say." Ranger X stood. He raked a hand over his face, moved toward the door. "I need some time."

Then, without another word, he set off from the bungalow and into the distance.

Chapter 16

Sometime later, the store opened. I robotically went through the motions of filling orders and chatting with customers. At some point, Gus appeared by my shoulder and worked silently. We didn't discuss anything except business.

As evening fell, I looked up, startled to find the stars and moon peeking out above us. The passage of time had seemed fluid this afternoon, some minutes dragging on for a lifetime while others slipped by like a flash in the pan. I was disappointed when the last customer left the bar—they'd been my distraction and had kept me from thinking about Ranger X, Poppy, Zin, or Mimsey.

"I need a breath of fresh air," I told Gus once the bar outside was clean. "I'm going to go for a little walk."

He just nodded. "I'll prep for tomorrow."

"Don't—" I hesitated. "Don't wait around. I'm sure you have other places to be tonight."

"I'll take off when I'm done."

While Gus took his customary spot in the storeroom, I grabbed the knitted sweater from The Quilter and threw it over my head as I slipped outside. I kicked off my tennis shoes the second I hit the sand and let my feet sink into the sugary texture. Cinching my eyes shut, I inhaled a deep breath of lake air tinged with the salt crystals that kept The Isle a hidden, tropical community in the middle of the Great Lakes.

The fresh air calmed me, but not as much as it usually did. I was angsty, on edge, and needed to do something. I hadn't heard from X all afternoon. He'd told me he needed time, and I owed him that much. But sitting around would drive me insane.

Ironically, as I strolled along the lake shore, I found myself thinking I wouldn't mind a bit of help from The Quilter at the moment. After the events of the morning, my Muse blanket appeared to have stopped working. I'd kept it wrapped around my shoulders for a good long while after X had left the bungalow, and I'd been rewarded with nothing. No epiphanies, no lightning strikes—just the warmth of a well-made blanket.

"I'm right here, darling," a familiar voice said. "I knew you'd come around."

I glanced up through the darkness but saw nothing.

"Over here." The Quilter's voice rang familiar, but it was difficult to place her. "Out on the water."

I turned toward the shore and blinked at the sight before me. The Quilter appeared to be standing on the water, hovering above the lake. Her feet were bare, her skin pale and shimmery where it met the surface tension of the water.

"What do you mean?" I cleared my throat. "I mean, thank you. I appreciate the Muse blanket, but I still think it was wrong of you to give me the second gift—I don't know what to do with it. I don't want it."

"I'm not here to discuss past gifts." The Quilter's teeth glowed white under the moonlight. She took several steps toward me, alighting onto the sand. "I prefer to look toward the future—which brings me to your next gift. You, my dear, are keeping these weary old fingers busy lately."

I reached for the proffered blanket. "Thank you. What is it?"

"You'll have to figure it out."

"I'm hoping it will fix everything," I said, pulling the fabric closer to my chest. "Is it another Muse?"

"Don't be mistaken—my gifts don't fix anything. They just help you to help yourself. When all is dark and you need brightness, I give it to you. But I don't light the flame, I don't guide you out of the tunnel. You already know how to do all of that, Lily Locke. My work just gives you the confidence to see it."

I glanced down. This time, the blanket was made from deep, navy blue fabric dotted with streaks of silver and bursts of white that made it look like a clear night sky. "Please, can you tell me what this one does?"

The Quilter just smiled. "May the stars guide you, Lily Locke."

I examined the soft fabric, my fingers running along the thin ridges. "Guide me where?"

When I looked up, however, The Quilter was gone.

I was left alone with only a blanket and a shimmer of starlight over the water.

MY LEGS WERE TIRED by the time I stopped walking.

I took a look at my surroundings and was surprised to find I recognized the location. However, despite the familiar destination, I hardly remembered the journey. Something, or someone, must have been watching over me during my time after leaving The Quilter. Somehow, I'd made it from the safety of my beach into the depths of The Forest.

One glance down at my feet told me I was near the volcano that rose high above the northwest corner of the island. Fire Birds bloomed around my shoes, red and vibrant under the glow of the moonlight. They grouped together in thick swatches and laced the side of the grassy green pasture that extended as far as the eye could see.

A small path loomed before me, not made of dirt or stone or pavement, but of the grasses, the flowers, bending out of my way to reveal an earthy route forward. Which could mean only one thing: The Witch of the Woods had anticipated my arrival.

With a breath of relief, I hurried along the path, smiling as the flowers bowed out of my way. I paused to grab a Fire Bird and depressed its petals, causing a flame to burp from its lips as I held it against the top of the walking stick I'd enchanted to become a torch. I held my torch high and broke into a jog.

"You made it," The Witch of the Woods said with a smile when I came to a breathless stop before her. "Last minute trip?"

"I didn't expect it at all," I said, shrugging the blanket from The Quilter higher onto my shoulders. "I sort of... just started walking. And I ended up here."

"Well, I'm glad you did." The Witch of the Woods threw her arms out, and I fell into her hug. "It's good to see you, Miss Locke."

"You too," I said. "Was that you watching out for me tonight? I didn't hear a peep in The Forest. I was so lost in my own thoughts I didn't realize how dangerous my trip could have been until I got here."

"I sent out a few of my friends," the witch said, taking my hand gingerly and pulling me toward the huge rock face that signaled her castle. "They told me a lost young woman was looking for me. I used my crystal ball and saw you."

"Is any of that true?"

"Not really," she cackled. "But I'm glad you made it all the same. And yes, I always have my little birdies and lions and tigers looking out for my friends. I'm glad you saw safe passage tonight."

The Witch of the Woods, also known as the Grandmother of the Woods, lived deep within The Forest and was known for her influence over all living things. The very earth bent toward her will, from the animals who ravaged the wilderness to the air we breathed.

She had a special connection with the earth itself, and in turn, she watched carefully over her small kingdom from a mighty perch carved into the side of the volcano.

We made the trek up an endless flight of stairs. Conversation ceased as I found myself unable to breathe and talk and climb all at the same time. I had to choose two of the three options, and I chose breathing and climbing.

The witch began chatting happily once we reached the top of the winding, damp staircase chiseled from stone, built into the darkest corners of the mountain and lit only by the faint flickers of candlelight.

"You'll remember the library," she said at long last. "I figure, if your mind is so ruffled you chose to walk The Forest at night instead of resting that pretty head on a pillow, you're looking for something. Am I right?"

"I don't even know anymore," I said. "I suppose I'm looking for something, but I'm not sure what. Information would help. Closure. Alternative options for a future I can't seem to escape."

The witch rested a hand on my shoulder, her wizened face cracking into a smile. "Don't worry so much, dear. The future will play out as it should."

"Maybe, but I don't like the way it's playing out. I want to change it."

"Okay, then." The witch squeezed, happily grinning as if she knew something I didn't. "That sounds good. Can I help you find something in particular?"

I shook my head. "I haven't figured out what I'm looking for yet, or why I came here. I guess it felt safe to me. Or essential. Or something."

"Or a bit of both," the witch cackled. "Or maybe you just wanted some of my famous pumpkin spice tea? It's all the rage these days among the locals. I gather all the herbs myself."

"I'd love some tea," I said. "In the meantime, maybe I can peruse the shelves? See if anything catches my eye?"

The witch nodded, her eyes sparkling as if again, she knew a secret that I didn't. "I believe you'll find everything you're looking for through those doors."

I followed the witch's cryptic words and her ancient finger as it extended straight ahead toward a set of doors that, I knew from experience, led into a cavernous space so large the echoes didn't return. Sound was soaked up by wall-to-wall books of all shapes, sizes, colors, and topics. There had to be something in there to help me put an end to all of the questions.

With an already-exhausted sigh, I let myself into the Library of Secrets. The witch had disappeared elsewhere, presumably to concoct her newly famous tea. I pushed through one curtain which opened to reveal a long, pockmarked table and cushy chairs pushed up to the sides of it.

Suddenly, I understood the witch's cryptic words. Her promise that I'd find everything I needed waiting through those doors. She hadn't expected me to magically find the answers to the universe in a book that others had already scoured. Instead, she'd directed me to a man who might hold the answers to my greatest questions.

"What are you doing here?" I studied the figure sitting at the long table. "How did you know I'd be here?"

Liam considered his words for a long moment, watching me as I took deep, fortifying breaths. "I wasn't sure you'd come."

"I didn't plan on coming here. So why did I come here?" I pressed. "Did you talk to The Quilter?"

"You came here of your own accord, as did I. It's good to see you, Lily."

"I don't know about that. Every time you appear in my life, it only seems to bring trouble."

The sharp words brought a flicker of a shadow across Liam's face, but he recovered quickly. "These are dark times. But of course, I apologize for anything that I've brought on you myself. I believe it's time I give you some answers."

"I told you I'd direct you to all the answers!" The Witch of the Woods scurried in carrying a silver tray decked out with tea-serving supplies. She plopped it down on the table, shuffled around the sugar cubes and cream, then poured us each a cup of tea. "Whether you like it or not, Lily, you came here for a reason. Hear him out."

The witch whisked herself away just as fast as she'd arrived.

I sat down at the table and pulled a dainty teacup closer to me. I situated the blanket from The Quilter on my lap for comfort. I still hadn't seen or felt a single drop of magic in its clutches, but the sheer weight and warmth of it gave me confidence.

Wrapping my hands around the warmth of the tea, I looked up at Liam. "Talk."

"Not much in the way of a greeting."

"The last time I heard from you was when you told me my mother was an assassin," I said. "Then I found your name in the house of a murderer. What good have you brought into my life, Liam? Is it really a shock I'm not thrilled to see you?"

Liam looked his usual handsome self, but a bit weathered. A few more flecks of gray had appeared on his head, his face lined by layers of stress. Somehow, it made him look only more dignified.

"That's what I'm here to clarify," Liam said. "I want to tell you a story about your mother."

I raised my eyebrows, blew on my tea to cool it. "How do I know it's the truth?"

"Because I wouldn't lie about Delilah. I loved her."

The teacup rattled against the saucer as my fingers shook. "What?"

"I met your mother back when we both worked for MAGIC, Inc."

"My mother didn't live on the mainland," I said. "She lived here, on The Isle, when she met my father."

"We had a small satellite office here," Liam said. "It closed down a decade ago. Best to keep business off the island."

"How did you go from working at MAGIC, Inc. to doing... whatever it is you do now?"

"Your mother worked for the Agent side of things," Liam said, ignoring my question. "I did as well—we were partnered on a few cases."

"And you fell in love?"

Liam ignored the coarseness of my tone. "I did. We did, I suppose. But we worked together, and it wasn't supposed to turn into anything. We had a few nights together, and then someone found out about us. I was reassigned by my boss to prevent either of us from losing our jobs."

"You were reassigned?"

He nodded. "I lasted a year abroad. I was stationed in a Russian magical base, as far away as my boss could send me. No contact with your mother. I always wondered what might have happened if I'd asked her to wait for me, but I never did. I couldn't ask her to put her life on hold for me."

"What happened when you returned?"

"I'm sure you can imagine." Liam raised his teacup and paused for a sip. "I came back, looked her up. She was already coupled up with your father. That summer they'd met and fallen in love. I thought maybe when he moved away for school, they'd end their relationship, and I'd get another chance. But I hadn't anticipated..."

"Me," I filled in. "You hadn't anticipated a child."

"No." Liam's voice was a hushed whisper. "I hadn't anticipated you. And I would never break up a family. I never saw your mother again, Lily. I left The Isle."

"Where does the paperwork come in?" I asked Liam. "Was she an assassin for MAGIC, Inc.?"

"No. At least, not exactly," Liam said. "Your mother was involved in the takedown of the demigod who almost destroyed the Master of Magic during the second world war. You remember the story?"

"Yes."

"Well, your mother was part of the task force who brought him down. It's rumored that it's because of your mother, her work on the project, that the world is still spinning. If she hadn't managed to take down the demigod, then the world as we know it wouldn't be the same."

"And then, what? She graduated to assassin?"

"We had intel from The Faction that they assumed their demigod assassin had been taken down by one of our own indestructible assassins. There was no such thing—no such *person*. But your mother chose to take on the role. It put a target on her back."

"Why would she do that?"

"Fear," he said. "If we had an assassin who could take out a demigod, what couldn't she do?"

"And it got her killed," I said quietly. "They found her when she went to the mainland to bring me in for protection."

Liam hesitated. "It's not your fault. It was only a matter of time before they found her. If I'd known, if I had been closer to her, I would have done something, Lily. I promise you. I'd have tried to protect her, taken her underground."

"So, my mother was just doing her job," I said. "Trying to make the world a safer place, and my father's organization killed her."

Liam returned his hands to a folded position. "I've made it my life mission to get close to your father, to try and understand *how* he could do such a thing to a woman like her. A woman he loved."

"And?" I asked. "Any brilliant breakthroughs? Have you ever considered the fact that he's just plain evil?"

"Your father is a broken man," Liam said. "He was given false information. The Faction groomed him to take over; they set your mother up, murdered her, knowing she would be the only one who could hold him back from achieving great heights as a leader. They told him it was the humans, and that fueled his anger and furthered his resolve for their cause."

"That doesn't explain what's happening now. Why was your name at Melissa's house?"

"I don't know. I didn't have any contact with either Melissa or Ranger L"

"Ranger L was on a special assignment looking into my mother's life and death," I said. "You're sure you didn't run across him?"

"I'm positive," Liam said. "It's possible someone was trying to set me up. After all, think about it—if you hadn't caught Melissa when you did, who would have been your primary suspect?"

He had a point. If we hadn't discovered Melissa's lies, we would have turned our attention to Liam. We would have wasted valuable resources looking for him when the real murderer had been right in front of our noses the entire time.

"Melissa is still denying that she had anything to do with the murder," I said. "What if there's a chance she didn't do it? What if *she* was framed?"

Liam raised his hands. "If you're insinuating that I might have killed Ranger L, that isn't true. That's all I can tell you. I was aware that Ranger L was looking into your mother's files, but I didn't stop him. I was the one to give you the paperwork on your mother in the first place; if I'd wanted to keep it a secret, I wouldn't have given it to you."

I'd already considered Liam's argument and didn't have a good explanation. If Liam wanted something covered up, why would he have sent us information?

Melissa had killed her fiancé. The evidence was stacked against her. Wasn't it?

"I did keep apprised of L's work, though I didn't interfere," Liam said. "I hoped he'd help you find closure. However, I wonder if things went too far."

"What do you mean?"

Liam forced a smile. "I have found myself wondering if Ranger L could have been working for The Faction. If he'd been bought."

"That's impossible. Ranger X trusted him."

"He held meetings—I don't know with whom—in The Forest. It seemed to me as if he was reporting to someone."

"How is this supposed to help me now?"

"The meetings seemed to take place mostly on Sunday evenings," Liam said. "Tomorrow is Sunday. It's very possible that if he was meeting someone from The Faction, someone far away, they haven't heard of his death yet. They might still show."

"Everyone's heard of his death!"

"Everyone on The Isle," Liam said. "But The Faction doesn't keep residence on our island, at least not openly. There's a chance his partner will still arrive if they had a meeting scheduled."

"Where is this rendezvous?"

"Let me go with you," Liam said. "I'm not letting you go alone. It's far too dangerous, and if Ranger X ever found out I sent you to a meeting in The Forest unprotected, I'd be a dead man walking. I am already pushing the boundaries by telling you this."

"How do I know the whole thing's not a trap? For all I know, you could have made up this whole story to get me to trust you. To go willingly into The Forest with you alone."

A look of exhaustion crept onto Liam's face. "I'm beginning to doubt my ability to ever regain your trust. Alas, I suppose you won't know it's not a trap until it's over. All you have is my word. I promise you, I'll be at that meeting. If you want to come, you can join me."

"Why are you going?"

The exhaustion cleared, leaving behind an empty sadness. "I might have only had a short time with your mother, but I did love her."

"Are you saying you don't know who killed her?"

Liam gave a quick shake of his head. "I've been keeping an ear to the ground for years during my travels. It's a startlingly quiet topic."

I didn't realize I'd rolled my eyes until it was too late. I caught sight of Liam's face, which gave away a hint of dismay.

"For a man who seems to know everyone and everything," I said, "it just seems odd that you suddenly run into a wall when it comes to my mother."

"Yes, I thought the same thing," he said tersely. "But of course, you don't have to believe me."

"You're the one who betrayed me!"

"Did I?" Liam stood. "Did I betray you, or are you assuming I did? Lily, I will never run out of time or patience to try and prove my loyalty to you, but I am done for tonight. I am tired. I have been sick over your mother's death for years, wondering what-if. I can't change the past, and I'm sorry for that."

I glanced down, realizing the tea in my cup had gone cold before I'd even had the chance to take a sip. A part of me felt the urge to apologize, but my stubborn brain wanted to know why I should be apologizing when I'd done nothing wrong.

"Goodnight, Lily. The meeting is tomorrow at eight p.m. I'll be leaving here around four. It's a journey, and I want to be there early. If you'd like to join me, I will see you then."

Liam strode from the library and disappeared behind one of the many curtains flanking hidden walls, bookshelves, and who knew what other sorts of secret passageways. I stared at the twitch in fabric after he'd gone, turning back to the table only when I realized he wasn't coming back.

When a flame burst out from underneath the teapot, I looked up, startled. The Witch of the Woods stood before me, her expression passive though I'd no doubt she'd heard everything that had gone on in the library.

She snapped her fingers and the liquid in my cup disappeared. Reaching forward she picked up the steaming teapot and poured me a second cup.

"I can't believe you didn't finish your tea," she said. "It's legendary."

"I don't know what just happened," I said. "Did you bring me and Liam together on purpose? Did you know all of the things he told me?"

She tsked. "I don't bother myself with other peoples' business. Only the business of The Forest, the earth, and my animals."

"Well, I just find it hard to believe that we both ended up here on accident."

"I didn't say anything was an accident," she said. "I don't believe in accidents. Will you take a sip of the tea and tell me how much you love it, please?"

I curled my hands around the cup, lifted it to my lips. I took a sip and swallowed, feeling the warmth of the liquid as it slid down my throat and into my belly.

I smiled. "It's wonderful. And just what I needed."

"I thought that might be the case," she said happily. "Well, I'll leave you be. I imagine you have things to think about—your mind is even more ruffled than before, and that is quite a task. There is a bedroom behind the third curtain. You'll find it is stocked with everything you might need. Can I get you anything else before I leave?"

"Is Liam staying here?"

The witch looked at me curiously. "Does that change anything?"

"I suppose not," I said. "It's too late for me to head back, and—"

"You'll be perfectly safe as long as you are in my home," the witch said. "If I have to recommend anything for you, it's that you let yourself rest. Drink up, dear. Drink up. There's nothing better after a long day than a cup of tea."

Before long, the witch had disappeared, and I was left alone with the spirits of books and the swirling steam from my cup. I sat in silence and sipped until three cupfuls were empty, feeling my shoulders relax a bit with each pour from the teapot.

I briefly wondered if there was some sort of relaxation spell on the tea because the wonderings of my mind felt more muted than before. Dragging myself off to the room behind the third curtain, I found a small, cozy nook complete with a wire frame bed and a fat comforter. Fluffy pillows were stacked along the edge and pressed against a window with a view of the entire forest. It was beautiful.

A soft yellow armchair sat in one corner with an end table next to it and a teetering stack of books that reached almost a foot high. The seat begged to be curled into with a blanket. A weathered vanity with a foggy mirror stood against the other wall, and a closet opened to reveal fluffy slippers and a robe, along with towels, blankets, and other necessities for the traveling visitor.

Over it all, the faint scent of old, dusty books filtered into the room, and I realized with some pleasure that I'd never stayed in a library before, especially not one perched over the mouth of a waterfall, stories above the rest of the world.

I took a shower in the attached bathroom, prepared myself for bed. I climbed under the covers and sat for a long time with my legs crossed, the moonlight blinding as it pierced the window and streaked across my face.

I wondered what Ranger X was doing, where he was. I'd left a brief message on his Comm asking if he wanted to talk, but I hadn't heard back from him.

The empty bungalow popped into my head, and I found myself hoping that Gus had gone home to Mimsey as planned. I hoped he wasn't worried about my absence, or worse—I hoped he hadn't contacted Ranger X to say I hadn't returned from my walk.

I tried to picture where Poppy and her vampire hunter had run off to and figured just as quickly it was better if I didn't know. I hadn't wanted to be wrapped up in their star-crossed love affair, but the Muse had led me straight into the belly of the beast. Now, I was tangled up in it for better or for worse.

And finally, I wondered if my father knew that Liam had loved my mother once upon a time.

I tucked myself under piles of down comforters, keeping The Quilter's blanket wrapped tight around me beneath it all. I found myself thinking about family, about mothers and fathers and their babies. About how strange and beautiful and awful and utterly necessary families could be. And before I drifted off to sleep, I wondered what it would have been like to have had a father like Liam instead of a criminal like mine.

Chapter 17

I woke in a startled rush, confused by the sound of buzzing near my ear. It took a long second to find my Comm had slipped off my wrist. I found it vibrating under my pillow and hit answer before I could read the name on the display.

"Hello?" I asked groggily. "Who is this?"

"Lily," Ranger X said, his voice stiff. "You're not at home."

"No." I sat in bed, startled by the peek of sunlight in the distance. It was early still, the sun just barely creeping over the horizon. I felt like a queen surveying her kingdom, studying the tops of the trees, the specs of earth beneath. "I'm not. I left a message for you yesterday."

"Yes, but you didn't say where you'd gone."

"I hadn't known where I was going at the time. If you'd Commed me back, I would have told you."

"Are you safe?"

"Yes, I'm fine," I said. "Is everything okay? How are you?"

"I think we should talk."

My heart thumped hard. "Sure, of course. When?"

"Later tonight? I have things to take care of today. I came by this morning, but I missed you."

"Yes, that's fine. Ten o'clock?"

If Ranger X was surprised by the lateness of my proposed hour, he didn't show it. "That sounds fine. I'll see you then. You'll be coming home today, then?"

"I'll be back before our meeting. I'm sorry to have left, I just needed some time to think."

I could feel Ranger X's quiet understanding, though he didn't speak for a beat. "Please stay safe."

The thumping of my heart slowed slightly, the pit in my belly loosened. Surely, the concern in his voice was a good sign.

"Of course," I whispered. "You too. I love you."

"I love you," he said, and then disconnected.

I felt somewhat fortified by the softening of Ranger X's tone before he'd disconnected the Comm. Slivers of panic poked at me, but I pushed them away. For the next few hours, I needed to utilize my time in the library and learn everything I could about my mother, The Quilter, and my father's history with The Faction. And with it, anything that arose about Liam.

The day flicked by in a blur of manuscript pages, both published works and un-published. I devoured hand-scrawled notes in the margins and scoured faded pads of paper. The only interruptions were from the witch herself when she brought in plates of finger sandwiches and refillable cups of tea. Before I knew it, four o'clock had rolled around.

I headed for the staircase and made my way downstairs. I found the Witch of the Woods sending Liam off with a small traveling pack I assumed carried necessities like food and water.

I stopped abruptly at the sight of Liam. My arms were full, and I made no move to hide my magic. I'd spent the latter half of the afternoon Mixing a variety of defensive potions under the witch's watchful eye and helpful assistance. I had a Freeze Frame, a Halting Hex, and a Blinder ready to be used in case this mystery meeting in the woods went sour.

The Witch of the Woods handed me a travel pack as well. I slipped the potions inside, found some staple snacks already there, and thanked her for the hospitality. Without another word, Liam set off into The Forest, and I followed him.

We didn't speak for the first hour. It took us to the depths of the woods before Liam cleared his throat. "Are those potions for use against me or someone else?"

"We'll see," I said testily. "I'm still not convinced there's a meeting at all."

"Me neither," Liam said. "There's a very good chance that whoever was meeting Landon in The Forest has heard of his death and won't show. But there is zero percent chance I'm leading you willingly into a trap. Either there's a meeting or there's not, and I'll see you home after."

"Why are we going at all if the chances are so high the meeting is off?"

"We need to take all the opportunities we have. I don't trust anything when your father's involved—even things that appear to be the truth, iron clad, like Melissa's arrest. I'm still not convinced Landon wasn't working for The Faction."

I didn't doubt Melissa's arrest—the Rangers were the best at what they did—but Liam had a point. If there was a chance to get us more answers, if Landon had stumbled onto some findings about my mother's death that someone wanted hidden, I needed to be there. I didn't believe he was working for The Faction, but I did believe there was more to the story than the truths we'd uncovered so far.

"I have been a part of these types of meetings before," Liam said. "For both the good guys and the bad."

He watched me carefully for any sign of dismay, but I didn't give him the satisfaction of one.

"Most times, these meetings are set up by a third party. The attendees often are just messengers used to collect information—they don't know one another's names or identities. They meet behind cloaks and masks, or clouds of smoke. It is very possible that whoever was meeting Landon didn't actually know it was him—and therefore he or she would show up as planned."

I shrugged. "I don't know whether to hope you're right or wrong."

Liam gave a nod that bordered on agreement. "We'll be there soon."

Another hour into The Forest, and we'd made it to the destination Liam claimed to be the meeting location.

"We're early," he said. "We'll get set up before it gets dark. You've obviously brought some potions with you in case things turn dire?"

I nodded. "What about you?"

He gave a thin smile. "I have my ways. I've stayed alive this long, haven't I?"

"That's somewhat of a miracle considering your affiliations."

"Exactly my point," Liam said. "I think we need some height for our vantage point. Do you agree?"

"Yeah, I think that would be best," I said. "Are you thinking a tree?"

"I've got a better idea."

For the next hour and a half, Liam and I worked together in quiet harmony, setting up a small, bird's eye view of the clearing where Liam seemed certain we'd have a visitor shortly. Around the clearing on one side rose a rocky wall, and tucked inside of it, Liam had found a crevice that—with a bit of magical help—was the perfect size to hold two people in hiding.

The Forest was quiet this evening, but I added a touch of an Eavesdropper Charm and fixed it in our little cave. It would act like a radio of sorts and transmit any voices in the clearing up to our hiding spot while keeping us mostly out of sight and giving us protection in case things went south.

"I've got an idea," I said, fumbling in my pack. The Witch of the Woods had included all sorts of travel necessities including toiletries.

I took out a small compact. "What if we enlarge the mirror and mask it? We can use it to get a visual without sticking our heads over the cliff."

Liam took the mirror and examined it, slithering on his belly into the crevice. He held the compact out at an angle. A smile curved over his face. "I knew I brought you along for a reason."

I ignored his veiled compliment and completed the charm. "What's next?"

We surveyed our makeshift fort in silence. Mentally, I ticked off the protective spells and enchantments we'd scattered around camp as tiny safety precautions. We hadn't chanced using any powerful magic, just in case the people arriving did some sort of spell sweep to uncover hidden charms. The ones we'd laid wouldn't trigger much of anything, but they might save our lives in the event of trouble.

"Now," Liam said, "we wait."

THE TENSION ROSE IN our hidey-hole as the hour of the supposed meeting approached. It seemed the very earth flexed in wait, holding its breath for what was to come. I felt my muscles ache on high alert from two long days of journeying, worrying, stressing, and now... waiting. Waiting for someone who may or may not show.

"Relax," Liam murmured when a stick crackled deep within the woods. "I won't let anything happen to you."

I looked into his smile, one that had been so familiar weeks before. "I'll take care of myself, thanks."

Liam's smile faltered ever so slightly, but he recovered, slid deeper into his hiding position and squinted through the magnifier spell I'd fashioned onto the compact mirror.

After all this time spent preparing and waiting and hoping, I wasn't sure what I expected to happen. I wasn't sure what Liam hoped to achieve by bringing me here. I wasn't sure what I *wanted* to find.

All I knew was that I hadn't expected lightning.

The storm came swift and fast. The clearing, along with its immediate surroundings, was impaled with sudden high winds and ground-striking lightning. Soul-rumbling thunder clouds plowed through at rapid speeds. The flashes of white-hot light came in fast, jagged punches, cracking into the ground, the trees, the rock-face without abandon.

"What's happening?" I whispered.

From our perch in the rock, we were out of harm's way—for now. I could see the confined storm raging in a bubble before us, a defense mechanism for whoever was due to arrive. It would ensure the clearing was left empty—anyone inside the storm zone would either be frightened off... or left for dead.

Liam's face tightened. "I don't know."

"Is it coming for us?"

Liam just shook his head, his eyes calculating as he swept his gaze forward.

We discovered the answer to my question not twenty seconds later when the first of the lightning strikes hit the rock wall below where we lay, just inches from my outstretched arm. I rolled out of the way, watching as small fires flickered and smoked on the ground below, leaving a desolate wasteland behind. A few inches higher, and we'd be smoked out of our spot.

"*Stone and shield,*
Let danger yield—"

My initial Shield Spell was interrupted by a piercing shriek. One I realized was coming from my own mouth. The subtle build of thunder, the horrific flash of light, and suddenly, a jagged strand of intangible white power was shooting down at my half-formed shield as I raised a hand to cover myself.

I began to shift out of the way but found myself stuck in our small crevice, no room to move, forced to watch the strike that would finish me off as it shot toward me.

A rush of warmth as Liam rolled against me registered before his arm came up and over, wrapping around my body. He was muttering something in a language I didn't understand. He pulled me against him, our bodies surrounded in a wispy, silvery glow—some sort of shield or repellent I'd never seen before—just moments before the lightning struck us.

I felt Liam tense behind me. He emitted a low, pained groan as if stifling a worse sort of cry. I could smell blood suddenly, the sweet, metallic scent of it, and I wondered where it was coming from as the full force of the storm raged over us.

The lightning struck, rattling our bodies from the inside out. Our teeth chattered, electricity raced through us, and I felt as if my very body might short circuit at any moment. My arms went numb and tingling as thunder rocked over us and shook the rock wall on which we lay. And then, graciously, it all subsided.

I turned to Liam. And found the source of blood.

He offered a weak smile as he looked up, bleeding from a nasty gash on his forehead, his lip swollen and puffy, split from where he must have bitten down in his quest to save us both from the attack.

"I'm fine," he gasped. "Rock came loose above, hit my head on the way down."

"Liam," I whispered, my hands shaking as I fumbled at my travel belt for the Aloe Ale I always kept tucked there. "You're bleeding. We need to get you home, get you to some medics for proper treatment. I'm not a Healer, and I don't have much to work with."

He smiled, blood pouring down his face. "Do what you can."

With trembling fingers, I emptied the Ale onto my fingertips and smoothed it over the cut on his forehead. It didn't appear terribly deep; he would need stitches no doubt, but head wounds bled a lot.

They looked worse than they actually were—at least, that's what I kept telling myself.

"You saved me," I said, thumbing a bit more Aloe Ale onto my finger and spreading it over his split lip. "Why would you do that after all I've put you through?"

"You've put me through nothing," Liam said. "Nothing I didn't deserve."

"But I haven't believed you, don't trust you..."

"I'll do whatever it takes to gain your trust back," Liam said. "I've never stopped loving your mother, Lily. There are times I found myself wishing..."

"What?"

"That things had been different," he said, his voice weak. "If they had, maybe you'd have been my daughter."

My heart nearly stopped its rapid pounding at his words. I hadn't wanted to admit it, but over the course of the day, I'd wondered the same thing more than once. What if things had been different? What if Liam had been my father? A man who would have raised me as part of the magical world and told me the stories I longed to hear about the mother I'd never known. A man who would spend his energy trying to protect me, not control me.

I cleared my throat. "Well, things aren't different."

"I know," Liam murmured. "I've come to terms with it. I'm sorry about your real father, Lily. If I had the chance to go back..."

"I understand." I looked into Liam's eyes, held his gaze until he blinked to clear the blood away. I pressed my sleeve to his head, muttering an incantation to help the Aloe Ale burn stronger, to help solder the wound until he could be seen by a true Healer.

And somehow, I did understand. I understood Liam's loss and heartbreak, his pining for my mother and longing for a different outcome. And while the outcome could never be any different, it wasn't too late for us. For a friendship, for trust.

"I always knew," I said softly. "I might not have trusted you, but I always knew you cared. I didn't understand some of your choices, but maybe that's the way things had to be."

Liam closed his eyes, his face pale. "I'd do anything it took to keep you safe."

"I know," I whispered. "Stay still. Let me figure a way out of here."

"No. We've come this far, and now we wait it out."

"But—"

"Whoever cleared the area wants their space. I'd like to know why."

"You've got a nasty gash on your head."

"I'll live. Now, quiet—I hear footsteps."

We wriggled into place, keeping our line of sight to the clearing open through the mirror. Sure enough, a figure moved into place not seconds after we'd slithered deeper out of sight.

I glanced to my side, saw a smear of blood on the rocks where Liam's head had lain. The moonlight glinted off it, and I hoped it wouldn't draw the attention of the mystery guest.

"It's me," a man's voice called. "Show yourself."

He sounded familiar, though I couldn't quite place the voice. I frowned at Liam, unable to recognize the cloaked figure due to the hood pulled low over his head.

"It must be Landon's contact," Liam whispered. "Either an informant, or someone reporting in to The Faction."

"The Faction?" I asked. "How can you be sure?"

"Can you think of anyone else Landon might have been meeting once a week in the depths of The Forest?"

I raised my eyebrows. "Not exactly."

The crack of a twig sounded from the tops of the trees, followed quickly by the whizzing sound of an arrow cutting through air. A breath later, there was a *whoosh* as the weapon struck the mystery man in the shoulder. Cloak, hood, and body went down in a silent thud. He lay unmoving on the forest floor.

"Was that..." I hesitated, barely daring to breathe. "Is he dead?"

Liam's eyes were lit by the moon. "Don't move."

"We need to help him!"

"We need to wait for the attacker to clear out. He or she won't hesitate to kill us too—especially if they realize we saw everything."

We waited more than an hour with no sign of movement. My joints were stiffening when Liam shifted himself to a seated position. He looked downright terrifying with blood caked on his head and his lip blackening where it'd been split. His eyes showed no signs of kindness, only of cunning intelligence as he scanned the horizon.

A few muttered words from his lips, and I felt a slight gust of wind as Liam's spell spread into the darkness. We waited some more, until a second breeze brushed the hair away from my face and put a small smile on Liam's.

"It's clear," he said. "Let's go."

Liam and I scrambled toward the ground, keeping to the shadows where possible and leaving our feet firmly planted on sturdy stone. The last thing we needed to do was send an inadvertent rockslide down the ledge that would alert the entire forest of our presence.

Liam landed first in a crouch, closing his eyes for a moment as he pressed his fingers to the ground and listened. Another nod from him signaled we were still clear. The two of us crept across the clearing until we reached the fallen victim. There were no obvious signs of life until we got close enough to see the shallow rise and fall of the man's chest.

Liam gestured for me to stay back. He inched forward, his hand reaching toward the man's hood. Then, with impressive speed, he lunged forward and pulled the hood back while simultaneously rolling the man to his side.

Liam leapt back, keeping himself between me and our mystery man until we were both sure that he was unconscious. The man didn't so much as flinch, and if it weren't for his light breaths, I'd have thought he was dead.

I moved around, out from Liam's protective arm, and caught my first glimpse of the man's face. He wasn't, as I'd thought, a mystery informant. Or a member of The Faction. He wasn't a stranger at all.

My breath felt throttled in my throat as I struggled to inhale. "This makes no sense," I said to Liam as I stumbled back. "Why would he be here? He knew Landon was dead!"

"I've no clue," Liam said darkly. "But I think we can agree that this man had something to hide."

Chapter 18

"Is there any news?" I asked, looking up as Ranger X strode from the hospital hallway into the waiting room. I sat next to Liam, my hands clenched on the edge of the hard, uncomfortable seat. "Will he be okay?"

Ranger X had a hard look on his face. He gave a slight shake of his head, but I didn't take that to mean no. If anything, it meant that he had news—he just didn't want to share.

Liam and I had been waiting for several hours after returning from The Forest. We'd enchanted my gift from The Quilter to hover above the ground and had used the blanket to help us carry Ranger H's lifeless form with us as we made our way out of the wilderness. I'd Commed Ranger X directly, figuring it best if I kept news this big off the main dispatch line.

He'd met us halfway, helped us get Ranger H to the hospital and into a private room with two Rangers stationed outside the door. Liam and I had done what we'd been doing best all day: watching and waiting.

"He's coming out of a deep coma," Ranger X said. "He was hit by a mix of Pollycock Powder and a sleeper spell. Ranger H is allergic to Pollycock Powder, hence the near-fatal reaction."

"Well, it doesn't sound like an accident that someone used an arrow tipped with Pollycock Powder then," I said. "Normally, it's not harmful except to everyone else's nostrils."

Ranger X nodded. "Agreed. Someone who knew him, knew his weaknesses, fired that arrow. But who?"

"We didn't see anyone," I said for the third or fourth time. "I told you every detail. We didn't see anything until Ranger H hit the ground and we crept out of our hiding space."

Ranger X's jaw tightened. He'd heard our story in the waiting room two or three times, pressing both me and Liam to recount every detail we could muster from the journey. It wasn't much.

I could tell that Ranger X wasn't particularly happy with me on several levels, but he'd managed to swallow most of his frustration to replace it with stoic professionalism. It almost hurt worse, but I understood. There was too much at stake to get emotionally involved, especially in a public space like the hospital waiting room.

"We will be releasing Melissa," Ranger X said suddenly. "We had Detective DeMarco of the Sixth Precinct back today for an analysis. She confirmed a new suspect in the murder of Ranger L."

I swallowed hard. "Who?"

"Ranger H. He will be placed under arrest for the murder of his partner," X said blandly. "We found evidence of the murder weapon at his house."

"But what about Melissa's locker?"

"Detective DeMarco confirmed that there were indeed Mind Melter Residuals in Melissa's locker at Harpin's shop, but she also confirmed that they could have been moved there, placed there on purpose. We found the actual cannon at Ranger H's house."

"The one that fired the Mind Melter?"

"They're testing it for Spell Ballistics now, but Detective DeMarco said it was crawling with Residuals, even after all this time. She has no doubt it was fired recently. Once we have the match back from the lab, we'll know for certain. Ranger H's fingerprints were on it."

I blinked. "But, I don't understand. Why? What's the motive?"

Ranger X sighed, scratched under his chin. "We believe that Ranger H was—is—working for The Faction." Ranger X's eyes flicked ever so briefly over to Liam. "I had Landon looking into sensitive topics. If H caught wind of that, his contacts at The Faction would have wanted to stay apprised of Landon's movements."

"If he was feeding The Faction information," I mused, "then why would Ranger H kill his partner? What's the reward?"

"I don't know. There's a chance Ranger H was trying to convert Landon to work with him, to bring him over to The Faction," Ranger X said. "When he refused, Ranger H was forced to kill him. Alternatively, Landon found out that he was being reported on by H, confronted his partner, and was murdered for it."

"Which means Melissa is innocent?" I asked. "But that doesn't explain why she staged her own kidnapping."

Ranger X exhaled slowly. "When we spoke to her this afternoon, she opened up some. She claimed that she felt she was in danger—that she couldn't trust any of the Rangers after what had happened to Landon. She thought that by faking her own kidnapping and disappearing, she'd be removing herself from harm's way until the killer was found."

"She did place Ranger H at the crime scene," I said. "She said she greeted him as they were walking down Main Street."

"Yes," Ranger X said. "Zin listed that in her report from when she first spoke with Melissa. We obviously didn't dig deep enough into the lead." Ranger X clasped his hands behind his back, his face unreadable.

"Melissa looked like a good suspect. You had evidence that someone had carefully planted in her locker."

"But we were wrong."

"Then, who shot Ranger H? Why not kill him when they had the opportunity?"

"I think they did try to kill him," Ranger X said. "If you weren't there, he would have died."

"No wonder he was such a mess after Landon died," I said. "Drinking at The Black Cat like that. I thought it was grief."

"It looked like grief," X said. "We all thought so."

"What comes next?" I asked, feeling suddenly tired. "Where do we go after this?"

"Home," Ranger X said. "I need to make the arrest official first, and then I'd like to personally apologize to Melissa and deliver the news of her release. Finally, I'd like to speak with you. In private."

"Of course," I said. "I'll be at the bungalow. You know where to find me."

Ranger X nodded, then turned to Liam. "I think it's time for you to go."

Liam looked like he wanted to say something, but after one glance at X, he shook his head instead. Wordlessly, he left the waiting room without a backward glance. Once he was gone, I felt my stomach clutch. I hadn't even thanked him.

"He saved my life," I mumbled to X. "He didn't have to do that."

"He also wouldn't have had to save your life if he hadn't dragged you into The Forest in the first place," Ranger X said. "Do you trust him?"

I hesitated, looked out the window at Liam's salt and pepper hair as he turned up his collar against the wind and set down the path, a gauze bandage across the wound he'd gotten from pushing me out of harm's way.

"I'm not sure yet," I murmured. "But I'm getting there."

"IT'S A GOOD THING WE made enough Energy Elixir to refill the Atlantic Ocean if it ever runs dry," Gus said as I came through the door to the bungalow. "If I'd waited for you to fill the orders, you'd have customers winding thrice around The Isle."

"Sorry," I said shortly. "I had something to take care of."

"It didn't go quite as planned, I take it," Gus prompted. "I'm not one for small talk, but you are. And you're not talking at all."

"It's complicated." I sighed. "The Rangers arrested the wrong killer in Landon's murder."

"Melissa didn't do it?"

I shook my head. "They found the murder weapon in Ranger H's house."

"His partner?" Gus frowned. "I didn't see that one coming. Didn't think they would've turned on one another."

"Nobody did," I said. "But through this whole series of events, it turns out Ranger H was meeting someone in The Forest—probably a Faction informant—and we think Landon caught on. If Landon was investigating his partner on the sly, that would help to explain the random times he disappeared—possible weekends away or meetings that weren't otherwise on the books. He probably wanted to be sure before he went to Ranger X with his accusations."

"They were big accusations," Gus said. "It's just unfortunate that got him killed. So, I take it they're releasing Melissa?"

"Tonight," I said. "Ranger X is doing it now, just after he arrests H."

"Shame," Gus said. At my curious gaze, he shook his head. "I mean, murder of any sort ain't good. But brothers turning on brothers...Ranger X having to arrest one of his own..."

"It's hitting everyone hard. Ranger X, especially. Speaking of, he's headed over here after Melissa's release."

"I understand a cue to leave when I hear one," Gus said. "I'll get out of your hair before he arrives."

I eased into my seat at the table, rested my head in my hand. "I'm exhausted. When will this all be over?"

"I can't tell you if the end is in sight," Gus said. "But you'll get there if you just keep going. Stay strong."

"How?" I asked. "And why? Why can't I just let everyone else do their jobs and stay out of things?"

"Because you care." Gus hobbled toward the door, his cane thwacking the floor as he moved. "You'll figure it out, Lily Locke. You always do."

With that, Gus was gone.

I didn't want Ranger X to find me as Gus had left me, crumpled on the table, head held in my hands, defeat curling my shoulders to the floor. Pressing my knuckles to the table, I hoisted myself to my feet and flicked on the coffee maker. Once the smell signaled the brew was ready, I poured a cup, knowing I'd need the extra energy for the long night ahead.

I climbed upstairs to shower, and the journey felt just as long as my trek through The Forest over the last two days. After downing my coffee, I shed my clothes and slipped into the shower, letting the warm water wash over my body, drip from head to toe, snake down my back, trickle over my lips.

The journey with Liam had taken everything out of me. Physically, I was scraped over from head to toe from navigating the bramble and darkness while simultaneously guiding Ranger H's body toward the hospital.

Mentally, it'd taken every last ounce of my concentration, leaving me with a fuzzy focus as I let thoughts come and go like a breeze, unable to hold onto a single one for longer than a few seconds.

Emotionally, I wasn't sure what I could give to Ranger X tonight. Between Liam's plea for trust, the stories about my mother, the realization of Ranger H's betrayal against so many—I was worn thin. Not to mention my disagreement with Ranger X over his brother's visit and my requested spell—and the reason I'd gone seeking such a thing in the first place.

When my skin was red and my fingers pruned, I climbed out of the shower and toweled off. Wrapping myself in a fluffy white bathrobe, I hauled my clothes off to the laundry, taking care to unfasten my travel belt before bringing it into my bedroom.

I collapsed on the bed and spread the contents before me. I removed the empty Aloe Ale vial that I'd used on Liam, examined the defensive spells and hexes, along with the extras I'd brewed in the Library of Greats. I headed downstairs to return the vials to their rightful shelves, and that's when I saw it.

An unfamiliar vial with forest green liquid shimmering behind the glass. As I picked it up, tiny golden sparks twisted through the spell and made it seem alive. On it was a note.

Lily,

This spell will expire in one week. I trust you'll make the right decision.

B

My heart stuttered in my chest as I pulled the Spellbound liquid closer. Such a small jar for such huge problems. The clock was ticking down on how long it would be viable. One week wasn't a long time to think about a topic so large. But that's what I'd asked for, and he'd delivered.

Either way, this wasn't my decision alone to make, and when I heard the front door open, I shuffled the rest of the supplies back where they belonged. Save for the Spellbinder's vial, which I clasped in my hand and, at the last second, slid it into the pocket of my bathrobe.

Ranger X closed the door behind him and locked it. When he turned around, I was waiting for him, my hands tucked out of sight.

I sized him up, the way he moved, the look on his face, the tension in his jaw, but there was too much there to read. He was dressed in all black, the same outfit he'd worn earlier in the day to arrest Ranger H. He obviously hadn't stopped home to change.

"How did it go?" I asked. "Did you see Melissa?"

"I did." Ranger X's voice was a dead giveaway of his exhaustion. It was scratchy, like a gravel road. Free from any amusement, any softness that was usually there when we spoke. "She didn't say a word to me."

"She's probably still too upset."

"Maybe."

"What did you say?"

"I explained everything," he said. "Apologized to her, several times over. She just looked at me. There was this... expression on her face."

"What sort of expression?" I asked. "Sadness? Anger? She'll get over it, I guarantee it. She's just in shock. She lost her fiancé, and she was arrested for his murder. I'm not blaming anyone, but that would be a hard pill to swallow if she's truly innocent."

Ranger X's head jerked up, and he shot me a curious look. "*If* she's truly innocent?"

"I just meant... it seems like she didn't do it. But nobody has confessed, either."

"Lily, if you know anything, now would be the time to tell me."

"I don't. It was just a slip. I didn't mean anything by it."

"I can't help but think that I'm missing something." Ranger X ruffled his hair, stared out the window into the distance. "Something isn't sitting right with me, and I'm not sure what it is."

"You don't think..." I hesitated. "Do you think Ranger H is guilty?"

"How can he not be? The evidence is overwhelming. We found the murder weapon in his house with his prints on it. Confirmed by Detective DeMarco. Whatever I believe is off the table—we have to follow the facts, the evidence."

"Did he wake up in the hospital?"

"He was groggy, just coming out of the coma when I arrested him," Ranger X said. "He's under constant watch by Rangers while he's in the hospital. He'll remain there overnight, and then he'll be transferred to his cell early in the morning."

"Did he say anything when you arrested him?"

"He denied it, of course. But I expected that. What I didn't expect was the way he looked at me..."

I reached over, squeezed his hand. "You did the right thing. You had to arrest him."

"What a mess."

"I know, but it's not your fault. And, if you'd like, I could talk to Melissa for you."

Ranger X blinked, his eyes inquisitive as he focused on me. "Why would you do that?"

"I don't know if it will make a difference, but I could try to smooth things over," I said. "I could apologize again, give her a female perspective. I've already talked to her several times."

Ranger X stared outside. He was obviously bothered, and I hated that I couldn't help him more. When he shivered, I frowned in concern.

"If you're feeling guilty for arresting Ranger H, you shouldn't be," I said. "You followed the facts of the case and were just doing your job."

"I know."

"But?" I pressed, crossing the room. I let go of the potion in my pocket and raised a hand to touch X's face. "What's wrong then?"

"Melissa. She was just different in some way that I can't put my finger on from the last time we spoke. She didn't say a *word* to me this evening, even when I was apologizing. Not a single word."

"Look at it from her point of view. She's been on a bit of a rollercoaster these last few days. She lost the man she was going to marry. She probably needs time to process her emotions."

"Is that what you're doing?"

"What do you mean?" I glanced up at the sharpness in his voice. "Process what emotions?"

"Is this it?" Ranger X leaned forward, dipped his hand into my unprotected pocket and removed the vial from Banks. "I see my brother followed through on your request."

We both studied the swirling green liquid, shimmering with golden incandescent streaks. Eventually, I nodded.

"Please don't get upset with him; it's not his fault. He wanted me to talk to you about it first. All he wanted from me was to see you again, to talk to you."

"He knew exactly what he was doing when he made this." Ranger X's voice went flat. "He's a world renown Spellbinder—he doesn't manufacture any spells without thinking of the consequences."

"Maybe not, but—"

Ranger X raised his other hand and cut me off. "Banks shouldn't have been involved in this decision."

"He's not. I only asked him to create this as a favor to me, to family. I've had to create potions I didn't want to brew before."

X remained silent.

"I hadn't planned on taking it. Like I said—I was surprised by his visit." I inhaled a deep breath. "I was worried and stressed, and I thought this might be a solution, or at least one option to consider."

"Well?" He prompted. "Are you going to take it?"

"There's a week before the potion expires," I said. "We have a few more days to decide."

Ranger X raised an eyebrow. "We?"

"The right decision isn't one I can make alone," I whispered. "I know that. I'm sorry that I went ahead and commissioned the spell without your permission. I thought it might be an easy way out from my father's contract, and it was a moment of weakness."

"It wasn't easy, and it's not a weakness," Ranger X said softly, finally breaking from the stoic aura he'd worn ever since he'd stepped foot in the bungalow this evening. "It came from a place of strength. The part I take issue with is that you didn't trust me."

I sighed. The conversation wasn't going the way I'd intended at all, and we'd just begun. I glanced toward the hearth where Gus had left a warm fire crackling and made my way to the over-sized armchair beside it. My fingers trailed along the table as I moved, struggling to find a way to make things right.

"I do trust you," I said finally. "But when I've tried to broach the subject, you just shut it down. You tell me over and over again that we can't let my father dictate our lives. You're sort of stubborn when it comes to that."

Ranger X barked a laugh. "And you don't have a hint of stubbornness in you?"

"I do," I admitted. "But you don't consult with me about everything."

"Is this about Liam's files?"

"I had as much right to them as you did." I curled into the chair next to the fire, pulled my knees upward and wrapped my arms around my robe. The warmth of the fire cascaded over my body, but still, I trembled. "You didn't ask my permission before sharing the information with Landon."

"That was part of a work mission."

"No, it wasn't," I said. "You can call it work because you involved Landon, but that's not all it was. You didn't want me to know about it; you were afraid of what I'd say, just like I was afraid of what you'd say if you found out I'd commissioned a spell that would prevent me from having children."

"I'm sorry I made you feel that way."

"What sort of apology is that?"

Ranger X stilled. "What am I supposed to say? I believe I did it for the right reasons."

"And what reasons are those?"

"To protect you!" Ranger X's fist closed around the vial as he crossed the room, his footsteps loud and angry. "I didn't know what we'd find, and you're right—it *was* personal. Your mother's name was on those files. It stated she was an assassin, Lily. An assassin!"

"We know that's not true now!"

"No, but what if it was?" Ranger X's voice rose and he flinched, agitated, glancing into the fireplace as if it held the answers. "What if we found out that your mother was a killing machine? What if she destroyed families? What if she didn't give a lick for good or evil and was a killer for hire?"

"We knew that wasn't the case."

"You couldn't have known that, Lily," Ranger X said, an apology on his face. "You never had the opportunity to meet her, to really get to know her beyond your earliest year of life—which you can't possibly remember."

He was right, so I didn't respond.

"You trusted based on sheer hope," Ranger X said. "I couldn't base an investigation on *hope*; if I was going to look into it, if I was going to find the answers for you—the woman I love more than everything else—I needed a layer of separation between us."

"Because you didn't think I could handle it?" I felt small, shrunken in my chair. There was room for two of us on here, but X remained standing, too far away from me. "I'm stronger than you think, X."

"I know how strong you are. Stronger than me," X said. "And I wasn't strong enough to break your heart if the information from Landon came back painting a picture that wasn't what you'd hoped to hear. How could I have told you that your mother wasn't a kindhearted soul who'd fallen in love with the wrong man?"

"So, you would have hidden the information from me?"

"I don't know," X said. "But try to see it from my point of view. You already have a father who has disappointed you a thousand times over. If your mother turned out to be different than you'd thought..."

"She wasn't," I whispered. "I knew she wouldn't be. How could I have possibly come from two evil parents? I'm not evil, X, am I? I try to be a good person."

Ranger X finally collapsed forward toward me, falling to his knees on the shag rug before the hearth and taking both of my hands in his. "Lily, please, sweetheart. You can't ever think that about yourself. You have less evil in you than anyone I have ever met in my lifetime. This is why I couldn't bring myself to risk exposing your mother's secrets before I knew for sure that she was the woman you trusted her to be. The mother you deserved."

"She was," I whispered. "And she would have believed in me, too. She died for the good of the world, X. How could you doubt her? You might not know her, but you know me. Do you not believe in me?"

"It's my life's work to be skeptical, to question everything," Ranger X said, gripping me tighter and tighter. "I've seen brothers kill brothers. Parents do unspeakable things to their children. Families are complex things, Lily, and if I've learned one thing in all my career, it's that just because I wish for something to be one way, that doesn't make it so."

I heard the cry of desperation in Ranger X's voice and knew he wasn't only speaking of me and my mother, but of Landon and Ranger H and Melissa. If only there were another way to explain everything, but there just wasn't. No matter how much we wanted it.

There was nothing more to say. We'd argued and argued, gone over the same things time and time again. Talking in circles wouldn't make any difference.

I eased my hand out of Ranger X's grasp and reached for the vial he'd let fall beside me on the armchair. I held it out, examined it. Felt Ranger X's hand tense around my other wrist.

"What would you like me to do with this?" I asked finally.

"Do you want to take it?" Ranger X's voice was calculated, and he watched me scrupulously—in a way that had me feeling like he'd know if I spoke the tiniest lie. "The decision is ours, but the spell is yours."

I felt my eyes sting. "What I want isn't relevant. If you asked what I truly wanted, I would have told you that I wished my father died back in Olympia. But he's not dead, and we're not murderers, and I am never going to hand our baby over to him."

"He's in prison," Ranger X said. "He's not going anywhere."

"We are magically bound by the contract. You know as well as I do that there's no breaking a contract once it's been magically signed and sealed."

"I understand, but there's got to be another way."

"What is it? I've been hoping for one, praying, wishing on a star—whatever it takes. No path has opened for me."

"I don't think the solution needs to be so permanent," Ranger X said. "Do you trust me?"

"Of course."

"I promise you," Ranger X said. "I will find another way around the contract if that's what you want—if it's what *we* want. If things were different, would you want to start a family with me?"

"Yes, of course."

"Then wait, please." Ranger X leaned in, pressed a kiss to my forehead. "I love you, Lily. I'm sorry we argued. I'm sorry I went behind your back with the files to Landon."

"It's fine," I mumbled. "I'm sorry I asked your brother for help without talking to you first."

"I don't care about that." Ranger X smoothed my hair back. "Not anymore. I never did, I just worried about you, about us. I refuse to let our future be dictated by *him*."

"But—"

"Trust me," Ranger X said, his eyes pleading with me. "Lily, I will honor your wishes, whatever they are about having children. I love you, I am fulfilled in our life together as a family of two."

I sensed there was more to come, and indeed, Ranger X eased onto the seat next to me, pulled me on his lap. His hands came to play with the collar of my robe before sliding down to grasp the side and pulling it tighter around me.

I sat on his lap, my arms circling his neck and eagerly letting the comfort of being snug before the fire displace the tension that'd been wreaking havoc on me for days, weeks, months. I knew, as I always had, that as long as we were together, the rest would work itself out.

"I see so much death, so much evil in the world," Ranger X murmured against my hair. "Before you, that was everything I had. I had work, and I went home and tried not to think about work. Now, I have you. When I finish work, there is a light on for me at home, and that is you."

I inched forward, kissed his cheek. "I see the same in you."

Ranger X just shook his head, let the robe drape open as he pulled me to his chest, let my head fall against him so I could hear the beat of his heart as he held me like he'd never let go.

"It scares me sometimes, the way this world is going," Ranger X said. "The darkness, the murder, the greed. It terrifies me to my core, makes me wonder why I dedicate my life to a job that is impossible to accomplish. No matter how much good I do in this world, it will never be enough to offset all the evil. Then, I come home, I see your smile, and I have hope."

My heart swelled along with the tears pricking at me. I blinked and forced them back, closing my eyes and basking in the sensations of Ranger X's hands as they ran across my bare collarbone, across my sides, and sent shivers down my spine.

"When I think about the future in a general sense, I worry," Ranger X said. "I worry about what's to come, about future generations, what they'll have to tolerate. When we discussed marriage and kids for the first time, I felt excited, hopeful about the future for the first time in a while. The thought of having a family with you, bringing more of you into the world, is the thing I want most of all."

Through my lids, I felt the first tear leak down my cheek, cascade downward and drip from my chin to my bare chest.

"I feel the same about you," I said, letting my eyes flicker open. "But I worry—"

"Don't," Ranger X said. "Trust me to take care of you. Trust yourself to take care of our family. Whatever needs to be done—we'll find a way to do it. We always do."

Ranger X's words resonated hard, radiated someplace deep in my gut. I let my hands find the vial of stunning green liquid, the potion worth its weight in gold. I examined it, imagining one possible path forward. A life for Ranger X and me that would always be the two of us, no matter what.

Then I looked up at X, at the softness hidden behind the chiseled cut of his jaw, at the longing in his eyes, and I knew there was no other option.

With a flick of my wrist, I tossed the vial into the fire. Ranger X didn't move to stop me, nor did he show any sign of happiness. He just waited and watched as the flames licked the brick chimney in shades of blue and red and green and yellow, then faded to a thick black flame that bled white smoke into the air before finally returning to normal.

"I didn't ask you to do that," he murmured. "If you truly want—"

"You didn't ask me to do anything," I interrupted, turning back to face X. My hands reached out and cupped his cheeks as my throat clogged with emotion. "But it was clear what I needed to do."

"But—"

"I don't know what the future holds, Cannon," I said honestly, leaning in until my lips were a breath from his. "But I trust we'll figure it out together."

He closed the distance between us, pressed his mouth to mine in a hungry kiss that'd been so long in coming. The death, the betrayals, the awfulness that existed beyond our walls suddenly vanished and left behind just the two of us in our own swirl of reality.

Ranger X's hands were warm, confident as he slipped them under my robe, let his fingers trail down my arms, over my sides. I shimmied closer to him, let the terrycloth fall away from my body as X shifted me deeper onto his lap.

His mouth moved from my lips to my neck, draped a trail across my collarbone and over to the tender spot behind my ear. My hands slid under his shirt, helped rid him of the pesky material. It landed on the floor along with my robe, our eyes locking in a mix of desire and despair and love and need.

Hours later, when the fire burned to embers and we were curled naked around one another, a soft blanket draped over our bodies and X's fingers lazily running circles over my hip, I knew it would all be okay. Whatever the future brought, it would have us in it, and that was all I needed.

Chapter 19

"I haven't slept this late in some time," I said, stretching as the sun beamed through the windows into the storeroom. "I just hope poor Gus didn't walk in this morning. He'd be scarred for life."

I gestured to my body, which hadn't moved all that much from last night. My clothes were on the floor, and despite a night spent on the couch, I couldn't remember the last time I'd felt so rested. As I glanced over at X preparing our cups of coffee across the room, a calmness settled in my chest that hadn't been there for ages. If ever.

"You should know me better than that." Ranger X gave a big, shiny grin that crinkled his face into a stunning portrait that had my breath hitching in my throat and my heart skidding faster than usual. "I took care of Gus."

To my great relief, Ranger X looked happy. An emotion he wore so seldomly that each time it surfaced, it had me feeling as if I were the fortunate one to be witnessing it. Like a rare gem, a flash of rainbow in the inky blackness of an oil spill, a breath of fresh air after a long, frigid winter. If only I could capture it, bottle that smile. However, like all good things, it was fleeting. Soon enough, the real world would encroach on our private little life together. But I'd hold onto this moment as long as possible.

"Thank you," I said with my own smile. "Why don't you bring those mugs back here and climb under the blanket with me?"

"I've got a better idea." Ranger X was shirtless, wearing only a pair of shorts he must have grabbed from my self-populating closet upstairs. "For those of us who are too tall to fit on that couch, there's a bed upstairs that's just the right size for what I had in mind."

"But what about coffee?" I shrieked as he crossed the room, bundled me into his arms and held me against his chest. "Aren't you exhausted? We were up practically all last night, and—"

"Shh," Ranger X said through a smirk, kissing me to silence the burgeoning laughter in my own chest. "Don't speak. Just enjoy."

"Now, those are instructions I can live with."

"What did I just say?" He gave a playful shake of his head. "You're talking. That's against the rules."

He kicked open the door to my bedroom, laid me down beneath the covers.

"Cannon—"

"Shh," he murmured again, climbing in next to me. "You're not very good at listening. No wonder Gus is always grumpy around you."

I nipped at Ranger X's lip, dug my fingers into his shoulders and dragged him toward me. "I was just going to say that I love you. Is that so bad?"

Ranger X nuzzled against my neck, pressed his body against the length of mine. "Not at all. I love you too, Lily Locke."

Once Ranger X and I finally dragged ourselves out of bed and into the shower, and then finally into clothes, I was grinning so widely my cheeks hurt. X hummed as he poured himself a re-heated cup of coffee to go, and I sang along, off key, as he handed me my own.

"So," he said. "What's on your agenda for the day?"

I groaned. "Do we really need to discuss this?"

"I think so," X said with a smirk. "Unless you have something else you'd like to discuss?"

"I sort of liked when we had the no talking rule up in bed," I grumped. "I wouldn't mind going back to that. Maybe we can just seal off all the doors and windows and pretend the rest of the world doesn't exist."

Ranger X looked interested at the thought, but then his Comm buzzed from the storeroom table where he'd left it the previous evening while in the process of shedding his clothing and accessories.

"Damn," he said.

"You can take it," I said. "I know you're all cuddled out and antsy to get back to work."

Ranger X pulled me to him, pressed an exaggerated smoochy kiss to my lips. "It's a temporary hiatus. We'll resume soon enough. But I really should take this—I've been off the grid for longer than I intended."

"Yeah, well, get used to it," I said. "If we ever actually get married, I'm going to require some work-free nights with your wife."

"*When* we get married," Ranger X said with a wink. "Why do you think I'm working so hard now? Banking up that time for when my wife demands those nights off."

I smacked him playfully on the arm, then let him slip out of the storeroom and into the bar area to take his Comm. I fiddled with the vials on my shelves, pulling out refills for more Energy Elixir.

I glanced at the fireplace, which was now free of flames, and saw the sparkle of broken glass on the floor. I realized that while Ranger X and I had resolved the tension between us, I hadn't exactly made good on my promise to Banks. Unfortunately, Ranger X seemed to be completely uninterested in trying to refortify the bonds with his family, and I was hesitant to push him on such the subject when we'd finally achieved some semblance of contented happiness.

I pushed the thought away, telling myself I'd relaunch the conversation after the mess with Ranger H had been given time to rest. The case might be over, but it would still take time for everything to settle back into place.

When Ranger X reentered the storeroom, his expression was still upbeat though decidedly less gleeful. "Nothing's wrong," he said quickly. "But duty calls, and I will need to get back to work soon, as much as I'd like this morning to stretch on forever."

"I understand," I said, fingering several crushed rose petals. "I've been thinking, and I was hoping that maybe before you get started with your normal shift you could help me with something."

"What's that?"

"I want to speak with Ranger H."

X's shoulders stiffened. "Where did this come from?"

"I'm not sure," I admitted. "I thought about it briefly last night, but I hadn't really considered it. I know I'm just... well, I'm no one special, and I'm sure everyone and their mother wants to question him."

"You'd be surprised," Ranger X said. "Half the Rangers want to question him; the other half want him dead."

"Understandable," I said. "But I just saw something in his eyes at The Black Cat that I can't seem to shake. I'd kick myself if I didn't get the chance to talk to him—just a few minutes."

"I really don't think that's a good idea," Ranger X said. "I think it's best we leave the situation as it is and hope the wounds fade. They're still too fresh."

"Is there anything to stop me from visiting Ranger H on my own?" I pressed. "That would be best, anyway. I can keep you neutral and out of things while I go in myself. It's safe—I mean, it's at prison. I'll just talk to him for a few minutes."

Ranger X expelled a sigh before lifting a cup of coffee to his lips and taking a deep, fortifying sip. "Let's go."

"Excuse me?"

"I can see that I'm not going to deter you until you've seen H for yourself," Ranger X said. "I don't think it's a good idea, but I suppose there's no real harm in it. I'll take you."

"But—"

"Let's go. Final offer."

I nodded and grabbed my mug of coffee. On second thought, I grabbed the Muse blanket from the table and draped it over my arm. The whole situation was so convoluted, so confusing, I figured a little clarity and guidance couldn't hurt. And despite my best intentions, I found myself believing in The Quilter's magic whether I wanted to or not.

"I'm ready," I said. "Off to jail."

"You know," Ranger X said. "Other Rangers' girlfriends want to do things like cook dinner together or go stargazing. But not you, Lily Locke. You beg me to visit murderers in prison."

THE FAMILIAR CLANK of the lock sounded as the elevator cart began to rattle and descend to the lowest level of the prison—a level I knew all too well. Ranger X and I had checked in with the front gate, gone through security—a man who had thankfully blinked at the sight of my blanket and let the subject drop.

Ranger X had listed my father as the man we were due to see, but he'd pulled the guard to the side, murmured a few things under his breath, and the guard gave a second, more serious nod. A look of sadness and anger mixed on his face as he wished us luck. I didn't need to ask what had been said to know the gist of it.

The elevator hit the bottom floor, skidding to a shaky stop. The doors slid open, and I stepped one foot onto the earthen floor. The air felt damper this morning, cooler. Somewhere in the distance a drip sounded. Water leaked down the walls of this godforsaken place and into darkness, an all-consuming blackness. I shivered.

"Where to first?" Ranger X asked. "Do you want to see your father today since we're already here?"

I exhaled a sigh. "I wouldn't say I *want* to see him, but it's probably prudent we do. Just a quick visit."

Ranger X grabbed my wrists, pulled me close. "You don't have to do any of this, Lily. You don't have to see your father. You don't have to speak with Ranger H. It's all over—you can let it rest."

My eyelids fluttered against a stale breeze as it passed through the tunnels, artificial circulation in a place that was too deep below the earth's surface to ever grant the prisoners the feel of true wind or the sun on their faces. "I need to do this, and I think you know that, too."

Ranger X simply nodded, dropped his hands so his fingers clasped mine, and eventually let go. We walked next to one another through the familiar tunnels until we reached my father's cell.

When I rounded the corner, I was struck by his unusual silence. He prided himself on greeting me before we arrived, anticipating my first words. Mind games were his forte, and even when I knew he was playing them, it was difficult not to fall into his well-set traps.

"Good morning, Lucian," I said cautiously, stepping closer to the bars and studying my father through them. He sat in the back in a crouched bundle, his knees up to his chest and a wild grin on his face. I frowned. "Why're you so happy this morning?"

He gave the slightest shake of his head, but otherwise, it was as if he didn't hear me. He stared straight ahead, a somewhat wide-eyed gaze that was eerie due to its sheer blankness.

"Cat got your tongue?" I prompted. "Come on, Lucian. Don't tell me you ran out of words. We both know that's not true. What's going on?"

A high-pitched, guttural laugh came from deep in his throat, a laugh that grew in both size and proportion until it dragged Lucian to his feet and caused him to collapse forward into the center of his cage. He shook his head, as if the joke was on me.

A creepy feeling slithered down my spine at my father's unchar-acteristic behavior. Something had happened to him, someone had gotten to him. Charmed him, enchanted him, broken him. But how? And who? And more importantly, why?

I glanced at Ranger X and saw the alarm in his eyes, though he did a good job of masking it. His face was stoic, his arms folded across the front of his body as he waited for me to give him an order.

"What happened to him?" I murmured. "Something's not right."

"Even the strongest of minds have been known to break in here. Your father hasn't seen sunlight for months, Lily. He's not allowed visitors aside from those cleared with the Rangers—and the visitors he's gotten aren't bearing chocolates and flowers."

"It's not that," I insisted. "It's something else. He's different; fun-damentally different. Something in him snapped. But what? How? Who could have done this to him?"

Ranger X parted his hands, spread them in uncertainty. "Look around, Lily. There's nobody else here."

"I need—I have to clear my mind, to think," I said. "Let's go see H, but I want to come back."

Ranger X merely bowed his head and then tilted it to the side, gesturing in the direction we needed to go. I followed closely behind him, not speaking as we moved quickly through the tunnels.

My brain raced at top speed as I dissected my father's behavior, searching for any clue as to his breaking point—what had caused it, or how it had happened. All I knew was that something had trig-gered my father's mental collapse, and that would be the clue to un-raveling everything else.

Sometime later, Ranger X cleared his throat and stood to the side, letting me move into the lead position before gesturing around one last bend in the tunnel.

"He's just up ahead," X said. "Whenever you're ready."

I took a deep breath, which was all the preparation I needed. My guard was already on high alert. My shoulders were tense with the uncertainty of what had transpired in this prison, of what I'd find up ahead.

"His name?" I murmured quietly. "I assume his Ranger status was stripped upon arrest."

"Aiden," Ranger X said. "Aiden Munroe."

"Aiden," I repeated as I stepped out in front of the bars. "Munroe."

I let the name sit on my lips as I studied the former Ranger before me. A single night in this place had run him down nearly as much as my father had been run down in months—at least, before his new psychotic break.

"Lily?" Aiden blinked upward, his bleary eyes reminiscent of the evening I'd seen him at The Black Cat, except instead of a drunken stupor, this time it was exhaustion and sorrow that rimmed his eyes. "Lily Locke, Ranger X, is that you?"

"It's us," I said. "But we're not here for small talk. We want to know what happened. Why you did it."

"I didn't do anything," Munroe said wearily. His voice came out raspy, hoarse. Tired. "I told all of this to whoever would listen. I screamed all night long. The only person who heard me was the crazy prisoner cackling down the hall."

The thought of my father's weird new cackle raised goosebumps on my skin. Was it the sound of Munroe's distraught shouting through the night that'd caused my father to break? I doubted it—my father had endured a lot worse than a night of yelling.

"Well, the murder weapon was found at your house with your prints on it," I said. "Melissa placed you at the scene of the crime before you were ever a suspect."

"I know," Munroe said blandly.

"You were meeting someone in the woods last night. Who?"

"It's not going to make any difference," Munroe said. "I told all this to the arresting Rangers after X left last night, but they didn't want to hear it. I've used all my breath, Miss Locke. I'm tired. Once the murder weapon was found at my place, it was over. Nobody wanted to hear another word—I'm a Ranger-killer and will always be known as that first and foremost."

On an impulse, I leaned closer. "Then I'm your only chance."

"Chance at what?" The faintest hint of a gleam appeared in his eye, but it was distant, locked behind a night of sleeplessness, of realizing the future before him was bleak. Arguably the worst night of his life.

"I don't know exactly what happened out there," I said. "But something's not quite right yet. I don't know if you're innocent or guilty, but I might be the only one still listening."

Munroe shifted, inched closer to the bars, his hand coming up to run across his matted hair. "Why? Why would you do that?"

I bit my lip, gave a shake of my head. "Call it gut instinct. I saw something, Munroe. Something at The Black Cat."

Munroe closed his eyes, shook his head. "Not my finest moment."

"No, but an honest one," I said. "And I saw real, true sorrow at the loss of your friend. Why? Were you frustrated he wouldn't help you work for The Faction? Did he find out you were a snitch and planned to tell someone?"

A flash of anger in Munroe's eyes was the first real sign of emotion he'd shown all day. "None of that's true. I'm not a snitch—call me a murderer, whatever you want. But I'd never snitch, never turn on my partner."

"Not even if you found out he was working for The Faction?"

"Not without solid evidence and not before going to him directly."

His answer struck me as odd. "You've given this some serious thought."

"I had to," he said dryly. "I thought Landon was working for The Faction when he was killed."

I was vaguely aware of Ranger X behind me, his stoic presence comforting. "Why did you think Landon had flipped?"

"I didn't think he'd flipped, not necessarily," Munroe said. "But he was up to something. I think he wanted to tell me a secret, but he wasn't sure if he could trust me. He started acting odd, telling me bits and pieces of strange things, almost to see how I'd react."

"When did you get suspicious?"

"He'd disappear for hours at a time. Not often, once a month maybe. Sometimes he'd be on duty and just go off the grid. I was getting sick of covering for him—it's protocol that we know exactly where our partners are at all times. That was one of his tests, I'm sure of it. When I didn't go running to X and snitch, he got more daring. But I don't think he was doing it by choice."

"What do you mean?"

"He was nervous, uncomfortable. Shifty. I could tell he didn't like putting me through these stupid tests," Munroe said. "It was almost like he had to do it—was forced to do it. Blackmailed or something."

I chewed on that, wondering if this was a tall tale that Munroe had spun overnight in a last-ditch attempt to clear his name. "Do you have any idea who—"

"No," Munroe said. "I don't know who he met, who he worked for, who would have blackmailed him. The only people he loved enough to flip for would've been us—the Rangers—or his girlfriend."

"Melissa," I said. "And when she was arrested..."

"It made sense that she did it, at least in my mind. She could have easily been blackmailing him. I didn't come forward with any of the information because I figured, justice was served. Until it wasn't."

"You still think Melissa killed him?"

"I don't know. All I can say for certain is that it wasn't me."

"Why were you in The Forest last night?"

"I have access to Landon's calendar. He had one meeting set up, one of his secret little off-the-grid things. I scoured The Forest, set up some Trailer spells, and found the location where Landon had been going week after week. I figured maybe if he was meeting a Faction member from off-island, the other person wouldn't have realized Landon was dead."

I nodded, having thought the same exact thing thanks to Liam's intel.

"I wanted to try and pose as him, see if I could get this other person to talk. Or capture him. Or something. Landon, whatever he did, whatever he was forced into—he was a good man. He deserves closure, and his killer needs to be brought to justice."

"Did you see who shot you?"

"No."

"Who would have wanted to kill you?"

"I don't know. All I know is that it was planned," Munroe said. "Whoever was there knew me well enough to know about my allergy to Pollycock Powder. It wouldn't turn up on a tox screen immediately for poison. It would put me in a deep coma and, without treatment, I'd be left for dead in The Forest. Unless..."

"Unless what?"

"Unless someone didn't want me *dead*." Munroe's eyes glinted as he looked at me. "I got to thinking last night. What if someone knew you and Liam were there? Knew you'd find me?"

"That's impossible."

"Nothing is impossible," he said. "Think about it. Maybe whoever shot me actually wanted me alive. Pollycock Powder doesn't kill me outright—as you've seen. With proper treatment and time, it's easily survivable."

"Why go through the trouble of putting you in a coma but leaving you alive?"

"Think about it. It was *because* I was alive that the investigation resumed looking at me," Munroe said. "As for who shot me, I still don't know the answer to that. But I keep turning back to motive. The only person with motive to get someone *else* arrested for Landon's murder was Melissa. If I was arrested, she'd go free."

"But she was locked in prison during that time. She couldn't have been two places at once."

"I know that. Which is where I come up against a brick wall. Was this a plan in advance? Did she have access to someone on the outside while she was in here?"

"You realize this is all a huge leap," I said. "Very conspiracy theory for someone sitting behind bars."

"I'm trying to figure it all out, same as you," Munroe said. "I don't have any clue why I was framed except that I was the easy target. Really, what motive do I have? I'm not working for The Faction. I don't know how to prove that, but feel free to try. The murder weapon? Easy enough to plant. Fingerprints—easy enough to place. And if I hadn't flipped and didn't need to keep my partner silenced, then why the hell would I kill my best friend? And *why* would I keep the murder weapon at my place? I'm a Ranger. I'd know how to dispose of the evidence."

The words rang loud in the silent air. In the distance, a deep cackle began, rising until it sounded like a crazed animal beneath a full moon.

"Something is wrong with her," Munroe muttered. "She's been doing that all night."

"He," I said. "It's my father. He's... I don't know. Mental breakdown or something."

Munroe looked at me. "I'm sure it's a woman."

"No, it's just... I don't know what it is." I let out a huge breath. "I know his laugh is strange, but—"

"I heard her talking to someone," Munroe said. "Not doing that cackle, thing—but actually talking. It's definitely a woman."

My spine went rigid. "You heard him talking to someone?"

"It's a *her*, and yes," Munroe said. "Last night when I was brought in here."

"Were there any visitors to come down here last night?" I turned to Ranger X. "And was Munroe brought into prison before Melissa was released?"

"There were no visitors," X confirmed. "Visiting hours were over, and we always lock down the prison during transport of prisoners considered highly dangerous. We can double check with the guards, but I'm sure there was nobody down here except the prisoners and the guards."

"And the timing?"

X thought back. "Munroe was brought in about an hour before Melissa was released."

My blood ran cold. "X," I gasped. "It's her."

Chapter 20

A long silence followed as Ranger X digested the meaning behind what I'd said. Our footsteps sounded hollow against the earthen floor as we padded down the hallway toward my father's cell.

"It's her?" He finally echoed. "How can that be?"

"I don't know yet."

The Muse blanket hung heavy on my arm and, on an impulse, I shook it out and wrapped it around me as we came around the corner and stopped in front of the familiar bars. My father sat in the jail cell, hunched over at the back just as we'd left him.

I pulled the blanket tighter around my shoulders. The longer I stood wrapped in the Muse blanket, the stranger the image appeared before me. It began with a shimmer. His—her?—body trembled around the edges, a slight transparency to his features. The edges of his figure shook, and the longer I stared, the more convinced I was that what I was seeing was not my father, but the mere illusion of his physical form.

"How'd you do it?" I inched closer to the cage. "How'd you do it, Melissa?"

A slow smile crept over my father's face—the smile of a woman, of Melissa. The high-pitched cackle suddenly made sense, along with my father's mysterious silence—and Melissa's adamant no-talking-policy as she was supposedly released from prison by Ranger X.

"You haven't managed to swap voices, have you?" It came out more of a statement than a question. "How did you switch cells?"

The figure trembled more violently, shaking with the effort of holding onto a powerful spell that likely had sapped a ton of Melissa's energy. It was clear she wanted to share her genius with us, to bask in the knowledge that she'd thwarted us and rub salt in an already aching wound.

"Come on," I said. "Drop the act. I have a Muse blanket—it has recognized that you aren't who you say you are. And what's that behind you?"

A slight glimmer in the shape of an arch bounced off the cell behind Melissa. I wondered if that was how they'd switched cells, or if Melissa had more tricks up her sleeve that she hadn't exposed to us yet.

Melissa glanced behind her, the look on my father's face one of surprise as he studied the wall behind him. He jerked his head forward to face me, an ugly smile turning up his lips.

I went back and forth thinking of this *thing* as my father and as Melissa. He or she. If it was, in fact, Melissa, she was incredibly skilled at illusions—skilled enough to help a wanted criminal escape from the most secure prison on earth.

My father's figure caught me staring at the arch behind him, a mysterious half-halo that looked carved in the dirty stone wall and glowed with a brilliant blue-white light.

"Well done," my father's lips moved, but in an eerie twist of confirmation, the voice that emerged from his lips was high pitched with a feminine lilt. "Very good, Mixologist. Figuring things out before the guards."

"How'd you do it?" I pressed. "Switch cages?"

"Why, I didn't switch anything." Melissa raised her hands and closed her eyes. I lunged forward to stop whatever she was doing, but the magical bars on the cage were too good at keeping people in—and out.

"She can't do magic, can she?" I asked Ranger X. "I can't send magic through. I thought she couldn't send magic out."

"She can't do any spells to break the bonds of the cage," X said. "But she can use natural magic. She's obviously an illusionist, so she can..."

As Ranger X trailed off somewhat abruptly, the world began to spin around us. We both lurched forward, shaken off balance by the warping of the world as we knew it. Walls shifted and broke, disappeared and reappeared. The ground spun beneath our feet, swirling and morphing into an entirely new pattern. Before us, images changed in the blink of an eye.

Then, just as soon as it started, it stopped.

Ranger X and I were no longer standing where we'd been before the world had tilted. We were still in prison, on the lowest level, but we stood not before my father's cell, staring at my father, but at Melissa's cell, staring directly at the woman who had helped my father escape.

"But..." I hesitated. "You were released. Ranger X walked you out."

"It wasn't her," Ranger X said grimly. "It was all an illusion. She didn't even need to break out of her cage—it's genius, really. We did it for her. I walked Lucian Blackmore right out of this prison."

"That's why he didn't speak," I whispered. "His voice wouldn't have been disguised."

A flash of distress streaked through Ranger X's voice, but it was gone in seconds, covered by the hardening of his jaw and a burning in his eyes that would have anyone with half a mind running terrified in the opposite direction.

But Melissa just watched him easily, a smirk on her face. There was a sense of pride clinging to her that wasn't altogether unwarranted. An illusion of this scale—rearranging the prison's walls with her mind, then keeping my father cloaked until he'd made it to freedom, was no simple feat. It was something that had obviously been planned for some time.

"You're still trapped, Melissa," I snarled. "You'd better start talking if you have any hope of ever seeing the light of day again. It's not too late to work out a deal."

"Oh, it's much too late for me," Melissa said. "I knew what I was getting into when I moved to The Isle."

"You were blackmailed," I said, offering her an out in the event she wanted to take it. We could handle Melissa later. Now, the urgency was in finding my father before he got too much of a head start. "Let us help you. Where is Lucian going?"

"I didn't go through all this just to end up trapped," Melissa said with a haughty sniff. "Lucian appreciates me. He loves me like the daughter he never had. He hasn't abandoned me."

"If you think he's walking back into prison to save you," I said, "you couldn't be more wrong. He wouldn't do that to save his own flesh and blood, let alone *you*. He used you, Melissa. Did he make you kill Landon, too? Was that part of this whole ploy to get you locked up?"

"You wouldn't appreciate the finer details if I told you," Melissa said with a pout to her lips. "A shame really, because it's my greatest work. Ever. And there's nobody left to appreciate it. But Lucian will—he always does."

"Lucian is my father," I said, stepping closer to the cage. "No matter how much you try to please him, he will never love you like he loves me."

"Shut up!" she screeched. "You abandoned him in his time of need. You could have helped him out of prison, and then Landon would never have had to die. This is all your fault, you awful witch!"

"So, it's true," I said. "You orchestrated this whole thing as a prison break. You set Ranger H up from the beginning—mentioning he was at the crime scene even while I comforted you for losing the man who you supposedly loved more than anyone in the world."

"It wasn't always the plan to kill him!" A hint of defensiveness crept into Melissa's voice, and her eyes flickered with something close to dismay. "I didn't want to kill him. He loved me. I cared about him, but he didn't cooperate. He had to go."

"Didn't cooperate?"

"I tried to lead him to the way of The Faction, to explain to him slowly, carefully, how beneficial it would be to have an insider in the Ranger program. I thought that maybe, if he just loved me enough, he would come around. See my side of the story. Together, we could work as Lucian's eyes and ears on The Isle."

"But Landon would never have turned his back on us." Ranger X's fists trembled as they clenched tighter together. "So, you silenced him."

"He figured it out, finally," Melissa said. "He tried to convince me it wasn't too late to cut some sort of a deal. Promised me he'd help me become some sort of double agent for the Ranger program. I let him believe I wanted to do it, and then..."

"You shot him." My tone was dull.

"It didn't happen like that," Melissa said. "There was a lot of thought put into it."

A low growl came from Ranger X. He raised his wrist to his lips, presumably to Comm the other guards.

But I put a hand on his arm and gave a subtle shake of my head. "Not yet."

"I came to The Isle to gain intel for The Faction. I wondered if Landon might love me enough to see my logic and work with me. Work with *us*." Melissa shook her head. "When that was obviously not going to pan out, I needed an escape plan. The timing of the rest was just too convenient. Landon was getting suspicious of me... Lucian was in prison... the idea came to me one night, and ever since, I've been planning."

"Your boss isn't going to save you. You were duped."

"He's not my boss," Melissa snapped. "Lucian's a father figure to me."

"You can have him," I said. "But the truth is, he doesn't want you. He'll always want me more than you."

My subtle jabs were getting under Melissa's skin, I could feel it. Her rage was building, her figure becoming clearer and clearer as the illusionist magic drained from her body with her concentration focused on me.

"Shut up!" she said. "You're wrong. You don't show him respect. That's why he has none for you."

"Whatever you say." I glanced down at my nails, feigning nonchalance. "So, who fired the arrow at Ranger H in The Forest? Are you working with someone else on the island?"

"Wouldn't you like to know," she said with a slim smile. "Lucian has resources that extend beyond your wildest dreams."

"So, he didn't tell you who he hired to fire that arrow," I deduced. "He doesn't trust you, Melissa. He only used you to get out of here because you were silly enough to believe his lies."

"Of course he told me! It was just some stupid minion from the mainland," she said. "It didn't mean anything. It was just to get Ranger H in prison so I—or rather, Lucian—would be released."

"And this same minion planted the evidence in Ranger H's home?"

Melissa nodded. "He was just following orders. It was nobody important. Just a little weasel working for Lucian."

"You don't like Lucian keeping others close to him, do you?" I pressed. "Lucian owes a lot to this *minion* who helped him escape from prison. Maybe more than you. And this minion is free, while you're stuck here."

"Don't be stupid. I orchestrated this whole thing. I'm the mastermind behind it all. Who else cares enough about The Faction to incriminate themselves in a murder investigation? Nobody. That's who. *Nobody!*"

Melissa's hands flailed as she spoke. Her anxiety was palpable, a hint of crazed dedication radiating from her as she paced back and forth.

"It was genius. Genius! Your freaking boyfriend walked Lucian right out the front doors. I bet you never saw that coming!"

"Congratulations," I said. "You beat us all. Now what happens? You're still locked up in the most secure prison known to man, and nobody's going to be walking you out the front door. The only way out is with inside help—and nobody's left inside to help you."

"I am," she said, and an ugly smile spread over her face. "I've learned plenty about helping myself. I didn't come into prison without an escape route. All I needed Lucian to do was activate it."

"How do you know he's good for his word?"

"Because it's already activated." She gave me a smile. "So, I guess we should say our goodbyes."

"The key," I murmured to X as another flash of that bluish-white light blinked behind Melissa. "Get the key to her cell—she's got a portal inside!"

"That's impossible."

"No, it's not," I said. "You just said—natural magic can't be blocked by cell bars. If she set up a portal on the outside, knowing she was going into prison, she'd just need the connecting door to make it work—which can be anywhere. Including inside her cell. X, hurry!"

"Very good." Melissa's smile grew wider. "And Lucian has activated my portal and is waiting for me on the other end. I'll tell him you say hello."

Ranger X had already turned down the hallway, calling for the nearest guard. I stepped closer to the cage.

"Tell him this isn't over." I spoke through gritted teeth. "Tell him he'll never get what he wants from me."

"He doesn't want anything from you."

"I wouldn't be so sure," I said, feeling an awful grin spread across my face. "He's keeping something from you, Melissa. And it's something that only I can give him."

"Shut up, bitch!" Melissa turned, stormed toward the back of the cell and stopped just below the blue-white arch. Before stepping through, she turned back and gave me her own dark smile. "He'll kill you."

"I have no doubt he'd like that." My throat constricted. "Let him try."

With a last cackle of that high-pitched shriek, Melissa strode beneath the arch. For a split second, the illusion of the dirty wall faded away to reveal a portal shining with blinding white light. Two steps later, she'd disappeared for good.

I stared into the depths of the portal, feeling my eyes burn as if I were watching the sun. By the time Ranger X returned with a guard, the portal had begun to shrink, and within seconds, it snapped back into itself, gone forever.

"She's with him," I said. "We need to find her—find her, we find him."

"Lily—" Ranger X reached for me.

"It's not your fault. You couldn't have known. Without the Muse blanket, I would have never seen past her illusions. I wouldn't have been able to see the portal, either," I said. "Come on. We don't have time to waste. If we're going to track them, we've got to get started now."

"Lily, please," Ranger X said. "They're gone. We need to regroup, get a team."

"Go ahead," I said, turning away from him and marching toward the elevators. "I've got a different idea."

Chapter 21

I barely remembered the journey out of the prison. Ranger X caught up to me at the elevators and rode up with me, a silent and sturdy presence at my side. We didn't speak, nor did we touch. My mind blazed through different scenarios, what this all meant, but it was too much to handle at once. Too much bad outweighing the good.

As I reached the beachfront before my home, I was vaguely aware of the stormy skies rising in the distance, the whitecaps threatening to brush away the carefree spirit of our sugar-sand shores. Even the pink and purple shuttered building, a home filled with warmth and color and laughter, was now tinged with darkness. The whites of the porch were muted. The swing creaked as the wind battered it back and forth, and as I climbed the steps, they seemed to sag from tiredness.

I threw open the door and found Gus sitting at the storeroom table, his cane resting next to a pile of ingredients he was carefully measuring, separating, and preparing for use.

"Lily," he said, clearing his throat. "You're—what's wrong?"

I just shook my head.

Ranger X came into the room behind me and slammed the door shut. "They're gone."

"Who?" Gus asked.

Ranger X explained the developments from prison. When X finished, Gus looked at me.

"Now what?" he asked. "What will you do?"

Ranger X faced me, too. Waited.

"I have an idea," I said. "I need to work on it alone. Give me the afternoon."

"But—" Ranger X began.

"I'll need Gus's help," I said. "X, your time would probably be better used organizing your Rangers. If my plan doesn't work, it's best if we don't waste all our resources on it this afternoon."

"If it doesn't work," Ranger X echoed. "You'll Comm me before you begin the plan? What *is* your plan?"

"I'm using Melissa's logic against her," I said. "She is linked into a portal. Gus, what does *The Magic of Mixology* say about portal magic?"

"It leaves a distinct marker when it's active," Gus filled in. "It's based on Residuals—and it can be tracked. But Lily, you need a sample of the portal for use in a potion for it to work. Without a bit of the portal magic, you won't be able to match anything. And I imagine that the portal inside of the jail cell was manually wiped clear the second Melissa closed it."

"Maybe most people can't match a marker," I said, rolling up my sleeves. "But I'm the Mixologist."

Gus gave a deep bow of his head. "You are, Lily, but still—"

"My father had a hand in setting up the portal," I said. "He was on the other end of it. His magical touch will be on the exit portal. And, while I hate it, we're related."

Gus nodded, a show of understanding dawning on his face. "Ah."

Ranger X gave a shrug. "For those of us who haven't memorized the textbook..."

I grabbed Gus's knife from the table, pressed it to my palm. I winced as the skin sliced, a line of red blood appearing on my hand. I held it over the cauldron, made a fist, and squeezed.

"We share DNA," I said simply. "Residuals have traces of a person's magical DNA, if you will. I'll be able to help match mine against my father's. It might not work, but it's the only shot we've got."

"Then what?" Ranger X asked. "What happens after you trace the portal?"

"Just let me handle this," I said. "I'll let you know before anything happens."

"But—"

"I haven't figured it out yet, okay?" I sounded snippier than I'd intended. I took a deep breath, apologized. "I need to concentrate. It's the most complex potion I've ever made—transporting others through time and space. Just... give me some peace and quiet to think. Please."

Ranger X looked over my shoulder to Gus, exchanged some sort of sign that probably meant they'd stay in contact, and finally nodded. X crossed the room to me, opened my fist gently.

His hand glowed yellow as he held his palm over mine. He muttered something in a foreign language and, before my eyes, the skin sealed, leaving behind only a streak of dried blood to prove there had indeed been a wound before X's healing touch.

I felt my eyes smart with tears. Not of sadness, nor frustration, but of the sheer swirl of emotions battering around my chest. The desire for normalcy, the pressure of knowing that someone was out there with the will and the way to destroy my life at the drop of a hat. And knowing above all, that my father, a man who was supposed to be my family, wouldn't hesitate to leave me for dead once it was all over.

I pressed a kiss to Ranger X's lips. He grasped my arms, pulled me against him. My forehead pressed against his chest as he clasped me hard. His voice brushed against my skin as his fingers twined through my hair.

"I believe in you," he murmured. "But you don't need to do this alone."

"Thank you," I whispered, pulling back enough to meet his gaze. I forced a smile. "I'm not doing it alone. Since I've met you, I've never been alone."

X gruffly pressed a kiss against my forehead before stepping away, and without a backward glance, he left the room. Closing the door gently behind him, he cemented silence over the room.

I turned to find Gus watching the table with unabashed fascination. When he felt my gaze on him, he looked up, his eyes pale and focused.

"There's no spell for this," he said. "Your chances of tracking her are abysmal."

"Ranger X gave me the clue I needed," I said with a thin smile. "I don't have to do this alone."

Gus frowned. "I don't suppose this means you've figured out what you'll need for the potion?"

"As a matter of fact," I said. "I have. I'm going to use one of the only things I have that Lucian doesn't."

"What's that?"

I gave a broader smile. "Family."

"And if it's successful," Gus prompted, "and you bring Melissa back here, then what?"

"I'm not sure yet."

"I'll document." Gus pulled out the huge tome, *The Magic of Mixology*, and thumbed through until he found an empty page. "Do you have a title for this one?"

"Driving people through time and space," I said, leaning over and taking the quill from Gus's hand. "I think there's only one name that's fitting."

"SPELLDRIVER," I SAID finally. "It's almost complete."

"Almost?" Gus wiped sweat from his brow. "What's left?"

The sun had set, the moon had risen, the storm had pounded against the walls of the bungalow for the past several hours and prevented the store from staying open—giving us full concentration on the matter at hand.

"All that's left is asking for help," I said. "I can't do this alone."

"And for that, we need..." Gus waited for me to finish his sentence.

"Dried heart of palm," I said. "Ginseng, of course, and I think the final touch will be the thorns of seven red roses."

Gus pondered for a moment. "The palm to draw the attention of those nearest your heart, the ginseng because we'll need energy to make this spell work. And the thorns?"

I gave him a thin smile. "To represent family. Despite the thorns, the hurt and prickliness we have with one another, there's still something beautiful at the end of it all."

"And this is why we needed a female Mixologist," Gus muttered under his breath. "No offense, but your grandfather couldn't have come up with something like this."

"Did his father try to kill him?" I asked with raised eyebrows. "I didn't think so. Sort of gives a person incentive to think outside the box when I know it'll eventually come down to my life or his. Things tend to get personal when that's the case."

"There might be—"

"There's no other way," I said shortly, accepting the thorns gingerly from Gus's outstretched hand. "It is what it is, and I've accepted it. There. We'll wait a few minutes, and then we'll be finished."

"Shouldn't you let X know?" Gus asked. "Once this is activated, it will probably be good to have backup."

"If it works, the spell will draw whoever I need to be near me," I said. "That's the beauty of it. We don't have time to wait, Gus. The spell will only work as long as there are portal Residuals leftover on the exit, and it's already been hours since the escape."

"I'm Comming X," Gus said. "He should be here."

"Fine. It'll take a few minutes to work."

While Gus hopped on the Comm and alerted Ranger X to our progress, I prepared the incantation that would set Spelldriver into effect. I ladled the bright orange potion from the cauldron into a thin vial and studied it, watching the color twist and move with a life of its own. It felt right; it felt pure and good. The time was now. I knew that as clearly as if the Muse blanket had been wrapped around my shoulders.

"Calling those near my heart,
I ask of you to do your part.
In dire need of help from all,
May you heed this important call.
We must gather those who seek to harm,
Bring them before us without alarm.
To find the portal, match blood of mine,
And bring those who've gone through space and time."

I finished the incantation, watched as the potion gurgled, bubbled, then sparked at the top. A small flame sat at the lip of the tube, and only once it died down did I tip the glass to my lip and drink.

The potion went down easy, fruity with citrus overtones. I returned the vial to its stand just as Gus disconnected his Comm.

"I see you didn't wait," he said. "X is on his way."

"I'll bet he is," I said with a nervous smile. "At least, he should be if the potion worked."

"When will we know if..." Gus trailed off as the front door blew open with a gust of wind and in came Trinket, dressed in nothing but a nightgown and no-nonsense blue slippers that squeaked as she skidded to a stop inside the door.

"I guess it worked," I said weakly. "Though I didn't expect the spell would hit Trinket."

"What happened?" Trinket looked around. "I just knew I needed something upstairs, so I walked through my bedroom door, and I came out here."

"Huh," I said. "Interesting side effect. Listen, there's a spell I've Mixed that—"

Mimsey appeared seconds later, a plate of pancakes in hand. She blinked as she stepped through the door. "I just opened my fridge for some more syrup, and somehow, my fridge led me here. Is this your doing, Lily?"

I winced. "Sorry about that. This spell got a lot bigger than I expected. I was just trying to—"

The next person to interrupt me was Hettie. She stepped through the door looking a mixture of elegant and silly, dressed in a long white gown with lacy sleeves and a hat with white netting that covered most of her face.

"Well, ain't that something," Hettie said. "I just wanted to open my medicine cabinet and grab some lip gloss, and now I'm here."

"Ma, is that your wedding dress?" Mimsey took a bite of pancake. "Why are you wearing that out and about?"

"I was in my own bathroom!" Hettie said. "I didn't expect to be whisked away. Why the whisking, anyway? I imagine this is your doing?"

I nodded as Hettie's eyes swiveled to face me. "If it helps, you look quite beautiful."

"Thank you." Hettie curtsied. "Still fits! I don't fill out the bust quite like I used to, but it's nothing a few rolls of toilet paper can't solve. Now, who else are we waiting on?"

"I, um, honestly don't know," I said. "I just called those closest to my heart to help me disarm a woman who escaped from prison. I thought... maybe it would bring X and Zin here, or... I don't know."

"Shit!" The curse word came from the front door as a familiar bubbly blonde stubbed her toe on the lip of the doorway and stumbled inside, falling to a heap at the foot of her mother. Poppy looked up, surprise scrawled on her face as she clutched a floppy beach hat to her head. "Well, that's weird. They told me the towels were right around the corner, but I guess I must have gotten lost along the way."

"Oh, Poppy!" Mimsey flung herself at her daughter. "You're home."

"Not on purpose!" Poppy adjusted a two-piece swim suit to more properly cover her goods, and then she pulled herself up to stand next to her mother. "Can someone explain what's happening?"

"We're all just popping over here because Lily made a spell that asked us to be here," Hettie said. "I'm guessing she needs our help with something. Whatever it is, it's more exciting than what I had planned!"

"My father escaped from prison," I told the group. "He had the help of a young woman named Melissa. I'm trying to track them through portal use. I made a potion called a Spelldriver—it's supposed to drive people through time and space. It's, um, the most complex spell I've ever written. Hence the reason I wasn't sure exactly how it would work. I asked for help, and then I asked to track Melissa and my father. I'm not sure how the rest of this will play out."

Our next surprise came in the form of a large black cat leaping through the front door, claws outstretched, jaguar eyes gleaming gold. Zin, in her shifted form, crashed hard against the wall, sliding to the floor in a heap. She bared her teeth at the group, then shook her head, confusion in her eyes as she shifted back to her human form.

"I was hunting!" Zin said as her nails returned to normal size and her hair shortened to the severe bob she wore religiously. "I was just about to nab that uh—well, whatever. Then the next thing I know, I'm flying through the air into a wall."

She shook herself again, glaring around as she gathered her wits about her. Only a few vials had fallen, cracked, or shattered in the process. Gus was already on cleanup duty.

Suddenly Gus straightened, dropped the broom, and reached for his cane. He looked to me, a haziness in his eyes. "I have to go."

"What?" Mimsey asked, looking to her boyfriend. "Lily needs you more than ever!"

"I need to go," Gus repeated, shrugging and looking mystified. "I can't be here. Have to stop X, too."

Before anyone could comprehend Gus's sudden and uncharacteristic exit, he was gone, the door shut behind him. The room fell into chilly silence.

"I think this must be everyone," I said uneasily. "Apparently, it's supposed to be just us."

"What is?" Trinket asked, rubbing her head. "I've got children sleeping."

"And I've got a boyfriend on the beach and a pina colada with my name on it," Poppy said. "This is very inconvenient."

The group of women stared at me, and I could only raise my shoulders in apology. "I'm sorry, this is a long shot, but it's our only chance. I think this is everyone. Apparently, only the women are needed for this—why, I've no clue, but..."

"I think we have another visitor," Hettie whispered suddenly. "The last of us is arriving."

A hush descended over the room as we all turned to where Hettie's gaze was directed. There, hovering in the center of the room, was a hazy figure. It was definitely a woman's body, though her back was to me as she grew more solid with each passing breath.

Hettie spoke first. "Delilah?"

"Mom?" I echoed as the figure turned around.

She hovered just above the ground, an apparition more than a ghost. A faint outline in silvery wisps of air. Her features, however, were distinct—I recognized her from the Long Isle Iced Tea potion when I'd changed into her for a time.

My mother gave a nod, a soft smile spreading across her face. She looked real, so real—too real. I stepped forward, extended a hand. She raised her palm to meet mine, but we hesitated just centimeters apart. I knew if we moved a hair closer, I'd go right through her, and I couldn't bear to know that this wasn't real. For a brief snapshot in time, I chose to believe.

"What brought you here?" I asked. "How did you... how did you know?"

"You asked for help. And when my daughter asks for help from our family, we hear the call." My mother gestured wide, spread her arms to encompass the room. "You've been born into a family of amazing women, Lily—use them. You are never alone, darling. Even without me here to guide you."

I felt wetness on my cheek and brushed it away. I stepped backward. "But how... I don't understand. I didn't *try* to do this."

"Your powers as the Mixologist are growing," Delilah said, her voice whisper-soft, a comforting sing-song in the silence of the bungalow. "Your call was heard in all realms for help. You drew your family around you in your time of need. I'm so proud of you, Lily."

"But X—"

"This is a job for women," she said kindly. "X is better served where he is now. Sweetheart, I wish we had more time, but you will have another visitor coming soon, someone from the second half of your charm."

I looked knowingly at her. "I thought it might be too late. The Residuals must have faded."

"They have," my mother said with a faint twinkle of amusement in her eyes. "That's where I come in handy. I can travel between time and space and locate the portal magic which you seek. But once I'm gone, once I match the portal magic with the one you seek, there's no turning back."

"Without X, how are we supposed to capture her?" I asked. "I don't have time to make another potion!"

"No, but you've learned much from a Spellbinder, and you have the power of your fellow witches. Use it," my mother said, smiling around. "And trust in yourself, Lily."

I reached out, touching nothing but air. "But there's so much I want to ask, so much I need to know. Will you come back? Can I call you again?"

She just smiled. "I wish we had more time, but in the absence of it, I'll leave you with this: Trust your family, your friends. Liam can be counted among them. He's a good man."

"Mom, do you ever wish..." I trailed off, my throat constricting so I couldn't ask the question.

"I don't wish anything different," my mother said. "Even my death. It brought me you, and you're the greatest gift I could have been given—even for such a short time. Stay strong, Lily. I love you. And now, I must go."

"I love you," I whispered, but it was lost in the gasp of air as my mother disappeared.

The storeroom once again settled into an uncomfortable silence as my family looked at me, watched me for any sign of a reaction. Tears streamed down Poppy's cheeks, while Mimsey looked shell-shocked. Trinket's face was deathly pale, her mouth opening and closing with the effort of speaking, though no sound came out. Zin shifted her weight uncomfortably, gazing anywhere around the room but at me. Only Hettie looked at me with a pleasant smile.

"Well," my grandmother said finally, "I suppose we should heed your mother's advice. We have one more visitor to take care of tonight."

"I don't have time to Mix anything," I said. "I don't know if Melissa will come through here armed—or if she'll bring my father with her, or—"

"Girls," Hettie said, swiveling her gaze to Mimsey and Trinket. "Do you recall the spell I used on you both as children?"

"You're going to have to be more specific," Trinket said dryly. "You used plenty of spells on us as children."

"They were for your own good, dearies." Hettie smiled more sweetly. "The one I'm referencing is the Pain of the Past spell."

Mimsey shuddered. "I swore I'd never use that on Poppy. It's awful."

"I'm not suggesting we use it on Poppy," Hettie said. "And it's not actually awful if you haven't done anything awful."

"Everyone makes mistakes," Trinket said briskly. "It's always awful. Who in their right mind wants to relive the moments in which they've been most cruel to others?"

I glanced wide-eyed at Zin and Poppy, but they both looked stumped. This wasn't a spell found in *The Magic of Mixology*. It sounded like it might be found in some obscure parental handbook that had gone out of style in Hettie's era.

"It's not a spell to be used lightly," Hettie admitted, turning her attention to me, Zin, and Poppy. "But I think us girls might have been called here tonight because it's time to pass down a spell from one generation to the next."

"Um..." Poppy raised a hand. "I'm a vampire. No spellcasting powers."

"It's not about casting a spell," Hettie said. "We need to harness your power. There is strength in our family bond, and that's why Lily needed you here tonight."

"Whatever you need from us, you'd better talk quickly," Zin said, glancing toward the fire in the hearth which cracked extra loudly. "Lily's mother told us we wouldn't have a lot of time once she left."

Hettie nodded. "Pain of the Past spell. What it does is quite literally put the shoe on the other foot. My girls fought like cats and werewolves, and one day I got sick of listening to them. So, I enchanted two blankets with charms and placed one on each of the girls' shoulders. They were forced to relive the way they'd treated their sister—from the other person's point of view."

"But it's worse than it sounds," Mimsey said with a wince. "There's the awful truth to it—you see yourself in this ugly light. You have to watch yourself do or say terrible things to the people you love. It's why I swore I would never put Poppy through it, even if my mother had created it with the intent to be helpful."

"Exactly," Hettie said. "Lily, this Melissa—she killed her fiancé, if rumors are to be believed. Would you say she cared for him?"

I thought back to her defensiveness in prison, the way Melissa had fought to bare everything to me in an almost cathartic style. Like she'd needed to unload, defending her choices as if she hadn't had another option.

"She might have loved him at some point—it's hard to say," I said. "But I do believe she cared for him, even if she cared for The Faction more."

"The spell is crippling," Hettie said. "We'd just need a blanket. We can charm it in two seconds. Then, if and when Melissa arrives, we just need to get her to touch it, and she'll be pulled under the spell. We can have Zin—" Hettie paused, smiled—"Ranger Z, I mean—arrest her while under the influence."

"Of course," I said quietly. "I have just what we'll need."

I crossed the room to the armchair before the fireplace where The Quilter's final gift to me, the completely unmagical blanket, sat folded and neatly draped across the top. I gave a shake of my head along with a wry smile.

"Well," I said. "I guess Gus was right. She knew I'd need this."

"That'll do," Hettie said with a wink as she took the blanket off my hands. "Now, to make this spell powerful enough, we'll need all of you to hold onto the blanket. A family bond is stronger than one of an individual, and if this Melissa is as strong as I imagine, we'll need all the power we can get."

All six of us circled the blanket, grasping onto the fabric. We stood shoulder to shoulder, all eyes on Hettie.

My grandmother smiled around at us. "Family time," she said. "I love it. We should do this more often."

"Maybe we'll save the sentimentality for after we catch the bad guy. Or gal," Poppy said, glancing over her shoulder as the fire snapped and crackled again. "How does this chant go?"

"Pain of the past, we call you back.
Show us history from the opposite path.
Step into another's shoes to feel,
And teach us from the pain we steal."

At once, warmth shot up and down my arms, spreading from the tip of the fabric to my shoulders, into my neck, until my body tingled. Judging by the shifting of others around the blanket, they felt the same thing.

"Now," Hettie said. "We wait."

"Except," Poppy said, her eyes widening. "I don't think we have to wait long."

In the center of the room, a flame leapt through the storeroom in the form of an arch. It left scorch marks behind in midair the same shade of blueish-white that had signified the portal in the prison cell.

Someone was coming.

All of us in the room shifted a step further from the portal. It perched between us and the fireplace. Knuckles clutched the fabric of the blanket tighter, but nobody moved. Nobody backed away. Nobody flinched.

"Together, we can't be defeated," Hettie said. "Just wait until she arrives. We need her to touch the blanket. Then, Zin, you'll know what to do?"

Zin nodded from my side. "Are we sure there will only be one coming through the portal?"

"Nope," I said, at the same time the arch in the air before us turned into a full-on oval portal.

Melissa stumbled through, her face angry and shocked as she stepped into the bungalow and glanced up, surprised to find herself surrounded by people.

"What's going on?" she snarled. "Where am I?"

"Lily," my mother's voice echoed from beyond. "I've found them—hurry."

"Wait!" I said as Hettie raised the blanket slightly. "There's another."

A second figure was appearing behind Melissa in the portal, slowly gaining visibility. An arm, a leg, a flash of a torso, and then to everyone's shock and dismay, my father stepped through the portal and into my home.

Zin bared her teeth in a reflexive, animalistic instinct. Before any of us could say a word, she dropped the blanket and began transforming—whether on purpose or as a natural defense mechanism before her enemy, it didn't matter. She was on the ground as a jaguar, snarling at my father before the rest of us knew what happened.

"Zin, wait!" I said, holding out a hand to her. "Mom?"

I couldn't put my finger on why I didn't tell Zin to attack at once, as I wanted nothing more than my father out of my life for good—but my mother wasn't back yet. I needed to know she was safe—wherever she was—before we made our move.

"Lily," the voice said again, this time more faintly. My mother drifted through the portal, giving me a private look amid the chaos, a smile filled with the love of a mother, the smile I'd longed to see since I could remember. "I'm so proud of you, darling. But now, I must go."

"Delilah—" My father extended his hand toward her. His eyes were glazed. As my mother's figure floated out of the portal and across the room toward me, he took an involuntary step toward her. "Delilah? What are you... how are you..." My father turned an astounded gaze toward me. "That's her voice. It's *her*. How did you manage..."

He couldn't finish a sentence. It was the first time I'd seen my father speechless. The first time I'd seen his eyes widening with anything but malice. The first time he seemed vulnerable, softer around the edges.

"Shut up, Lucian!" Melissa cried. "Attack them! Kill the girl. You know it's what needs to happen!"

My mother's figure straightened at the cries, and she turned in the air toward her former love, her ghostly lips frowning in disapproval.

"Lucian," she whispered softly. "Would you murder the only flesh and blood you have on earth? Your *daughter*?"

My father stopped his forward movement. He just stared at my mother, a complex emotion in his eyes, something close to love and hurt and distrust there. "Delilah, you don't understand. Things have changed."

"You only get one family, Lucian." My mother's voice grew softer still. "It'd do you well to remember that."

"I'm your new family!" Melissa shrieked. "Kill the ghost! Kill the girl! You don't need her. You have a new daughter, and it's *me*!"

Hettie's fingers twitched on the blanket, but I shook my head. Melissa and Lucian were so focused on one another that I wanted to see how their argument would play out before we attacked. I sensed a fracture was near, but just how big of one, it was hard to say.

"This *is* my family!" Lucian whirled to face Melissa. "You are not my daughter."

With a start, I glanced at my mother, then through her, to Lucian. I realized that, for the first time, my entire family was together in one room. *What a warped family*, I thought. We gave dysfunction a whole new meaning.

"Delilah, I've never stopped loving you," Lucian said, pleading as he turned to my mother. "They took you from me, they stole you after she was born..."

"You know that's not true." My mother's voice cut out, her figure flickered. "I loved you, Lucian, but you've changed. You must know, it's not too late. Never too late, unless..."

"Unless what?" Lucian demanded, falling forward to his knees. "Delilah!"

My mother's figure flickered to nothingness for a moment. When she reappeared, she was next to me, her hand outstretched, her palm a breath from my cheek. "I'm so proud of you, darling. I love you, Lily."

I raised my hand to press her palm against my cheek, but it touched nothing but air. My hand passed through my mother as she faded for one final time, her silvery figure winking away into another realm. My palm landed on my cheek where I touched wetness.

I looked up, found the same streak of tears on my father's face. We watched one another for a long moment, a look too intense, too powerful, too strange to put into words.

Our connection was severed by a screech.

"Get out of here, Lucian!" Melissa moved toward my father, grabbing his arms and hauling him to his feet. "They're going to attack!"

"No, wait—Melissa." My father raised his hands in surrender, his gaze not letting go of mine. "I want to—"

"Don't be stupid!"

Melissa bent low, braced herself, and with a gigantic shove, she managed to knock an unsuspecting Lucian off his feet. He took one step backward, stumbling into the portal head first. Melissa gave him one final push while simultaneously muttering under her breath and raising a hand to close the portal.

"Stop her," Trinket shouted. "Or she'll get away!"

Hettie looked across the room, and upon my nod, the entire family raised the blanket in unison and muttered the incantation together. Before Melissa knew what was happening, we'd tossed the fabric over her head and engulfed her with it like a spider's web. As the portal snapped shut, Melissa fell to her knees—stuck with us in the storeroom.

Her eyes went blank, her figure frozen in place. She tugged the blanket closer subconsciously, staring at something in the distance, something beyond all of us. I glanced over my shoulder to see what she was staring at so intently, but there was nothing. Whatever hell Melissa was trapped inside was in her own mind.

And then the screaming began. The terrible, awful, soul-turning screeches.

It was eerie to see Melissa unable to react physically to whatever was happening inside her head. Whatever she could see was causing her intense, acute pain, and yet she posed perfectly still, her eyes wide open, screaming as if she was being murdered.

One by one, we turned away from her, unable to watch. We all knew this was a replay, her personal replay, of the moment she had killed Ranger L. Zin morphed silently back into her human self, and we waited together for the awfulness to pass.

Hettie moved to stand next to me, slipped one of her deceptively frail-looking arms over my shoulder. "I don't think your father will bother you for a while."

"I know," I whispered.

"And you do have family," Hettie said. "He's the one who doesn't."

"He has me."

"He had you," Hettie said. "He's losing you, if he hasn't lost you already."

"I don't know what to make of any of this."

"You don't have to say anything." Hettie hugged me close to her side. "Whatever he's done to you, he's still your father. There's bound to be conflicting feelings, and nobody will judge you for that, least of all your true family."

I leaned over and gave my grandmother a peck on the cheek. "Thank you for being here with me."

"Where else would I be? I couldn't miss out on the action." Hettie winked. "I'm proud of you. And so is your mother."

Melissa had stopped screaming by the time Hettie finished speaking, and as we turned around, I watched her body go limp from exhaustion. Melissa slumped forward to the floor, her arms sprawled on either side of her body, her spirit broken.

Zin stepped forward, somberly gathering Melissa's wrists and fastening the standard-issued magic-proof handcuffs over her wrists.

"Melissa Cross," Zin stated in a dull monotone. "You're under arrest for the murder of Ranger L." She leaned forward, whispered in a coarse voice. "This time, you're going to rot in prison—forever."

As Zin wrapped up the arrest to a near-comatose Melissa, the front door to the bungalow burst open, and in flew Ranger X followed closely by a cane-thumping Gus. Their eyes were clear of the haze from the Spelldriver potion, but the confusion was rampant on their faces.

"Lily, are you okay? I tried to find you but..." X scratched at his head, looked around at the crowd gathered in the room. "I got lost?"

The poor man sounded so distressed it was almost comical. He obviously wasn't used to having his plans foiled. Hettie hid a grin and Poppy smothered her own smile as she scooted closer to Mimsey, who had a death grip on Poppy's shoulder as if her daughter would vanish the second she let go.

"What happened?" Ranger X finally asked. "Is that Melissa?"

"It is," I said. "Zin—er, Ranger Z—just finished arresting her. I trust there's a special cell for lockup where she won't be able to work her illusions?"

A satisfied look came over Ranger X's face. "Most certainly. There's a cage with her name on it. Ranger Z, would you like me to accompany you to drop her off?"

Zin shook her head no, but then hesitated. "Per protocol, that would probably be best. I don't think she's going anywhere, but I'd hate to take any chances."

Ranger X gave a nod, his face beaming with approval. "Very well. Lily, a word?"

Ranger X grabbed my hand and led me out the back of the storeroom to the bar behind the bungalow. There, we found ourselves alone, the stars twinkling happily above us. The storm had cleared.

"Do you feel like sharing what happened in there?" Ranger X asked. "I don't—I'm sorry I couldn't make it sooner. I don't know what was wrong with me."

"It's my fault. Or rather, the spell I made. It, um, backfired a bit."

"I'm not sure that's true." Ranger X toyed with a piece of my hair that had slipped out from my ponytail and pushed it behind my ear. "You're the best Mixologist this island has ever seen. I think your potion did exactly what it was supposed to do."

"You might be right. I do think we ended up with everyone there who needed to be present."

Ranger X let his hand drape down my side, hooking lightly into the pocket of my shorts. He tugged me closer. "And your father?"

"He's..." I hesitated. "I'll tell you the full story later. I'm not sure exactly what happened, but I think it will be a while before he bothers us."

"You wounded him?"

"Sort of. Not physically, but when my mother made an appearance," I said, watching X for a reaction, "I think it affected him. In a strange way, I think he's always loved her. His love has manifested itself in a crazy, extreme way, but I think seeing her spirit, hearing her voice, shook him all the way through."

"So, you're saying we have some time." A soft smile curved over X's lips. "Where it's just me, you, and nothing to worry about aside from getting married."

"I'm not sure if that'll ever be true when I'm marrying the Head Ranger," I said with a light laugh, "but close enough. For now, we can breathe easier."

"The contract?"

I just shook my head.

"We'll figure it out," Ranger X said. "I promise you, Lily. I promise."

"I know we will," I said with more confidence than ever before. "But for now, I think we need to get Melissa locked up. Get our wedding sorted. Move on with our lives."

"I can't agree more." Ranger X pressed a long, lingering kiss to my lips. Only when he heard the sounds of a scuffle coming from the main room did he pull back, his eyes clouded with the desire to stay exactly as we were.

"And X, can I ask you one more favor?"

"Anything."

"I know..." I hesitated. "Well, I don't know the full situation between you and your family. But when I met with your brother the other day, it seemed like he really wanted to reconnect."

"Lily—"

"I'm not going to pressure you into rekindling a relationship if you're not ready, but just think about it," I said. "We're getting married, and I thought it might be nice to have your family there. I'd love to have my mom there, but..."

Ranger X's gaze softened. "Let me think about it."

"Of course," I said, tugging gently on his shirt. "Thank you. Anyway, hurry home tonight—I'll be waiting up for you."

He tucked his finger under my chin, raised it, and smiled. "You better be."

We returned to the storeroom and discovered the sound of the scuffle to be Zin hauling Melissa to her feet. There was a haziness to Melissa's expression that told me she was still shaking off the jitters from the Pain from the Past charm, along with the shock of everything that had transpired in the last half an hour.

Ranger X nodded toward Zin, and together they led the prisoner out of the bungalow. Once they were gone, the rest of us shifted in uncomfortable silence.

"Well, I have children to get home to," Trinket said. "Goodnight, everyone."

"Mimsey," Gus said, the second Trinket had left. "Let me walk you home."

"But—" Mimsey clutched Poppy tighter. "Where will you be? Are you going back to... wherever you were?"

Poppy blinked, tears pooling in her eyes. "I have to go back. Chase is waiting for me."

"Are you..." I glanced at Poppy's finger. "Did you get married?"

She shook her head, gave a bright grin even as she wiped her eyes and sniffed. "It's too soon. I realized the second we left town that I couldn't make that sort of commitment without my family around me."

Mimsey collapsed onto Poppy's arm in relief. "That's great news, Poppy."

"I'm sorry I dragged you into this, mom," she said. "I never meant to hurt you."

Mimsey kissed Poppy's cheek. "I know, dear. You followed your heart. You always were the most passionate of us, and I would never change that about you. Just... be safe, okay? And come home soon."

"What will happen to Chase?" Poppy asked. "He can't come home. They'll arrest him on sight. And I love him—I can't let that happen."

"I'll talk to Ranger X," I said. "I can't guarantee anything, but I'll push for a fast and fair trial."

"Oh, thank you, Lily," Poppy said. "That's all he's ever wanted. He *wants* to work with us. He's changed, and I really think he could be an asset to the Ranger program."

"We believe in second chances." Mimsey stroked her daughter's hair. "And maybe he can help us. His skills could turn out to be useful."

Poppy nodded. "Just wait until I tell him, mom. I'll be home before you know it."

"In that case," I said. "I suppose we should get you back. Except... I'm not exactly sure how? Or where?"

"That's easy," Mimsey said. "Do a quick spell reversal on Poppy, and it'll cancel out the remaining Spelldriver charms and send her right back. It'll send me back, too."

I nodded and took a deep breath. I put my hands on Poppy and Mimsey.

"*Your time to help has come and passed,*
Send them back to their places, last."

I blinked, and then both Poppy and Mimsey were gone. Gus and I were alone in the bungalow.

"Well," Gus said. "You've captured a murderer. You've cleared Ranger H's name. And your father is free, but according to what I've heard, he won't be bothering you for a bit."

"It's almost too good to be true," I said, allowing myself a small smile. "Except for poor Landon, of course."

"He went down for the right side," Gus said gruffly. "It's what he would have wanted."

"So," I said, bumbling toward the center of the storeroom. "I hate to ask this, but what's next?"

"Next?" Gus asked. "Oh, I dunno. Give it a few weeks, and I'm sure you'll have another crisis on your hands."

"What if I don't want another crisis?"

Gus allowed himself a genuine, crooked grin. "Then stay out of trouble, Miss Locke. Maybe you'll even find time to get yourself hitched."

EPILOGUE

F*our weeks later*

"What do you think?" Wanda asked, her red lips smacking over a piece of gum as she studied the latest design she'd draped over my body. "Sexy, huh?"

"Um," I hesitated. "Where's the rest of it?"

"It's siren-inspired," she said. "What do you expect, a woolly sweater?"

"No, but I did expect a little more than this." I weakly snapped at the thin bra straps that held up a sparkling top. My stomach was bare, and a tight skirt began at my waist and flared over my ankles. "This exposes more skin than my swimsuit."

"It might be nice for the honeymoon," Poppy said kindly. "You know, to lay out on a beach. A private beach where nobody will ever see you."

Zin just snorted.

Mimsey sat next to her daughter, still soaking in every moment with Poppy since she'd returned. Chase hadn't yet appeared on The Isle, but Poppy assured us he was just taking care of some outstanding business before he turned himself in, gathering the proof he'd need to clear his name. Poppy swore he'd come back, but only time would tell.

"I dunno," Hettie wheedled, snapping one of the bra straps. "I rather like it. If they'd had something that flashy in my day, I might have gone for it."

"Thank God they were going the traditional route in your day," Trinket said. "Wanda, next, please."

Wanda sighed and then clapped her hands. "Go change, Lily. I'll be right back. I'm running low on options. Most of my clients aren't this picky."

I didn't think it was particularly picky to have a requirement that a gown cover my full body, but Wanda marched to the beat of her own wedding band.

Exhausted, I slipped back into the dressing room, stifling a yelp at the sight of the woman standing among all my leftover dresses and scattered undergarments.

"What are you doing here?" I asked The Quilter. "How'd you get in without anyone noticing?"

"It's great to see you, Lily." The woman smiled, pushed back hair that looked like a Brillo pad back from her face. "As it turns out, I have one last gift for you."

"Hold on a second—I'm still trying to digest your other gifts," I said. "I understand the sweater and the Muse blanket. But what about the other blanket? The one with the sparkles that led me through The Forest?"

"That old thing? It's completely unmagical," The Quilter said blithely. "You needed the confidence to grow. To add your own sparkle to potions. To take charge when nobody else would do it. And, look what happened. I give you a blanket I knit from plain old yarn, and you arrest a murderer."

There was a compliment somewhere in there, so I tucked the new information away for later when I could properly digest it. "And the baby blanket?"

She just smiled. "I know you don't want it, but it's yours. It belongs to you—that's all I can say."

"I can't keep it."

"Let me give you my final gift," The Quilter said, changing the subject. "I truly hope you'll like it."

Before I could tell her that wasn't necessary, she whisked a covering away from a hanger. There, against the white wall, glittered a dress. *My* dress. The gown I would wear down the aisle to meet Ranger X.

I knew it the second I laid eyes on it. My fingers reached out, touched the gorgeous fabric. A warmth flowed through me. Long, delicate sleeves in lace hung at the sides, narrowing to a slim waist before fanning out into a train that looked to extend for miles and miles.

Every inch of the fabric had been made with the gentlest touch, the most intricate of details. Bits of diamonds and crystals sparkled under the lights, tucked into patterns that wound their way from top to bottom. It was the most beautiful piece of art I'd ever seen.

"For me?" I gasped.

"I hope so," The Quilter said. "This time, it's your choice. But, I hope you'll accept. It's my gift to you, a blessing for a long and happy marriage."

"I love it," I whispered. "I want... may I try it on?"

"I'd be honored. Let me help you. It's form fitting, though I left a little extra room."

"Extra room?"

The Quilter just smiled as she helped me into the dress. I'd forgotten her comment by the time she pulled the back tight and laced up the corset. Her gentle face beamed from over my shoulder at me in the mirror.

"It's perfect," I said, turning to The Quilter and throwing my arms around her. "Thank you."

"Congratulations," she said. "You all will be so happy."

"All?"

"Show your family. Go on, see what they say."

The Quilter pushed the curtain open without further ado, revealing the gown to my family. Their sharp inhalations said it all.

Mimsey burst into tears. Poppy spontaneously began to clap. Hettie had to sit down, leaning against Zin who, to my great surprise, blinked and smiled. Even Trinket's lips turned upward in appreciation.

"It's beautiful," Hettie said. "That's the one."

"Well, I have a few more options—" Wanda came to a dead stop, looking up at me from behind an armload of dresses. "Where'd you get that?"

I turned to look behind me and found The Quilter had all but vanished.

"I'm so sorry, Wanda," I said. "But I've found the dress."

"But where did you get it?" she pressed. "I've never seen it before."

I smiled. "Let's just call her my fairy godmother."

"Well, I think you're ready to get married," Hettie said. "When's the wedding?"

"Um," I hesitated, frowning as I rested a hand on the loose fabric over my stomach. "Next month. We decided not to draw things out. We're ready."

"That's fabulous! But, Lily, are you okay?" Hettie asked. "You look a little peaked."

"Just overwhelmed with the dress," I said. "It's nothing but excitement, I'm sure."

But as I slipped back into my street clothes, I couldn't help but wonder about The Quilter's words. *You all will be so happy... I left a little extra room...*

There was no way...

But as I thought back and calculated, I knew there was a way.

There was the possibility, a chance that I was pregnant.

And if that were true, then we faced a world of trouble.

THE END

Author's Note

D ear Islanders,
        Thank you for joining me on another segment of Lily and Ranger X's journey! I hope you enjoyed spending a little more time on The Isle. To be notified of the next release in this series and others, please sign up for my newsletter at www.ginalamanna.com[1]. In the meantime, stay tuned for an all new series to release this spring!
    Thank you for reading!
    Gina

Now for a thank you...
To all my readers, especially those of you who have stuck with me from the beginning.
By now, I'm sure you all know how important reviews are for Indie authors, so if you have a moment and enjoyed the story, please consider leaving an honest review on Amazon or Goodreads. I know you are all very busy people and writing a review takes time out of your day—but just know that I appreciate every single one I receive.
Reviews help make promotions possible, help with visibility on large retailers and most importantly, help other potential readers decide if they would like to try the book.
I wouldn't be here without all of you, so once again—*thank you*.

---

1.   http://www.ginalamanna.com

x

List of Gina's Books![2]

Gina LaManna is the USA TODAY bestselling author of the Magic & Mixology series, the Lacey Luzzi Mafia Mysteries, The Little Things romantic suspense series, and the Misty Newman books.

List of Gina LaManna's other books:

The Hex Files:

Wicked Never Sleeps

Wicked Long Nights

Wicked State of Mind

Wicked Moon Rising

Wicked All The Way

Lola Pink Mystery Series:

Shades of Pink

Shades of Stars

Shades of Sunshine

Magic & Mixology Mysteries:

Hex on the Beach

Witchy Sour

Jinx & Tonic

Long Isle Iced Tea

Amuletto Kiss

Spelldriver

MAGIC, Inc. Mysteries:

The Undercover Witch

Spellbooks & Spies (short story)

Reading Order for Lacey Luzzi:

Lacey Luzzi: Scooped

Lacey Luzzi: Sprinkled

Lacey Luzzi: Sparkled

Lacey Luzzi: Salted

Lacey Luzzi: Sauced

---

2. http://www.amazon.com/Gina-LaManna/e/B00RPQD-NPG/?tag=ginlamaut-20

Lacey Luzzi: S'mored
Lacey Luzzi: Spooked
Lacey Luzzi: Seasoned
Lacey Luzzi: Spiced
Lacey Luzzi: Suckered
Lacey Luzzi: Sprouted
Lacey Luzzi: Shaved
The Little Things Mystery Series:
One Little Wish
Two Little Lies
Misty Newman:
Teased to Death
Short Story in Killer Beach Reads
Chick Lit:
Girl Tripping
Gina also writes books for kids under the Pen Name Libby LaManna:
Mini Pie the Spy!